LEFT RIGHT LEFT IN TEXAS

A STORY BY

STEPHEN LEON WHITE

CONTENTS

CHAPTER ONE

The sky often painted itself a cloudless blue, hanging on lazy afternoons over our town of Brentwood, California, a part of Los Angeles close to the Pacific Ocean. Whenever I looked up, the whole horizon appeared to be flat and gray - a mirror of my life.

As a rather talented procrastinator, I usually made my New Year's Resolution shortly after summer vacation began, determined to turn over a new leaf. The year before my senior year in high school, I began to honor these resolutions by driving to Santa Monica to get a haircut, changing my appearance, tucking in my shirt, and wearing my pants around my waist, secured by a belt. My cool motorcycle boots found a place in my closet beside my slippers. With my new look and New Year's attitude, I began the quest for a summer job.

A week passed. Every day, I looked for an opening. Each morning, with my coffee, I poured over the want ads in the Los Angeles Times, all to no avail. When I managed to get a couple of interviews, I showed up only to learn they had just hired someone else. I had lousy luck. I retired from serious job-hunting after a week of frustration, and still had no job. Then, I turned to my favorite pastime. Lounging at the pool in the center of the building, hoping to meet chicks. I read during the day, and lying on the fashionable beige couch in our apartment living room, I read at night. Sometimes, I remembered to take my shoes off before stretching out on the couch. With time, my shirttails began to hang loose once more, my hair grew longer, and my jeans, sans belt, dropped inches closer to my crotch.

I took to spending more time in my room. I sat at my typewriter, sometimes for hours, writing little stories about people I knew. To write impressions like that felt like great fun and passed the time.

Also, books from the library had piled up: Freud, Menninger, Jung, Nietzsche, Darwin, Kahill Gibran's, *The Prophet*, and the thick *Magic Mountain*. After staggering through the Mann opus, I recovered by reading the hottest book around, *Bonjour Tristesse*. The author was only eighteen, and reading her passionate volume inspired me to start writing more. After Darwin, I feasted on *Charlotte's Web* by E.B. White. I'd read a review of it a while ago, and had taken it out of the library. Though nobody examined the books I read, I had to be careful with this one, knowing that my brother would tease me to death if he spotted it. I know it's a children's book, but the story of a spider saving a pig just hit me. I love animals, and one day, when I'm on my own, I'll have two dogs and a cat. Ruth, my mother, thinks they are dirty. A month passed, another two weeks, and I grew tired of lying around the pool, reading, and being yelled at by my mother.

We lived in a cool apartment building on a street called Montana, a recently built modern building with colored shapes across the front representing the ultimate hipness. We'd moved here about a year ago after mother's most recent divorce. The apartment had enough space, though the walls were too thin. My brother and I each possessed a smallish bedroom, while my mom took the largest for herself. The petite balcony overlooked the interior pool area and had a small grill in the corner for summer barbecues. My bedroom window looked out on a scene fit for a contemporary artist, a white stucco wall of the apartment building next to ours.

Each day, I seemed to bring a new and challenging confrontation with my mother. I didn't measure up, as she often informed me once I mastered puberty, so these confrontations came as no surprise. Halfway through the summer, I had grown tired of the constant squabbles, as I had with the books and pool life, and decided the time had come to confront the problem. My psychology books had informed me that being constantly beaten down was not healthy for one's psyche, and I intended to keep mine as healthy as I could.

One morning, before my brother joined us to stick in his two cents worth, I came to breakfast prepared to bring up my issue. Once Mom, clad in a bathrobe with curlers in her hair, appeared, the cornflakes arrived. As I poured milk from the container, I opened my mouth with the words, "Mom, we have a problem." Just then, the phone rang, and Mom vanished into another room to carry on one of her long-winded conversations. I sat patiently, stirring my spoon round and round in my bowl of increasingly soggy cereal until she finally reappeared, sporting an expression that immediately raised my curiosity.

"My brother Sid in Houston called," she informed me. I found her comment odd, as she rarely shared information about whom she spoke to. She poured herself a second cup of coffee from the electric coffee maker next to the sink.

"Mom, I need to talk to you."

With a familiar expression, I might call, "What again?" she sat down across from me and poured cream from the creamer beside her on the table into her coffee. "Are you all right here, or do you want to sit in the living room?"

That suggestion tempted me to escape eating the soggy cereal, but I feared another interruption. "This is good. Mom, listen, I need a car desperately. I'm sure all that time I went out to look for a job, if I'd had a car I could have got one."

"Gotten one," she corrected. "Better obtained one. You mean the week you looked for work before you retired?"

"Yeah," I agreed, ignoring her sarcasm. "I'm sure I could have got hired on a couple of jobs. Others, I didn't go after because they were too far away."

"Been hired, Cal. For someone who loves to read, your use of language is pathetic."

"Been hired." I knew that. I knew bad grammar bugged her, but here, I used vernacular when I knew how to express myself clearly. What made me bug her at the moment I wanted to get something from her?

"How many times have we been through this chicken and egg business?" She asked, for if the truth be told, I'd had issues with her before this one.

"Dozens, I know. Your position is that of the chicken; we can only discuss a car after I have a job, but honestly, I feel like the egg, so how can I get a job without a car?"

How did your brother get a job?" Mother laid out the usual

retort number 3.

"By looking, I guess, though if truth be told, he got hired by his girlfriend's dad. But, even before he started working, you bought him a car for his sixteenth birthday. I'm like already seventeen and I have no wheels. I don't need a new car like you bought him, just a car to run around in."

"What happens if you get a car and then don't get a job?"

"I don't know. But I'm probably the only kid going into senior class with no car. If Keith didn't drive me, I'd have no way to get to school. You have a new Caddy, and Keith has a new Chevy. I just want an old something. And don't say we can't afford it."

"I didn't say that," my mother snapped. She absent-mindedly stirred her coffee with a spoon and took a sip before she said more. "I just don't think you do anything to deserve a car. Keith made 10th grade President, straight A's and now he's working part-time. What did you do?"

"Let's not go over that again. I've told you what they teach in my school is a bore. I learn a lot more on my own."

Her expression showed her ongoing frustration with me. "That attitude is precisely why you don't deserve a car. A car is a reward for effort and accomplishment. You are not interested in high school, not interested in working, and have no goal or ambition. You read a lot, but you don't apply what you read to anything."

"That's not true," I retorted. "I write character studies. I analyze people and makeup stories about them. That's something."

When she didn't respond, I added, "I want to work. Just give me a chance to prove myself. One day, I promise, you'll be more proud of me than Keith."

Though I believed my words, her expression told me she didn't. "You've had chances, Cal, lots of chances. You don't take advantage of opportunities. Look at your appearance. For a week, you dressed nicely. You cut your hair. Then, once you didn't find a job, you reverted back to your old behavior. How do you expect to find a job with that long hair and those baggy clothes you wear?

I didn't answer.

"Look how your shirt is hanging out, even now. Your hair is a bird's nest. And you need to shave. Why would anyone hire you? You look more like a hoodlum than a prospective employee."

"I'm not a hoodlum, Mom. I'm a teenager. Can't you see there's a difference? Lots of us dress this way to express ourselves. My psychology books say there's nothing wrong with expressing oneself. We have our own music, our own way of dancing, and the custom cars we drive around in. They are cool things and forms of expression."

"Maybe they are, Cal," she acknowledged. "I know you like to be different. I've seen all those psychology books you've read. I guess you understand your generation, but I sure don't. I would think all that understanding would make you act more mature. If teenagers are the way you say, then why isn't Keith like that?"

"Oh, Mom, What I could tell you about Keith." That thought

flashed through my mind, but I knew better. Instead, I said, "Keith doesn't need to be cool. He has a crew cut, and no one dares to tease him because he's tough. He wears a white shirt and slacks to school, and no one makes fun of him. He's popular with kids. He doesn't need to seek recognition; it just comes to him. Girls are fighting to go out with him. He lives by his own rules and people just accept that, including you. Some people are just luckier than others."

Mom sat silent for a moment, thinking over what I said. "Maybe you're right. You are just trying to figure out who you are. I just worry about you. That's what mothers do. But I don't think you're developing in the right way, which leads me to what your uncle Sid and I spoke on the phone about. He thinks that there is a military school in Texas that could be a really good learning experience for you."

"Why would that be good for me?"

"Because you could learn self-discipline that could help you all your life."

"I doubt that. Anyway, next year is my final year of high school. When we moved to this side of the mountains, you said I could stay in the same school until I graduated. Every day Keith and I drive all the way to the Valley to go to school there. Why would I want to switch schools now?"

"Sometimes change can be good," she suggested. "You might come out of the experience a different person."

"You know a lot about change," I agreed, referencing her five husbands.

She got the message, as her glare indicated.

"I don't think that is such a good idea. Let's just drop the idea, okay?"

"Sid has promised to send me some more information about the school he has in mind. He said the place is close to where he went to college at Texas A & M. Let's talk again when we have more details."

I stood up. The conversation had headed in the same direction as all the others, nowhere.

"I'm going out for a morning swim. As far as I'm concerned, that's a nowhere idea."

I turned to leave the room, intending to head for my bedroom, where I could change into my trunks. Mother's words followed me as I left the room. "We'll talk more about this, Cal." When she got an idea in her head, the idea often sat there and wouldn't depart until she turned that idea into action.

CHAPTER TWO

Another week passed with two more books digested along with a slightly deeper suntan.

Each week that passed brought me another step closer to returning for my final year of high school in North Hollywood. Best news. Mother hadn't mentioned the military school business again. Not that my current school experience had been so great. The thought of finishing high school excited me; to be rid of the grey-haired biddy who wore her braids wrapped around the top of her head and taught Spanish, the dull math and confusing science course; of course, if I'd concentrated more and kept up with my homework…

On Saturday morning, Keith joined me at the pool, as he had weekends off work. His arrival imitated the appearance of an Adonis, with rippling natural muscles, blue eyes, and blond hair; all female eyes turned towards him when he arrived poolside. As he lay there soaking in the sun, he told me how he had plans for the evening: a date with a Las Vegas showgirl. Don't ask me where he meets them. He told her he was eighteen, but he was only sixteen, a year younger than me. Maybe his swagger made him appear older. When we were together, people usually assumed I was the younger brother. I tried to tune him out as he started to brag about his conquests during the week. After a few minutes of this crap, I jumped into the pool, the only way to escape.

As anyone could guess, Keith and my mom get along really well. They were like two peas sitting in the same pod. She believed him to be an angel, a virgin, and future presidential potential. Maybe she had a point… right. Anyone who could so totally con my mom the way Keith did can probably do the same con job on the American people.

I knew better. I knew the real Keith. He had sadistic tendencies. He proved that earlier in the summer, soon after, we got out of school for the year. There's an alley behind our apartment building. I had taken out the garbage when I spotted him smoking in the alleyway. When I brought the garbage can back to the kitchen, I told my mom to follow me down the back stairs, as I had a surprise for her. I ached to blow Keith's cover because she continued to have this ivory tower image of him. I took her to the very spot I'd stood when I spotted him puffing on the coffin nail, but when we reached that location at the foot of the stairs, angel Keith looked hard at work, polishing the paint job on his car in the alley.

"That's your surprise?" Mother asked, turning back up the stairs. I tried to follow her, but Keith nailed me. He froze me in place by the intimidating way he called my name, "Cal," with his deep voice that, while changing octaves, never seemed to crack. He had it all: the commanding voice, piercing blue eyes to go with his tanned skin and firm physique, the complete package. Even though I came out first, I somehow ended up with all the leftovers.

He walked over to me, and put his face up against mine. "What's the idea, Pal?"

"You are full of shit," I informed him. "You con Mom constantly. I wanted her to see the truth about you. She's always calling you a goody-goody, when I know better.

You're a manipulating rat."

"Oh, yeah." He pulled out a cigarette, lit up, and blew the smoke in my face.

"Yeah," I responded, wiping away the smoke.

"You're a bastard, Cal."

"Drop dead," I said as I turned away from him, intent on climbing the stairs.

"Hey, Cal, see this."

As I turned, a right hand nailed me right in the jaw. I must have a glass jaw or something because I found myself flat on the ground. I almost bounced my head against the bottom stair.

"Rat on me again, and there's more where that came from."

With his foot alongside my head, he dropped his cigarette and snuffed it out with the bottom of his shoe. Then he walked back to the car to continue to polish it. As I sat up, rubbing my jaw, he informed me of his future plan. "You know, Cal, I'm going to tell you every rotten thing I do. You will know about the women I make, the nights I get drunk, and the drag races along Sunset Blvd. And if I ever hear you mention even one word to our mother, I'll break every bone in that very brainy head of yours. Get it?"

I just stared, as I righted myself. My jaw hurt like hell. I needed to go into the refrigerator and make an ice pack for it without Mom seeing me.

So, this became my summer to hear about all of Keith's

exploits. I guess, in a way, he needed an outlet, someone to brag to about his self-proclaimed talents and skills. According to my psychology books, he felt really insecure underneath. Unfortunately, for him, he picked the wrong party to mouth off to because I told him that his girlfriends were ugly. I smiled when I said it, of course.

Once I'd taken a swim and returned to my lounge chair, he started mouthing off about his date with the showgirl again. "She's supposed to be firecracker hot. I know a guy who did her and he claims she was the best piece he ever had."

"You are so vulgar," I informed him.

"I know why you don't want to hear about any of this. Because all you've done with a girl is get to first base. And that's nowhere."

"You'll learn, little brother, that sex isn't everything. There are more important things in life."

"How would you know, you horny little turd?"

I really had begun to sense that Keith didn't like me. And I knew I'd have to suffer him for a long time, or at least until I grew up and could escape.

"You seem to be the horny little turd, not me," I informed him.

"You idiot. Don't you think I know there are more important things than getting laid? That's why I work so hard in school. I'm going to be a great lawyer, maybe even a judge. You, on the other hand, are going to be a loser. No doubts there."

"And I suppose you'll go to college, join a frat house, and

become one of the boys. Then you'll go out and make lots of money, get married, raise some kids, and spend the rest of your days playing boring golf at some country club."

"So?"

"So that sounds so mundane. Just another idiot American materialist."

"You should know," Keith shot back. "You are an expert on idiots. All you do is waste your time on poetry and all that psychology crap that screws up your head. You'll either end up in the poorhouse or the nuthouse."

"If going there got me away from you, it'd be okay."

"Even Texas, buddy?"

That comment caught me off guard. "How did you hear about that?"

"Word gets around. Are you gonna go?"

"Not if my going will make you happy."

"Oh, go, Cal. I'll miss you so much, and you'll make a great cadet."

"Drop dead." I jumped up and dove back into the pool.

Without me to badger, Keith looked around and spotted a girl in a two-piece who had come down the stairs to the pool while we were arguing. I had seen her several times but had never spoken to her.

"Hi, Carol," he said.

"Hey, Keith," she answered sweetly.

"Whatcha been doing?"

"Not much. It's been so dull since school let out," she told him. He got up and moved close to her. "This apartment house sure gets lonely when there's nobody around," she went on.

"Yeah, I guess so," he said, sitting up and staring directly at her.

"Gee, there hasn't been anyone around in a long time," she continued in an inviting way. Her words directed at him cut straight through me. "I guess I just have to stay home again tonight and watch television."

Keith shook his head. "I'd love to take you to a show or something, but I've got a date. Maybe tomorrow. Hey, watch," he said, jumping up and heading for the diving board. In one quick motion, he executed a perfect backflip. Carol looked impressed.

"Hey, Cal," he said, and as I turned toward him, he rewarded my efforts with a face full of water.

"Let's have a water fight."

I ignored him and decided to climb out. I couldn't figure out why he wanted to impress Carol, who he claimed had been chasing him all summer long.

"Aw, c'mon, sissy," he taunted. Playfully, he scooped a small handful of water and threw it at my face.

"No."

He ignored me and began his all-out offensive, scooping

water with both hands.

I retreated, aiming for the stairs at the shallow end of the pool.

As I waded through the water, I could hear Carol laughing.

Keith dove under the water and grabbed the top of my trunks just as my foot started up the first of the underwater stairs. I went under, came up sputtering and coughing with one hand, trying to keep my trunks up. Gasping for air, I pulled away and headed back to the stairs. With a loud laugh, Keith let me go this time, followed me out of the pool, and, while I dried myself off, headed over to sit next to Carol on her chaise lounge.

Hanging my towel over my neck, I left the pool area without looking back. He always made me feel so damn small, and this time proved no exception. Suddenly, the idea of going to Texas didn't sound as far-fetched as when my mother brought the subject up.

CHAPTER THREE

Sunday arrived as no big deal, just another day like Monday, Tuesday, or Wednesday, because every day is like every other day for a person surviving a long summer with no work.

I tend to like to read my books lying upside down. I had sprawled out across an easy chair in the living room, my legs splayed across the back, my butt on the seat, and my head resting against the edge of the cushion, with a book held up in the air. This may not be the easiest way to read, but I find the position relaxing.

Just then, my mother walked in. She sat down on the sofa and seemed to be examining her upside-down son. Judging from her expression, I picked up that she planned to resume the discussion we'd had a few days earlier.

"Cal, what do you hope to do when you finish high school?"

I back-flipped the book over my head, where it landed with a thud on the ground, twisted my body around, and splayed the legs in a different direction, each over a side of the chair. "I can give you the same answer as the last time you asked. Probably go to college, or maybe junior college, but I don't know where or what I want to study yet."

Though the hour edged towards lunch, Mom still wore her blue bathrobe over her pajamas. Her hair needed a bit of brushing, but then again, this was a quiet Sunday morning, and the Sunday LA Times still lay spread out across the breakfast table. Mom's natural beauty showed, even without any make-up. Her small, well-proportioned body, delicate face with large brown eyes, high cheekbones, and styled hair drew men faster than flies to spilled syrup. Her mouth screwed up as she faced me and sought her next words. "Let me see if I can phrase this properly. What I am trying to ask is, what do you hope to obtain out of life?"

A shrug of the shoulders offered my immediate answer, but then her eyes warned me they expected more. "I don't know yet. That's an important decision. I'm working on the answer to that myself." She didn't know the truth behind that statement. All these books I read, all those nights I laid awake in bed trying to figure this crazy world out. All the hours spent at the typewriter writing little stories on this and that. How did I fit in? What could I do? My brother had received all the gifts from whoever gave him those gifts. I felt something lurking inside, maybe even some important contribution to make this world better, but that gift remained a mystery shrouded in darkness.

"You say you do want to go to college?"

"For the three hundredth time, yes, more than anything. I can't wait to get out of high school and go someplace that offers challenging courses taught by smart people. I feel positive that once I'm in college, I'll identify which direction to move in."

"Do you have any idea what you want to study?"

"Mom, I'm seventeen. I just explained that I don't know yet."

"Your brother is sure already that he wants to be a lawyer."

She took a sip of coffee, which made me realize she'd been

holding a full mug all the time.

"Well, there are many choices; maybe psychology or English, creative writing is fun, philosophy, history, something like that."

"Don't you think you could use some help finding your direction?"

I smelled a direction to her conversation, but I didn't plan to help her get there.

"What I am trying to say, Cal, is I think you need some guidance. You seem to be headed down the wrong track. I think with proper discipline and help, you could think much clearer than you are now."

"And how would I achieve that, dear Mother?" I reached down and picked up the book off the floor. Her eyes followed me.

"This military school your uncle has told me about could do wonders for you."

"As I said last time you raised the idea, I'm not interested in discussing the subject. I'll struggle through my last year in North Hollywood and then go to a junior college or a four-year school, depending on where I can get in."

"I worry about you," she said, with just the slightest drawl coming through. Only on a rare occasion did her Texas past slip through, but that sentence revealed it. "Keith is following in the footsteps of your father. He has ambition. I want you to have the same thing." She spoke the words "your father" with a certain tone of reverence, as she always did when she spoke of my real father, her first of five husbands. She appeared to have had great respect for him, which surprised me, considering she doesn't speak highly of any of the other men she married.

I prepared to continue my defense when the phone rang. She left the room to answer the call, and I opened my book again. Now I couldn't concentrate. I stared at the words on the page, but they did not speak back as my mind wandered away. I felt so bummed out that I even sat up straight in the chair. What she said about direction bothered me, even though I thought the problem was somewhat her fault. She'd already been married five times, and I'm only seventeen.

My real Dad was no more than a sniff of memory. He attained holy status because he died in his thirties, and he'd made enough money by then for Mom to raise us in comfort, with or without a husband. I can't figure out why she continued to marry so often after his death. She grieved for a while, that period of our lives I kind of remember, but two years after we buried him, she married a doctor.

To her credit, Mother never married a bum. All her husbands after the first one possessed one common asset. **Each had lots of money**. I was only seven when she married the second time. That marriage lasted about six months, followed by a surgical split. All I remember about that guy is he liked to give Keith and me checkups. Mom took us to Las Vegas for six weeks, and he vanished from our lives.

Three years later, she'd found number three. In those years, between husband two and husband three, came an assortment of temporary faces. She went out so much that the baby sitter could have retired early on what she earned. Number three had an insurance company. He looked like one of those comic strip characters: short, almost bald. What did she see in him other than he followed her around like a puppy? Whenever she wanted him to do something, off he went. He gave her jewelry, brought her presents. When I think back, I wonder if she'd handed him a gun and asked him to pull the trigger, he would have shot himself, going out with a smile. I had no doubt he would have pulled that trigger. Well, that ended fast, a year and a half later. She went down to Mexico to get a quickie divorce. He cried like a baby when she told him to pack his bags.

Number four arrived shortly after three. As a matter of fact, when I think about four, now that I'm older, I wonder if he became the reason she dumped three. Four looked like a hunk, Tarzan dressed in a polo shirt and denim pants. She met Carl at a party. A big, muscular guy, brainless, but the type of person who makes a house interior attractive, like some of the modern furniture carefully placed around our apartment. I have no idea where Carl got his money or even what he did for work. They honeymooned in Europe while Keith and I were shipped down to Grandmother's house in San Mateo, near San Francisco. I must have been about twelve and Keith a year younger. We didn't even meet Carl until they returned home.

They had rented a nice house in an area called Brentwood, the same area we live in now, very plush. So we returned to a new stepfather, a new house, a new school, and Mother sporting a new look as if she'd removed a few years to make herself equal to Carl in age.

I'll never forget our first night in that new house with the four of us. The house had a pool in the backyard and many rooms. Carl brought us into one of them, a library with shelves but no books. Boxes were stacked on the floor, and we had no place to sit. Hulky Carl stood across from us while my twelve-year-old eyes stared through him. He looked the part of a picture-perfect god. His broad, tanned face maintained a very serious expression, and his blue eyes took us in for a while before he spoke.

"Men," he said in a tone that made me want to laugh. "As you know, your mother and I are married now. I am, therefore, your stepfather. I want us to become good friends. We can go to movies, and football games, swim in the pool out back, horseback ride, whatever you men like. All I ask in return is that you listen to me when I ask you to do something, be respectful, and if you'd call me Father or Dad, that would please me."

What a crack-up. I wanted to break out in laughter. Carl looked about twenty-five. I didn't utter a word, but Keith, even then being the clever kiss-ass, spoke right up.

"That will be swell, Carl, I mean Father. I would love to do all those things you told us about."

Carl's eyes turned to me. "How about you, Cal? You on board?"

"I wouldn't call you Father, not on my life. You're not my real father. He's dead. You're not even old enough to be a father. So that's that. Excuse me." I turned and marched out of the room, proud that I had spoken my piece.

There's an expression I heard one day about shooting oneself in the foot. That's another way of saying you are your own worst enemy, and you did something stupid. First, Mom bawled me out for being insolent to her new husband. Second, Carl and Keith went to football games, horseback riding, and other places. He taught Keith to play tennis and how to hit a golf ball. They had a great time the entire time Carl remained around.

My memories of Carl were interrupted when my mother returned after her phone call.

" Helen wants me to meet her for brunch," she informed me. "I have to go change clothes. But I want to continue our talk soon."

"Anytime," I said, wondering if my sigh of relief sounded too obvious.

After she left the room, I remembered the day when Carl left the house. He certainly was a jerk. I don't know how she put up with him for two years. She kept trying to culture him, but that didn't work. And then she learned he had some girl on the side. She didn't share the details with me. I just know that after two years, one day, Carl had departed.

Finally, after a year of living on her own in the house we'd shared with Carl, she married Hugo, a psychiatrist. Hugo had his own home in the hills above Studio City. We gave up the rental house and moved in with him there. I gave them a swell wedding present. They were married during the day but couldn't go on a honeymoon because he had to work. The night of their wedding day, I got bored and went over to my friend Joey's house. His parents had gone out for the evening, and he pulled out a bottle of whiskey he had swiped from their liquor cabinet. I was fifteen and had never had a drink before, the same as Joey. We decided to take a glass each. We had one. Then we tried another one. My lungs were on fire, but I felt swell, like I could take on the world; before we knew how the contents of the bottle were empty.

To hide the evidence, we buried the bottle in the backyard. Then we decided to go over to Joey's girlfriend's house. We had decided they should get married. We climbed on Joey's bike, but I kept falling off the back. Finally, we staggered the two blocks to her house. By then, the time was late, and the lights inside the house had been turned off. That didn't stop us. We rang the doorbell continuously. After a while, her father came to the door.

"What do you punks want?" Her daddy asked.

"Wanna see, Joanie," Joey mumbled, finishing off the demand with a hiccup. Tired, I stretched out across the porch.

"You punks, get outta here now," came the angry voice through the screen door.

"Wanna see Joanie," (hic) Joey insisted.

"I'm looking for God," I mumbled, turning on my side enough to roll down the stairs onto the walkway. I landed on the cement with a thud.

"I'm calling the cops," the voice informed us before the door slammed shut.

"God, God, where are you?" I called across the lawn.

"Joanie, I want to marry you," Joey called out, slamming his flat hand against the wooden frame of the screen. Joey dropped to his knees while I closed my eyes.

The next moment I remember occurred inside the police station. Joey and I sat in a cell for juveniles. I felt cold, and my head ached. I kept looking for God through the bars on the window, then under the bed, but the guy didn't show up. Then, I puked in a bucket in the corner of the cell. Joey offered no help. Joey wanted to know where Joanie was hiding. He kept calling her. We made quite a pair.

My mother arrived with my stepfather for a few hours. They both seemed terribly embarrassed, as if they had produced a monster. My first words to my new stepfather were about God. Had he seen him? I insisted I had been looking for God, and if he didn't show himself, I'd had it with him. When they took me from the cell, I left Joey behind, waiting for his parents. He mumbled something I couldn't understand as his parting words. In the car, I really pushed this God thing. My mother kept asking how I could do this to her on her wedding day. She sounded terribly upset, but Hugo didn't say a word. We were off to a great start.

The next morning, my head hurt like hell, like a hammer keeping up a rhythmic tattoo on my brain. I didn't want to crawl out of bed. I didn't want to see anyone. I particularly did not want to see my mother.

I knew I had to rise, even if I wouldn't shine. I turned on a cold shower, which helped in clearing my brain a little. I dressed and went into the kitchen for breakfast, fearing the worst. Hugo sat at the breakfast table reading the morning paper. He had a cup of coffee in front of him. I poured a cup from the percolator and sat down across from him. I had no appetite.

Hugo lowered the paper enough for me to see his face. "What happened last night, Cal?"

He asked me.

"I don't know."

"Why did you drink like that?"

"We were being stupid. His parents weren't home, and we wanted to see how liquor tasted. I guess we overdid it."

"Do you always cater to your impulses?"

Nobody had ever asked me a question like that. "Huh?"

"What I'm asking is, do you always do what you feel like at the moment?"

"No, not usually."

"Have you ever been drunk before?"

"No. And never again, believe me, my head's on fire. The whole thing shouldn't have happened, it is stupid."

"I'm glad to hear you say that. But what you do is up to you. We may as well get things settled, Cal, as we don't know each other. I'll not interfere with your life unless you ask me to. I know you've had a pretty rough time up until now, and if there is a way I can be of help, I'll be more than happy to try. Beyond that, I'll keep out of your way. Is that fair enough?"

Headache and all, Hugo's words showed respect, and they encouraged me. "You bet."

After that morning, we became close friends. Through friendly talks, Hugo developed my interest in psychology. I started reading Freud, though I probably didn't understand a lot. I read some other easier books. Some nights, he would drive me to C.C. Brown's on Hollywood Blvd., and we would both have a hot fudge sundae or go to Wil Wright's for ice cream or some other place. We would carry on long discussions. I came to like him far more than any of Mom's other gallery of husbands. Best of all, he seemed to see through Keith's phony act. He treated him with respect but kept him at a distance. I sensed he didn't trust him.

When Mom started divorce proceedings a year later, I couldn't understand why. She charged mental cruelty, but I never saw them fight, or him being nasty, or anything like that. I wondered if maybe Keith had filled her head with lies about Hugo. Unfortunately, she often listened to him. Hugo was the best thing that came into her life, but despite that, she began looking for a new address. She reverted to using my father's bland last name and once more became known as Mrs. Carter. I think she liked the anonymity of that name. Even though she and Hugo were both Jewish, she never followed either the religion or the customs. The little I learned about the Jewish culture, Hugo taught me.

We moved from Hugo's house into the apartment we lived in now almost two years ago. I've often wondered what Mother wants out of life other than seeing Keith and me succeed. Maybe she doesn't know. But she is seeing a psychiatrist now, and she hasn't married again, so maybe she'll get some insight into what she's doing.

The day promised to be a hot one. I contorted myself upside down in the chair once again and continued to plow through the book in my hand.

CHAPTER FOUR

Five fingers, five days, and just like that, Monday morphed into Friday night. I had put some pomade in my hair to smooth it down and put on my coolest shirt, a white short-sleeved shirt with a pattern in the front like some kind of knight's crest. Purposely, I let the shirt end hang out over my black denim. I sat in the den, waiting for my best friend, Ray, to show up. Mother hadn't raised the military school issue all week, which put me in high spirits. I hoped she had finally forgotten about the warped idea.

At dinner, I received my ten-dollar allowance. Keith didn't need one because he made good money bagging groceries for the place his sometime girlfriend's father managed. I had tried bagging groceries once last year. But then, after a week, the manager called me into the stock room, put his arm around my shoulder in a fatherly way, and said, "Son, you'll never be a box boy." I can't tell you the sense of relief that came over me when I heard those words.

I could feel the ten-dollar bill burn a hole in my pocket, and just the thought of getting out and doing something fun with Ray had me bouncing around worse than a nervous bride. Ray had arranged for us to pick up his friend, Jack, and for the three of us to see a movie and, afterward, "cruise the Boulevard."

In Hollywood, "cruising the Boulevard" occurs mostly on Friday and Saturday nights and is as much a religious tradition for us teens as going to church on Sunday. The "Boulevard" is Hollywood Boulevard, and we cruise its length between Vine Street and Highland, maybe a mile long, driving back and forth, looking around for some action. We don't usually find any, but you never know. There are hordes of teens that show up to show off their souped-up cars, both to impress each other and the girls. Each of those nights, the cars drive at a snail's pace, bumper-to-bumper, a parade of cars going three miles an hour. There are many people filling the sidewalks as well. There are restaurants, the new Cinerama theatre where I saw the first Cinerama movie, the Egyptian theatre, book and record stores, and a lot of cheap stores to buy junk in. The "Boulevard" is hopping on those two weekend nights with neon lights and shops open late on every block, with people doing everything from picking up chicks to fighting, getting drunk, and making a nuisance of themselves. There are many cops around, so you have to be careful.

Ray and I have been going down to the "Boulevard" ever since we were old enough to drive, almost two years now. To an outsider, bumper-to-bumper traffic, noisy kids, and honking horns have no special significance except to encourage disgust, cursing, or both. As a compromise for taking the street over on Friday and Saturday, we teens have let the tourists and locals enjoy it during the rest of the week.

The doorbell rang just as I felt ready to climb the wall.

"Come in, " I yelled. "It's open."

"Hey," Ray said, walking into the den. He wore Levis and a sloppy blue shirt open just wide enough to show off the hair he proudly cultivated on his thick chest. His upper body, more solid than mine, gave him the kind of torso a football coach dreams about putting on the front line to protect his quarterback. Ray didn't play football. Nor did he ever bother to read a book. He barely passed his classes. His mother called him a lazy loafer, a no-good bum, and a few other choice terms. His dream job is to make a living by betting on horses at the racetrack. The two of us go when we can. All we need is the drop of a hat to get the two of us there. When we have the urge, no matter where we happen to be, we will agree we are in the general vicinity of Santa Anita or Hollywood Park, depending on which one is holding races. The general vicinity can be up to a hundred miles away.

 "Can I raid the refrigerator, or is your old lady home? "

"Help yourself. She's gone to a play. And Keith's not around either."

Ray went into the kitchen to try his luck in the refrigerator. Like me, he believed greatly in luck. When we went to the racetrack together, we counted on luck to let us come out ahead. As two oddballs who found each other, lady luck had cemented our friendship and brought us together. We played weekly poker games with our high school club, visited the racetrack together, and often shared bets, for Ray appeared old enough to pass for 21 with a fake ID. Ray had heavy stubble covering his face and equally thick dark hair, both of which made him appear older. He even flashed his fake ID the one time we went to Las Vegas, and they let him gamble. They looked at mine and booted me out. As different as we were, these shared pleasures kept us together.

He returned from the kitchen, where, with good luck, he'd scored a chicken leg, which he held in his favored left hand

and chewed.

"Ready to cut out?" He wanted to know.

"Good chicken, huh? We ate most of that bird for dinner."

He grunted approval, grabbed my arm with his free hand, and pulled me up out of my chair. "Let's go," he said, then added as I closed the front door, "I didn't tell you what happened yesterday. I picked four winners on paper. Even caught the daily double. Remember the last time you and me went out? I bet this nag called Arthritis. Stupid name, stupid horse ran way out of the money." His voice had deepened with excitement as we headed to his car, a souped-up '48 Ford with headers. He waved his now naked chicken bone dangerously close to my nose.

"I remember," I said, retreating to avoid a collision.

"Then you might remember the nag was due to win and how she led until the stretch, then folded faster than a fan."

"Yeah."

"They ran her yesterday up in class. So, she had long odds. Guess what happened?

"She ran the wrong way."

He slapped the chicken bone off the back of my head. "Arthritis led wire to wire and won by two and a half lengths. Paid over thirty bucks."

"So? Unless you had a bet down, that and a quarter will buy you a burger."

Ray liked to babble. He could pick a hundred winners on

paper. "So what?"

After his usual complaint that we always took his car, a moot point at best, we climbed in and headed over to where Jack lived, somewhere near Farmer's Market off of Fairfax. Then we headed toward the "Boulevard," each of us excited about the possibilities the evening ahead offered.

Jack had dark brown hair slicked back into a ducktail. He looked tough. I didn't know him at all, nor did I know how he and Ray had palled up. Though the evening air felt warm, he wore a leather jacket. Jack couldn't wait to tell us about a nineteen-year-old office girl he'd picked up; Ray wanted him to know all about Arthritis while I sat back quietly, enjoying the enlightening discussion in the front seat.

We hit the "Boulevard" at Highland and cruised to Vine, then back and forth a couple of times more. At eight o'clock, the street had just begun to wake up. Most of the action came after ten when the shows let out. We waved at the girls driving in the other direction and whistled at some other girls on the sidewalk. Occasionally, we got a smile.

"I have this plan," Ray said, seeking our approval. "I thought when we see a car in front of us with chicks in it, I would pull up and lightly tap the bumper. We'd pull over. I'd get out, check the damage, which would be none, and tell her I needed her phone number for insurance purposes." He looked around at Jack, then turned to seek my approval from the back seat. "Lame," Jack told him.

I nodded in agreement.

The time came to find a parking place; never an easy task on a Friday night. A discouraged Ray drove down a couple of the side streets. We had decided to go to a movie.

As he searched for a space, I thought this might be a good time to float my mother's idea. "Hey, I haven't told you guys. My mom wants me to go to school in Texas next year."

"Texas, where the hell is that?" Jack asked.

We all laughed.

"What for?"

"She thinks you're a bad influence, Ray, and she wants me to get away."

"Did she say that?" The hurt came through in his voice.

"No. She just thinks I need discipline. I need to find myself."

"Are you lost?" Jack asked, turning around to look at me.

Ray located a parking place and began slowly trying to maneuver his car in. He treated this car like a baby. Finally, he shut off the engine. We had parked a couple of blocks away from the "Boulevard."

"I wouldn't do it," Ray said. "I heard they hate foreigners down there."

"Last I heard, they've decided to let California stay in the United States." Then I added, "I won't go if I can avoid it."

Jack cut in. "I heard they've got some really hot babes down there."

"At a military school?"

"You didn't say anything about that," Jack told me.

The topic ended as we exited the car and started along the street that led us to the "Boulevard."

"Let's hurry," Ray said. "You know how full the movies get on a Friday night."

We walked three abreast as fast as we could without looking ridiculous until we reached Hollywood Boulevard. Movies were playing at several theatres along the "Boulevard," and we wanted to find a good double feature.

Just then, Jack announced he had an idea.

"That's a surprise," Ray teased.

"Why don't we sneak into a theater?"

"What? That's crazy," I told him.

"No, it's easy. I have done it once with another guy." Jack's voice grew animated. "Hey, all we do is find a show that's having an intermission. I sneak in and then find some ticket stubs for the three of us. You guys stay out with the crowd smoking. Then come in. If the usher wants to see your stubs, just say your friend inside has them. I'll be close by, and I'll come up to find out what is wrong. I'll show him the stubs. Can't miss."

Ray thought it sounded cool, but I couldn't be so sure.

"No sweat," Jack assured us.

We walked past several theaters that were quiet until we came across one not too far from the Egyptian Theater that had many people standing in front smoking. Jack disappeared. Ray handed me a cigarette, as I didn't usually smoke, and we mingled with the crowd. When the smokers returned to the lobby, we carefully doused our cigarettes just outside the entry doors so the usher could see us and walked in.

"Did you fellows sign out?" The usher asked.

"Sign out. What for?" Ray asked.

"When you go outside, you are supposed to sign the list so you can return."

"We didn't know there was a check-out list," I said. "We just didn't see it."

The usher wore one of those fancy costumes that resembled Johnny, the midget guy who goes around yelling, "Call for Phillip Morris." He frowned at us.

"If you aren't on the sign-out list, I'm afraid I can't let you back in."

Ray pretended to blow his stack. "That's crazy. We paid our money to see two pictures, and now we want to see the other one."

He had screwed up his face to look angry - the flushed usher went off to find the manager. Meanwhile, Jack, in a corner close by, waved some stubs and smiled while we waited nervously.

A jovial-looking man wearing horn-rimmed glasses appeared beside the usher. "What seems to be the trouble, boys?" He asked, though he damn well knew the answer.

I presented our case.

He made a sincere face. "Sorry, boys. I can't let you in, either. Policy."

Just then, Jack appeared, our knight in shining armor, waving three tickets in the air as he approached the manager.

"What's going on?" He asked.

"They won't let us back inside," Ray informed him. "You've got the stubs, don't you, Jack?"

"Sure do," Jack answered, waving the stubs in front of the manager's face.

The manager examined them. "All right, since you have stubs, I'll make an exception and let you in. But please remember to sign out in the future."

Victory!!

We promised to do just that as we walked through the lobby into the theater where the film had already started. Patting each other on the back, we took three seats on the left side toward the front.

We weren't seated more than a couple of minutes before the usher in the Philip Morris costume came down the aisle to where we sat. "Would you boys come out in the lobby for a minute?" He asked.

Confused and wondering if they had caught on, we followed him up the aisle and into the bright lights, backed by a chorus of popping popcorn. The manager, grim-faced, stood next to the snack bar with his hands on his hips.

"Get out of here," he said, waving the stubs at us.

"Why?" Jack wanted to know.

"These stubs you gave me are no good. One stub sold two hours later than the other two."

Jack blew his top. "You can't make us leave. We paid to see this movie, and we're going to see it."

"I think we should go," I said.

Ray nodded in agreement.

"What do you mean?" Jack asked. "We paid good money, and now you want to walk out?"

"Don't cause any trouble, boys," the manager said. "I don't want to have to get the police."

"Let's go," Ray told Jack, tugging his sleeve.

I didn't know this Jack, but I could see he wasn't like Ray and me. His face turned red, and he jerked himself away from Ray's grip. I thought he might swing at his friend. "You go if you want. I'm going in to watch the movie."

"Look," the manager's voice rose.. "Either you go now, or I'll have the usher call the police."

"I'm not going anywhere," Jack answered.

"Come on," Ray pleaded, looking scared. I began edging toward the front door.

On the way over, Ray told me once he hung out with Jack in a park when they exchanged words with three tough-looking guys who challenged both of them to a fight. Ray wanted to take off, but Jack stood his ground. He challenged the biggest guy, one-on-one and got his ass whipped. But they admired his toughness, and he ended up becoming friends with them. Jack and I were as different as night and day.

"You go," Jack told us. "I'm standing my ground."

"Clarence, call the police," the manager ordered the usher.

"Yes," Jack mocked. "Clarence, call the police like the big man told you."

They had a phone behind the counter at the snack bar. Clarence picked the receiver up and dialed the number without looking it up.

"That's just a bluff," Jack said with confidence. "The police won't come for this." Ray and I listened, both of us frozen in place.

Clarence talked for a moment and then came back to inform the manager, "They said they'll send someone right away."

"If you won't refund our money, at least let us watch the film until the cops come," Jack demanded.

"I'll do nothing of the kind," the manager said sternly.

Jack ignored him, and walked toward the theater entrance even aftdr the manager had refused entry.

Rushing over to stop him, the manager grabbed him by his shoulder and said, "You can't go in there."

Jack swung around, yanking away from the man's grip, both fists ready to pounce. "You don't touch me."

The manager backpedaled as he repeated, "You can't go in."

The usher and two people who stood at the counter to buy popcorn before they entered the theater stopped to watch this exchange. Jack folded his arms. "You touch me again, and I'll clobber you."

The manager bit his lip and looked out, hoping the police would arrive soon. Everything and everyone seemed frozen in place, and the only sound came from two gawkers eating their popcorn, watching an entertainment they suspected could exceed the pictures being shown inside.

The manager suddenly bolted for the door to let in two LAPD cops in uniform, one tall and the other average height. The tall one asked the manager to explain the problem.

"These kids tried to sneak in, and they got caught. These two," and he pointed to Ray and me, "are all right. This one is threatening to hit me and causing trouble."

The manager had positioned himself behind the police so that they stood between him and Jack.

"Did you threaten him?" The tall cop asked Jack.

"Only after he grabbed me," Jack said.

The cop hadn't expected this answer. I could see his confusion from the expression on his face. He didn't know exactly what to do. Now, half a dozen people, who appeared out of nowhere, surrounded us.

The tall cop asked each of them to explain what happened. Jack repeated his phony story, and the manager explained the difference in the stubs. Then Jack, who I admit could think on his feet, said Ray and I had come in at six, and he'd joined us two hours later. He actually had the cop believing him. I could see the way he glanced at the manager, who began to fidget and bite his lower lip.

The cop was about to demand the manager return our money when a guy at the snack bar walked up to the cops and said, "I saw these kids. I saw them all come in together around 7:00."

We had lost. The cops had us each fill out a card and ordered us to leave the theater.

By now, too much time had passed to go to another movie. We walked back to Ray's car and drove to Burbank. Bob's Big Boy, a coffee shop and drive-in being the usual meeting place for those of us who attended North Hollywood High. Jack came along for the ride.

In retrospect, I don't know why we did such a crazy thing. Between the three of us, we had over fifty dollars. I never saw Jack again, which is probably a good thing. I think people can influence me too easily.

CHAPTER FIVE

One of the odd aspects of life is how you just know something will happen even when you really know nothing. All the next week, life continued at a normal pace, but I just sensed the Texas issue would return. I had resolved over the past weekend to try to find a job, as that would strengthen my case against moving to Texas. But by now, over half the summer had vanished, and the weeks moved by quickly.

Sure enough, Saturday morning came. We all ate pancakes for breakfast. Whatever else I might say about my mom, she's a damn good cook. The pancakes tasted super good with real melted butter and maple syrup on top. She knew how much I liked to eat these for breakfast. She probably thought the melted butter would melt me as well. That's probably why she made them because halfway through the meal, she said, "Cal, I'd like to continue our talk from last week."

I looked at Keith, who had a smirk on his face.

"Not in front of him," I said.

"There is nothing I'm going to say that Keith can't hear."

"But there may be things I have to say that Keith shouldn't hear."

Mother agreed to talk in her bedroom after breakfast. We finished the rest of the meal in silence, with Keith tossing me looks like, "You are in for it, brother, as you'll see." I just stared down at my pancakes as they vanished from my plate.

Mother's bedroom had been painted and decorated in what she calls muted colors. They are soft pastels, and they blend in what I would say is a pleasing way. A large modern painting hangs on the wall across from her double bed. I don't know which of the husbands gave her that painting, but she claimed the painter who made the piece was important. Light curtains covered the windows, but they had been pulled back to let in the morning light. I flopped down on top of the baby blue bedspread, and she sat in a chair across from the bed and for a moment, she just stared at me.

"Cal, I know you've been avoiding the subject, but I wonder if you've given that school in Texas any more thought."

"I have. I keep asking myself why you are so eager to get rid of me. I can't be that bad, can I?"

She shook her head. "I love you. But ever since that night, you and your friend got drunk and ended up at the police station, I've been worried about you. That's all."

"Mom, that happened two years ago. And on the day of your fifth marriage."

The number seemed to bite her, an irritation, like a little mosquito that took a nip on the back of her neck. "I understand you haven't had the most stable upbringing. I've been talking to my therapist about that issue, about how Keith handles situations so well, and you seem to have so many problems."

"You mean, other than not finding a summer job?"

"Yes, take your room, for instance. You keep the place like a pigsty. Clothes are strewn all over the floor, the bed is unmade, and uneaten food is left on the desk. Poor Charlotte has to clean up your room more than any other in the apartment when she comes. Cal, this is no way to live."

"But I'm comfortable with myself that way."

"Eventually, you will have to live with other people, whether roommates at college or a wife. Do you think any of them will want to run around picking up after you?"

I shook my head.

"I've said many times your appearance is more like that of a hoodlum than a clean-cut high school senior. You haven't improved there either, though I confess you looked better this last week when you went out job hunting. We live in a nice neighborhood, have a nice car, and have lovely furniture in our apartment. You generally dress like you live in the slums. I remember what you said about being a teenager, but I don't see how that can justify your overall appearance."

We were skating across thin ice as we danced in the usual circles in that conversation. "God, Mom, I'm not some thirty-year-old man working in an office. I'm still a kid. I'm not perfect."

"I understand that."

"If you do, then why so much concern? And why all this pushing on a military school?"

"Because the problem goes beyond what I've mentioned, it's an attitude you seem to have developed. You appear to be lazy and unfocused. I know you read a lot of interesting books, and you sound intelligent when you speak, but your grades are dismal. You don't put that knowledge you acquire to good use."

"Many kids my age are just like me."

"Maybe." She punctuated the word with a sigh. "But all I have to go by is you and Keith, and Keith shows me what a winner can look like. I want you to be a winner like Keith but in your own way. Could you try this school? I think a year there could teach you the qualities most important to your future; order, self-discipline, and becoming goal-oriented. Won't you at least try it?"

"No."

"Think about what I'm saying, Cal. I only want the best for you. The school certainly can't hurt you, and you may find yourself emerging as a different person after the experience."

I did not doubt that. I would be a different person after emerging from a torture chamber, too. "Anything else?" I asked, standing up.

"Yes, one thing more. Keith has gotten a week off work. Tomorrow, we are driving up the coast to San Mateo to your grandparent's house. So please pack your clothes and be ready."

"Okay," I said on the way out of the room. Ruth knew her method of persistence usually succeeded in getting what she wanted. My resistance had already weakened. Persistence always wore me down. When she gets my grandmother to side with her and Keith, I am a dead duck. My fate hung before my eyes. Normally, I'm never hot to visit my grandparents' place; days are so boring there, but this time, I had more incentive than usual to find a way to stay home.

I've never understood why anyone is expected to love his relatives. People think just because they share your heritage, you are supposed to love them. I don't know how some people put up with relatives they can't stand. Most of my relatives aren't the type of people I'd want to hang around with. But I'm stuck whenever we see them because they're relatives.

I decided to go for a swim. On the way to the pool, I wondered who, if anyone, I should notify if I ended up leaving town for a week. Ray, of course. Who else? I tried to think of someone, anyone else, who might care that I had left town, but no one came to mind.

This is the essence, the perpetual story of my life. The only times I've left the house with a friend were evenings Ray and I and some of his friends decided to go somewhere, like that night with Jack. And what would we do on those nights? We'd follow the same routine; poker, movies, Bob's Big Boy, or, for a daytime activity, the racetrack.

If I went to a play or concert, which I liked to do, I went by myself. Since I'd gone to the same high school for two years with a lot of the same kids, I sort of knew them, but not in a friend's kind of way where we would do things together. Everyone else in the school seemed to have many friends. Even the club I belonged to hadn't brought anyone other than Ray close to me. I wanted a girlfriend but still didn't have one.

By the time I reached the pool, I had reversed my mental course. Texas could prove to be an adventure, and I wouldn't be leaving much of anything behind. Maybe a change would be a tonic. Maybe my mother had a point about where my life was at and what I needed to change directions. But I didn't intend to tell her that or go easily.

Early the next morning, excuses not accepted, my bag packed and in the trunk of the car, apartment locked up, we set out for San Mateo, a small town between San Jose and San Francisco, about 400 miles up Highway 101 from Los Angeles. Mother asked me to drive the Cadillac, and I proudly sat behind the wheel and carefully made my way over the Sepulveda Pass and west along Ventura Blvd headed in the direction of Santa Barbara. I wondered if this had anything to do with my mother's melted butter psychology, putting me behind the wheel of her beast. Usually, Keith took the wheel when we went anywhere. She claimed she let Keith drive because he drove more carefully than me. She had never been in a car with him when he drag-raced along Sunset Blvd.

The Cadillac purred like a kitten out on the open road. Whatever psychological impact she anticipated by letting me stay behind the wheel worked well. I felt ten feet tall. We passed through Santa Barbara, one endless light at a time, then continued along the highway to San Luis Obispo. There weren't too many places to stop to eat, but we found one in King City. After lunch, Keith took over and drove like an old lady the rest of the way.

We arrived in San Mateo an hour or so before dinner. My grandmother met us at the door with kisses. She looked more wrinkled and heavyset than I remembered, her grayish hair permed, horn-rimmed glasses covering her eyes, and wearing an old housedress partially obscured by an apron around her waist. Since she was my mother's mother, I couldn't help but wonder if one day my beautiful mother would answer the door looking just like her.

During our arrival, Grandpa remained sound asleep in his favorite green chair. Every time we'd driven up for a visit, for as long ago as I can remember, Grandpa greeted our arrival with loud snores. The chair he slept in didn't actually look all that comfortable, but he'd been parked there for so many years; chair and man looked as if they were wedded together. Grandpa, who smoked cigars and liked a bit of bourbon before dinner, was an okay guy. My grandparents weren't rich, but they lived okay. Grandmother worked for some kind of lender's exchange. I tried to understand exactly what she did. She explained the procedure once. She kept records for different loan agencies around the Bay area. She had a list of who had loans open or paid off with each agency. If someone applied to borrow money, the potential lender would call Grandmother to see if he had any outstanding loans from another agency. She had a room full of files and cards with people's names all over them. I don't know how she kept track of who had a loan, who didn't, and who had paid his loan off. But she must have been okay at the job because she'd been doing this since I first visited as a little kid.

Grandmother led us into the living room and woke her husband up. She told him we had arrived and dinner would be ready soon. He got up to wash, waving hello as he passed by and stopping for an instant to place a kiss on Mother's forehead. One could never accuse my Grandfather of being overly sentimental. Though he was seventy, he still ran a small trucking firm, and he claimed to be active in different civic organizations. His hair had remained mixed black and gray, and his face hadn't wrinkled, all of which made him appear younger than Grandma, though they are the same age and have been married forever.

Grandmother loved being artistic. She went to San Francisco a lot to the museum or to take in the theater or a concert. She also did much civic stuff and was in the women's club, on top of working full-time. When I think about how bossy my mother is, I don't have to look very far to find out where that bossiness began. You know that business about the fruit not falling far from the tree? Grandmother orders Grandpa around like a drill sergeant. "Morris, do this, Morris do that." He gets his marching orders whenever he is home. Of course, he's gone most of the day.

The house they lived in on Isabel Street was a two-story white frame house. They had two bathrooms, one up and one down, and three bedrooms upstairs, as well as a small maid's room behind the kitchen. That's the way they used to build houses before the war, someone told me. Happily, I got the room behind the kitchen every time we came. You would think that would piss me off, but actually, I liked being away from everyone else. I had a bathroom to myself, while the others shared. And even though I had a small room, it looked out to the backyard, and I loved the location. During visits like those, I could spend hours lying on my bed, or spread out on the throw rug on the floor, reading a book.

A book can take me far away from San Mateo or the rest of the world. On this trip, I had brought my current read, a book called *Tap Roots,* about a family with anti-slavery sentiments who lived in a county in Mississippi that had seceded from the South during the Civil War. They were living in Mississippi, in the heart of the rebellion, and fighting the Confederates. The book had me hooked. Crazy story. If we read interesting books like this in history, I might be doing a lot better in school.

Grandmother had made a great dinner of Southern fried chicken, mashed potatoes, and biscuits. She loved having her family visit, though she didn't have much time for them during her workday. Grandpa never said much when we ate. All through dinner, Grandmother and Mother caught up on news about the relatives, most of whom I didn't know or care to know.

After dinner, Mother helped Grandmother clean up while the rest of us returned to the living room. Grandpa dived back into his favorite chair. I talked Keith into a game of gin rummy just to pass the time.

As we played, I wondered what they were talking about while they did the dishes. Probably me. I'm sure my mother had enlisted her mother's support.

"Hey, Cal, are you playing or what?" Keith asked.

A minute later, he threw all his cards on the table. "I'm bored," he said. The gentle sound of Grandpa's snores played in the background. "Let's borrow Mom's car and see if we can find some girls."

"I'm too tired."

"You're too tired. That's a laugh. You're just afraid we'll

score a couple of chicks, and you won't know what to do with the one you have."

I wanted to use a word that would get me in trouble if anyone heard me. I stayed silent.

Keith continued on. "I wish I knew where I could find some action around here. At home, I wouldn't be playing boring gin with my boring brother."

"You're not home, so pick up your cards and shut up."

He looked at the cards in his hand and then slammed one down. "Gin."

"You cheater. You haven't even gotten more cards. If you had gin before, why didn't you call it?"

Keith took his hand and threw it up in the air. Cards went flying in all directions. He walked off, and headed toward the small den which had a small table TV.

"You jerk," I called after him.

"Drop dead, Calvin," he answered, hissing out my full name, the name I hated. Ever since I'd read *East of Eden,* I had shortened my name to Cal, and I wouldn't answer to any other name. Cal sounded cool, while Calvin sounded like some loser. Ray and I had just seen the film as well, one of the most beautiful films I've ever seen starring this new young actor named James Dean who played Cal. I definitely felt like a Cal and not a Calvin.

Furious at my brother, I began picking up the cards that had fluttered all over the room, landing on the rug, the couch, and even one that landed on the top of Grandfather's head.

After I restored the deck, I said goodnight to the ladies, as I passed them plotting over cups of coffee at the table in the breakfast room beside the kitchen. A week of staying here felt similar to spending a week on an archery range where my head would be used each day for target practice.

Each of the next three days seemed to drag on forever, every hour moving as slowly as a century. I finished all 600 pages of *Tap Roots.* I also watched the small TV in the den, slept, and went to a double feature. Keith remained as bored as me, but every time we found ourselves in the same location, we ended up fighting over a ridiculous comment or issue. My mother hadn't mentioned the military school again since we arrived, though based on past experience, I knew that day would come.

The fourth day fulfilled my brilliant prophecy. Grandmother had finished work. She and Mother were sitting together in the breakfast room drinking a cup of coffee, as they so often did when I passed through the kitchen on the way to my room.

"Cal, we would like you to join us," Grandmother said when she spotted me. I took a cup from the cupboard, poured a cup of coffee for myself, and sat down at the breakfast table in the small room adjoining the kitchen. While I poured my coffee, Grandmother cut me a piece of her homemade apple pie and placed the enormous slice in front of my empty chair. The full press had begun.

"Mother and I have been talking," my mother said. "She agrees with me that the school would be an excellent opportunity for you to turn your life around."

"You are persistent," I told Mother. "You are good at strategy. But unfortunately, the product still remains the same. Send me to Paris for a year, and I promise to come back a changed young man." This evoked a laugh from Grandmother.

Mother remained in that serious mode. "Cal, your grandmother and I feel you need a bit more encouragement."

"Ah, a bribe. Just what I've been waiting for."

"Call it that if you wish," Mother said. "But if you agree to go to Texas, and you graduate the military school there, we both feel you deserve to have a new car as a graduation present."

The ante had now been considerably raised in this poker game. I already held the winning cards and had played them close to the vest to my advantage. "Oh. What kind of car?"

"We thought you should choose what you'd like," Grandmother said.

"Let me think your offer over."

"Let me know by tomorrow," Mother said. "I have to find out if they still have space available."

"All right. Excuse me."

I finished off the pie, a piece of which alone might have enticed me to go to Texas, and drank the remainder of my coffee before I left the table and went into my room. With the door shut, I clenched both fists and did a silent scream of WOW. I mean, WOW! To get a new car, one I could choose, exceeded all expectations. One of those little foreign jobs could be fun, a Jaguar or an Austin Healy. I'd read somewhere that Francoise Sagan, the eighteen-year-old author of *Bonjour Tristesse*, had bought a Jaguar with the money she earned from the book. I sat down on the bed but couldn't stop thinking about this unexpected twist.

I'd already psyched myself up for going. I'd read enough popular psychology books to know that I didn't have much confidence in myself. Worse, I didn't know where my talents lay or if any existed at all. I really had no specific idea about what direction I wanted to go in after finishing high school. Mother had a point about all that. In my mind, this school had become a challenge. What could be worse to attend than a military school? I hated the whole stupid idea of the military. I hated the idea of the draft. You bring people to boot camp and train them how to kill people. What good does that do? Now, I could infiltrate the enemy camp where the military mind would reveal itself to me. The students and faculty would make an interesting psychological study. Exactly, I wondered, what kind of people have a desire to train and learn how to kill other people? No doubt, I would return from school a year later, wiser, a different person, stronger for having conquered adversity. Maybe I would come out of the experience with a whole new outlook on life, a stronger, tougher me who could stand up to Keith and other phony types. Maybe the new me would be able to find a steady girl. At the very worst, this would be an adventure, and I felt ready for a challenge. The possibilities seemed endless, and all through the dinner and the rest of the evening, I couldn't stop thinking about what might change in my life.

I woke up early the next morning, lying in bed and thinking, wondering what the school would physically look like. I didn't even know its' name or the location of the school in Texas. As soon as the clock struck nine, I dressed and went upstairs to knock at Mother's bedroom door.

"Come in," Mother answered in a sleepy voice.

I burst through the door. "You wanted to know about my decision. I've made one. "

Before I could say more, she cut in, "I just want you to know that no matter what you've decided, I won't bother you about this further. "

"You're going to have to, though, because I've decided to give the place a try."

She sat up in bed, and her face lit up brighter than a flash bulb on a camera.

"I couldn't be happier, Cal. I know the school will be good for you. I just have to telephone them to make sure they still have openings."

"We'll see how good the place is for me. I'm not convinced, but I'm willing to give my best shot and see what transpires. By the way, does this military school have a name?"

"Roxwell Military Academy," she announced as she climbed out of bed. "I'm going to go downstairs right now to call your uncle Sid. He said he would get you enrolled and act as your guardian while you are there."

I made what I thought represented a smart salute, like one I'd seen in war films. "Yes, Ma'am."

Mother, still in her nightclothes, went off to make her phone call, and I trailed after her all the way down the stairs. Grandmother was already at work. She always woke up early and had a pot of coffee ready on the counter. Each breakfast had become a do-it-yourself affair. I put two pieces of toast in the toaster and kept my eyes peeled for Keith.uk I couldn't see him around, probably sleeping in as usual, I concluded.

A short while later, Mother joined me at the breakfast table. She could look radiant when happy. This morning, she looked radiant. "Sid said there wouldn't be any problem. He promised to get you enrolled today. You should be happy."

"That remains to be seen," I told her. She seemed to have put all her faith in that Texas school, the last hope for someone who, she had convinced herself, would remain a loser otherwise, which was obviously me.

"I didn't tell you, but earlier in the summer, I spoke with Mr. Roxwell personally about you. I had a concern that the school might be too difficult for you since you are not from Texas, but he assured me that students come from all over the country, and even places like South America." That she had called the school and talked to the head of the place didn't surprise me.

 Sid called back from Houston, where he lived and had worked as an engineer, later in the morning to say that he had enrolled me over the phone. He also had Mom write down a list of articles I needed to bring. As soon as she talked to him, she knocked at my door and gave me the "good" news. "So if you have no plans today, we can go shopping for the items. School starts at the end of August," she informed me.

"I'm free. What do we need?"

She reeled off a list that included sheets, pillowcases, blankets, towels, undershorts, and undershirts. "I may need some new pants and shirts," I added.

"No, the school provides you with your uniforms."

The first wave of shock settled over me. Of course, military school, military uniform. I hadn't even thought about what I would wear there. *Duh.*

She read my expression and placed her hand on top of mine to reassure me. "Don't worry. You'll get used to wearing those clothes. Everyone does."

"I hope you're right." Though I'd gone a long way out to convince myself to go, underneath, the old fears hung around like bats in a cave.

"What else did the guy say?" I asked. "Did he mention anything about holidays? Will I be able to come home?"

She shook her head. "I didn't ask. I thought for Christmas, you might stay in Houston with your aunt and uncle."

Suddenly, being home for Christmas became urgent.

"Can't I come home if I want to?" I asked her.

"We'll see, Cal," she said. "If, when the time comes, you think coming home is that important, we'll find a way to bring you home. Let's not worry about that now. I'm going to get dressed so we can go shopping for what you need."

An hour later, Grandmother, who had taken a day off work, Mother, Keith, and I were on the road to San Francisco. At Union Square, we split up. The two ladies left to shop while Keith and I rode a cable car all the way out to Fisherman's Wharf. We had lunch there in a place full of wood and fish symbols overlooking the water, a restaurant much too crowded and noisy for my taste. Keith liked seeing young female tourists all around. He tried to hustle a couple of them, but they ignored him. Did that shake his confidence? Not one bit. He rationalized that they were dogs and not worth the pursuit.

The last few days of our visit proved as boring as the first three. I had bought a couple of books in San Francisco and finished them both before we left. On the way home, I once again got to split the driving with Keith. As I sat behind the wheel of the Cadillac, rolling down the 101, I understood the feeling of power that comes from power, especially when I put my foot down on the gas and the car responded; that sensation, above all, provided the highlight of the week.

CHAPTER SIX

The pace to move me out the door accelerated the moment we returned to our Los Angeles apartment. Mom called the airport to arrange a non-stop flight to Houston, and she arranged for my Uncle Sid and Aunt Esther to meet me at the airport. They assured my mother I could stay a few days with them, and they would drive me to the school.

My thoughts began to dwell on the city I would leave behind. A big, sprawling place, the City of the Angels remained the only home I'd known. I knew parts of the sprawl pretty well because we'd moved around so often, and I'd been to a variety of schools, grammar (3), junior highs (2), and high schools (1). Constant movement could explain the reason I developed so few friendships.

When I think of LA, the city reminds me of an oversized baby, one whose body has grown much faster than its legs. A lot of cities have subways and other mass transits, but not LA. We have buses and the red car that runs on tracks, but the city itself is so spread out, that many places are still difficult to reach. Freeways make some difference, but a lot of the city doesn't have any freeways nearby, and those locations are only accessible on surface streets. Los Angeles doesn't have the culture of San Francisco, and though we have ethnic neighborhoods, the city isn't a melting pot like New York. Most of the people here came from the Midwest or South after the war to look for jobs and sunshine. A lot of refugees streaming in from lousy climates don't produce a city of brainiacs. When I think of LA, I think of Brentwood, where I live, Santa Monica, Culver City, Burbank, and Beverly Hills; little suburbs woven like a mosaic through big Los Angeles, melting into one another like pieces of cheese spreading out across the top of a pizza in a hot oven. Some of these small cities and towns have their own governments, like Santa Monica or Burbank. They may be independent, but they don't cooperate much with each other.

What I like about LA is the parks, great parks like Griffith Park with its observatory, playgrounds for kids, outdoor sports, and even if we don't have a major league baseball team, there is a pro football team, the Los Angeles Rams. My favorite baseball team is the Los Angeles Angels, who play in the Pacific Coast League and are fun to watch. The best part about living here is those days you can go skiing in the mountains in the morning, then drive down the mountain to the beach for a swim in the afternoon. Where else can you do such a crazy thing?

Since my plans were now settled in cement, the first move I made after we came home was to call Ray to give him the big news. He immediately felt sorry for himself. Who would he go to the racetrack with? Who would cut a class with him or go off behind the bleachers to join in the dice game played during nutrition? I had to say, "Hey, feel for me, punk; I'm the one going off into the Texas army. Cool it." Anyway, we made plans for a final day at the track and for a last cruise of the "Boulevard" on the Friday night before I left. Ray promised that just the two of us would go.

The most amazing change came from my brother, Keith. Mr. Perfect backed off for once in his miserable life. He couldn't believe I would actually leave town. He kept telling me it took guts to do something like this. "You amaze me, brother," he told me, even before we left San Mateo. "I didn't think you had the balls to take on something like that. I wouldn't."

All of a sudden, I began to feel nostalgic, as if I had already left everything behind and had relocated to Texas. What kind of trade-off had I made, I wondered, leaving behind a beautiful place with great weather, with horse racing almost year around, with beaches and beautiful girls, for a uniform and a rifle in an unfamiliar town called Cullen and a school that specialized in training people how to kill? In Los Angeles, you remained free to do what you wanted. You could get rich and famous or live quite well as poor and unknown because used cars were cheap, as were gas, apartments, food, and almost everything. Maybe Los Angeles seemed like just another city to most people, like Chicago, Minneapolis, or Baltimore, but LA was MY city, and that meant a lot to me.

I still had a couple of weeks remaining to say goodbye to my hometown. I decided to use the time to enjoy every moment. I talked my suddenly cooperative mother into letting me use her car as long as she didn't need to drive somewhere herself. Certain parts of the city felt special for me, and I wanted to bid those places a fond farewell. A year, or more accurately nine months away from home, sounded like an eternity. These familiar landmarks I had taken for granted as always being there when I wanted them, but perhaps they wouldn't be here when I returned. They needed to be imprinted in my mind so if the school became oppressive, I could remember what I would be returning to: the Los Angeles I loved.

A couple of days after we returned from San Mateo, I borrowed Mom's car to drive to the beach in Santa Monica. I had only visited there on occasion since we'd moved into our apartment with the sparkling, kidney-shaped pool in the center of the building. I reached Pacific Coast Highway, which ran alongside the endless expanse of the blue Pacific and sat for a moment in the parked car to enjoy the lapping of the waves and the ocean spread out before me. Nothing looked more impressive. I exited the car only to encounter a slight breeze and inhale the smell of the ocean, which felt like inhaling an elixir. My whole body began to vibrate. I walked down to the shore, removed my shoes, and stood with my feet in the sand, watching the waves beating down along the shore beside the Santa Monica pier. As a kid, one of my stepfathers had taken me fishing off that pier, and now, as an almost adult, I stood beneath those pylons, ready to take my first dip into the ocean of life.

I'd read that Texas had a body of water somewhere, the Gulf of Mexico, but how did that compare to the great Pacific Ocean? From what I could tell when I checked Cullen, the town that housed Roxwell Academy out on a map, the school looked extremely distant from the Gulf.

The salt air must have stirred my brain cells, for I remembered back a year when an incident took place on the beach right below Ocean Park Pier, a pier about a mile from this one in Santa Monica. Two guys in my club, Larry and Sandy, and three girls we knew from school who were in a corresponding girl's club all went to the beach together. Ocean Park Pier housed a big amusement park that recently closed, but last year, they had a roller coaster, whirligig, carnival games, and a merry-go-round for the kids. We were having a great time going on rides, playing the games, and eating lots of junky food.

About an hour or two after we arrived, we ran out of money. Since we'd come on a Sunday, the pier was packed with visitors. Sandy came up with a plan to get some more bread. He told the three girls to go around asking for pennies, nickels, and dimes, saying they were being initiated into a club and the group that got the most money earned a special reward. Larry, Sandy, and I would hang out in the background to make sure they didn't have any problems. The girls thought this sounded fun and agreed to become sexy panhandlers.

Half an hour later, the three girls, after prancing around in their bathing suits, had collected two and a half dollars. The plan seemed to be working well. Then, they made the mistake of approaching a group of guys hanging out in a corner of the pier. To me, these guys looked like dope addicts, the kind of losers you see hanging around amusement parks looking for trouble. As the girls wiggled past them, asking for money, the guys kept shaking their heads. But when the girls left, these guys followed, and the three of us looked at each other, anticipating trouble. When the girls looked back and saw these guys following, they ran to us for protection. The guys continued in our direction.

"Hey man," a heavyset guy with tattoos said to Larry, "Those chicks with you?"

"Yeah," Larry answered, trying to hide his fear.

"Then why are they coming here wiggling their asses like

they wanted it?"

He must have been their leader because the others hung back. Frankly speaking, he looked bigger than the three of us put together and looked as if he ate nails for breakfast.

Larry attempted to explain our fundraising scheme.

"So, how much bread did those chicks collect?"

The girls cowered behind us. The three of us stood side by side a few feet from this midway monster. "About fifty cents," Larry said, pulling a fistful of change from his pocket.

"I could sure do with a beer, man," the leader said, approaching Larry. "How about you lending me enough to get one?"

Quickly, Larry handed him some coins. The man looked down at them and, apparently satisfied, turned to lead his pack away, though several muttered bitterly he should have taken more.

Shook up, we didn't stay longer but headed straight to the car and as far away from the pier as possible. This had been a wake-up call.

That had been my first sort-of date, and the smell of the ocean stirred the memory. In a sense, that date had been a failure, as was the second one I had a few months later, the only other one during my junior year. I asked this girl to our club dance and party. She looked attractive, pretty, but not too pretty, a brown-haired girl who sat behind me in my English class. She had a beautiful voice that purred like a kitten. She agreed to go with me. When we arrived, and I confessed I couldn't dance, instead of offering to teach me, she asked me to take her home early. She claimed she had to study for a test.

I stayed at the beach a while, then drove back into Hollywood to go to my favorite hot dog stand, Pink's, at the corner of Melrose and La Brea. Pink's sold the best chilidogs in LA. I bought two of them, feeling the chili spread in a mess across my cheeks after each bite, a process that required the serious use of napkins. I sat alone on a bench and tried to decide what to do next on this day reserved just for me.

I drove East on Sunset and headed toward Griffith Park. I hadn't been to the zoo in years. I'd always loved going there as a kid, particularly the snake house. Snakes have always held a fascination for me. One summer, about three years ago, my Mother had sent Keith and me up to San Mateo on the train to spend a week with our grandparents. One day, I saw a cage of snakes for sale in a pet store. They cost a quarter each, garter snakes about two feet long. I bought two of them. During the train ride home, I kept them in a box under my seat. Keith wanted to let them out in the railroad car for exercise.

This was during the time Mom was dating Hugo, the psychiatrist, and the three of us were still living in the rental house she'd shared with Carl until she tossed him out. I kept the snakes in my room, much to my mother's disapproval, and fed them what I'd been told to feed them. We became good friends. They were green, and they used to wrap themselves around my hand when I picked them up. Their heads would rest right on my index finger, and I would stroke the top of their heads with my thumb. Then everything changed. One day, I came home to find eight little baby snakes crawling around in their box. My mother found ten snakes, ten too many, and she pushed me to get rid of the lot of them. Imagine a mother having no appreciation of another's motherhood. I argued with her that they were harmless, and in the end, she let me keep them as I had promised to make sure they stayed in the box.

I couldn't believe what happened next. About a week after the eight babies arrived, another batch appeared with another nine snakes, making seventeen babies with evidently two mommies. I fed them and watched over them after school, and all went well until, I don't know how this happened, a hole opened in the bottom of the box (Keith was the prime suspect here), and all the babies vanished into an exploratory mode, poking around the house. Over the next month, the baby snakes would appear, sometimes in the breakfast room or the living room. One of them ended up in Keith's bed (I wonder how he got there), and my mother was pissed because none of her friends would visit her until we moved in with Hugo, the psychiatrist.

This whole snake episode came to an unhappy ending. The first time I took up one of the snakes after the babies were born, she bit me. The bite didn't hurt that much, but I became upset because I thought we were friends. So I unwound her and tossed her onto the grass in the backyard. The next day, the other one also bit me. Now, I had no big snakes and lots of little ones running about the house. When we moved months later, my snake breeding days came to an abrupt end.

Though the afternoon heat beat down on everyone, I walked around the zoo paths for a long time. I mentioned how I have always loved animals, and as I stared at the cages and outdoor areas containing monkeys, elephants, and giraffes, I wondered what they must think when they see us. Do we look like gaping idiots to them? How do they feel about being locked up all day and night? Do they even know there is a place on this earth where they could live free? I know being locked up would drive me nuts. Did they know they were captive, or had they been raised that way and therefore didn't know any alternatives? I sat down at a refreshment stand with a cold coke and tried to sort out my feelings about wild animals living in a zoo setting.

As the afternoon waned, I headed back across town to have dinner with my mother and Keith. I couldn't get over how nicely they treated me, almost as if they suddenly realized I would soon be gone and they would miss me.

After dinner, I borrowed the car once more to go to the Hollywood Bowl. The Hollywood Bowl is a summer institution during our warm summer nights. On Tuesday nights, the night I went, they played classical music. The bowl-shaped amphitheater accommodates thousands of people, with tiered seating in the back and boxes in the front closest to the stage. You can sit up in the bleachers for seventy-five cents. I parked on a side street and took the long walk over to the bowl. Hugo started the habit of my going, for he'd take me to hear classical music a couple of times each summer when he was around. We would often sit in a box and have a fancy box dinner before the program started. On my own, I bought a ticket that gave me access to the nosebleed section. From my vantage point, the bowl looked dwarfed, with the musicians barely visible, but the music washed my soul as they somehow piped the sound loud enough for the entire audience to hear. An evening breeze reduced the heat. Above the bowl, with lights illuminating the stage, stars shined. I closed my eyes and, listened to the music flow, and wondered how I could find anything to match this experience in Texas.

I just need to say that classical isn't the only kind of music I enjoy listening to. I grew up on a program called The Hit Parade, and I like both popular and new rock and roll music. Chuck Berry, Fats Domino, and Little Richard are great musicians. Every week, there seems to be some hot new song out on the airwaves.

After the concert, I drove home along the Sunset Strip, passing Ciro's and all the famous nightclubs where actors and actresses hang out. What a treasure that day had been, mine with the freedom to do whatever I wished. Who could ask for more?

All the next day, I just hung around the pool. That evening, Mother's new friend Sasha came over to take us out to dinner. I had asked to eat at the Samovar, our favorite little Russian restaurant near Paramount Studios.

Sasha, a Russian guy, had slicked-back black hair and puffiness below his blue eyes. He moved like a heavyweight boxer. He played the cello in an important studio orchestra. On occasion, he would come over to join us for dinner, and when he did, he usually fell asleep in the living room after the meal, snoring loudly and cracking up Keith and me with the sound, which registered like a deep tenor snore.

The couple who ran the Samovar, Alexi and Olga Pushkin, like Sasha, were real Russians. They took great interest in their restaurant and patrons. An older couple, small, very nice, they particularly loved to talk in Russian with Sasha. They always scurried about during dinner, making sure the food was all right. Keith had skipped joining us, having another date to deal with, which worked okay for me. The owner, Alexi, came over to visit and sat down with us for a few minutes. I ordered my favorite dish, cabbage borscht, with big chunks of beef in the soup. In the background, the jukebox played some bouncy Russian polka so that we had to raise our voices to speak to each other. When I told the Pushkins I was going away for a year, they brought me a special dessert, a Russian apple cake that tasted delicious. The husband and wife hovered over the table as I ate it, making sure that I enjoyed every bite. They walked us to the door and, over the noise of the jukebox, wished me a good trip. I felt great when they said they'd miss me.

The following day, Ray and I had scheduled to make a pilgrimage to the racetrack. We drove almost 100 miles to Del Mar, on the ocean near San Diego, as they have the August meet there "where the turf meets the surf" every year. The day grew hot, but by the time we reached the track, a cool ocean breeze made the afternoon comfortable. All the way down, Ray babbled about which horse he thought looked good and which one didn't, and he kept pushing me to reveal which horses I planned to bet on. I only had twenty dollars that I'd saved up, so I had to bet carefully. On the way home from the Russian restaurant, I'd bought a racing form and pored over each race at home, trying to figure out who had the best shot at winning.

We arrived a few minutes before the first race. I bet two dollars to win and two dollars to show on the horse I'd selected. Since Ray had to place our bets, he knew which horse I'd chosen.

While he waited in line, I noticed an odd situation, one I'd never thought about before. Post time (when the race begins) was two minutes away, and the lines at the betting windows stayed long. People at the back of the line, afraid of missing a betting opportunity, approached those closer to the front and asked if they would place a bet for them. What fascinated me is that old ladies approached old ladies, Negroes asked other Negroes, and Mexicans or Asian people sought their own kind.

The day's races provided limited success, and by the time we left, neither of us had done very well. I came out five dollars ahead, and Ray lost ten dollars. We decided to leave before the last race in order to beat the crowd traffic on the long ride home. We walked out of the track passing grounds littered with discarded losing tickets and racing forms, the residue of people who thought, like us, they knew the right way to bet. As we made our way through the parking lot toward the car, we spotted a small group of men shielded behind a car toward the rear of the lot. Ray and I edged close enough to see they were shooting dice. A few of the men wore suits, which reassured me this probably wasn't a crooked game. Crooked or straight, a few rolls of the dice, and I'd lost my five-dollar profit while Ray went another ten dollars down.

A frustrated pair of young gamblers drove back to Los Angeles that afternoon. We got home too late to go anywhere, so I just stayed home and watched TV.

Friday, I spent running errands and buying a few odds and ends I'd need for the trip. I drove Mother's car into Hollywood and parked the beast in a lot. I walked over to Hollywood Blvd, close to the corner of Cahuenga, and stopped for a moment to contemplate all I would be leaving behind. Here, I stood on the most famous street in the country, except for maybe Broadway in New York. For a moment, tears clouded my eyes, but I quickly brushed them away. Real men don't cry, or so I'd been told.

What set me off was a girl who passed by where I stood. She wore a pair of tight black Capri pants and a bright red sweater. When I say tight, these pants looked as if they had been sewn around her legs. She had a voluptuous figure that fought to burst out of the clothing that imprisoned her body, and her natural blond hair hung halfway down her back. In true LA fashion, she kept her eyes hidden behind a pair of sunglasses. I began to follow her as she walked along the street, intrigued about of all things, her sunglasses. Were they drilled into her head? What kind of brain dwelled behind them?

Nor was I the only one to notice her, though, from the tilt of their heads, I guessed those male viewers focused on areas below the sunglasses. As she walked along the sidewalk, those other faces, also hidden behind various brands of sunglasses, turned to stare. I backed away just as a couple of walking sunglasses began to fall in step behind her. From across the street, a pair of sunglasses put two fingers in his mouth to let out a loud wolf whistle. I began to wonder if Hollywood was nothing more than a solid mass of sunglass commercials with a few thousand heads attached for the purpose of promoting them.

Now as I walked in the opposite direction from the girl, I couldn't help but notice how all the people that passed wore sunglasses. A whole family of sunglasses appeared: mother, father, three children of varying sizes, each sported his or her own pair. A pair of sunglasses dressed in a suit rushed by carrying a briefcase. Tourists sporting Hawaiian shirts and suntan lotion wore sunglasses. They were easy to identify, always recognizable by their red sunburned skin or pale white skin.

My head wanted to explode. I retreated into a service station bathroom. With a sudden, unexpected motion, I ripped my own sunglasses off my face and smashed them against the bathroom floor. Never again would I hide from the world beneath a pair of dark green glasses.

Seething, but without understanding the source of my anger, I retrieved the car, drove back to the apartment, and dived into the pool to calm down.

Ray picked me up at eight o'clock that evening, and we cruised a very different-looking "Boulevard" than I'd visited earlier in the day. Back and forth we inched from block to block several times without any success. We headed for Bob's, where we hadn't been since the night we'd gone out with Jack and been tossed from the movie theater. Bob's had a fat kid, their "Big Boy" logo, standing in front of the restaurant. Inside, the booths and counter were usually full, and in the back of the restaurant, a large parking area offered curbside area service where carhops would take your order and bring back trays that attached just below your car window so you could eat in your car. I loved to go to Bob's because this seemed to be our own little teenage city. Other kids from other schools ate there, too, but I would always see people I knew, those who had been in a class, club mates, people I recognized but whose names I didn't know. We could be content knowing that if any problems arose, there were a lot of high school classmates to help out. Even though Bob's is a long drive from my mother's apartment in Brentwood, I still found myself continuing to come here. I don't think I've visited more than three other drive-ins in my whole life.

Ray and I parked in the lot and walked inside. We found an empty booth across from the counter and sat down. The booths are orange leather or fake leather; I'm not sure which. The tabletops are made of Formica. I ordered the Big Boy special, a hamburger, which arrived with the help of an aging waitress, on a plate with fries and a salad. Ray got the same, except he ordered a cheeseburger. A couple of kids I knew passed by, and we exchanged hellos and "How's your summer?" and all that. I'd been saying hello to kids like these for years. If they never saw me again, they wouldn't give the loss another thought. People are like that. If you're there, you are there, and if not, well, who has time to remember? The world seems to stop for no one.

That reminds me of what is odd about my relationship with Ray. If we're not talking about horse races, or girls on the "Boulevard," we don't have much to say. We actually ate our meal in silence at Bob's, and then he drove me the long distance back to my house. He promised to stop by the following Monday so we could play tennis.

The next day, I went to get a haircut. My mother convinced me a crew cut would be wise in the Texas heat, and in addition, I'd look much neater than usual. I asked the barber to give me a crew cut but not to cut the hair too short. Evidently, he wasn't the military type because he didn't pay much attention to my orders. He almost scalped me. I doubt if he left more than about a quarter of an inch anywhere on my head. Though I seldom swear, I did all the way home from the barbershop. I should have refused to pay him, but I didn't have the guts. I sure didn't tip the jerk, though.

I went into hibernation like one of those bears you read about in *National Geographic* magazine. How could I expose myself to the world looking like an army recruit who had just finished boot camp? I couldn't stop staring at that new person in the mirror. My head could have passed for a large egg with two brown yokes for eyes, one placed on each side of my nose. If I lived anywhere but LA, I wouldn't have cared so much. Most people, in most places, look and dress like bumpkins. I would have fit in as just another bumpkin. But here, the cool people would laugh at me, and the tourists would gawk. That's what tourists do. They run all over town looking for movie stars and taking pictures of whatever they can find. I didn't intend to expose myself publicly and have a dumb tourist take a snap of this bald-headed guy and paste it into his scrapbook about his trip to Hollywood. An even worse fear: what if one of those tourist types came up to ask me to pose, thinking I was some strange local type?

Ray came over Monday to take me out to play tennis. A weekend spent at home had made me stir-crazy, so I didn't cancel our play date. As soon as he walked into the house, he spotted my new look and started laughing.

"What's so damn funny?" I asked, acting as if I didn't know.

"Who scalped you? An Indian?" He burst out in hysterics at his brilliant joke.

"If you'll drop dead, I'll be happy to call the funeral home," I told him as politely as possible.

"You didn't have to pay for that, did you?"

"Oh, no. The place had a free haircut day."

"You're not too bright, are you?" He sounded his favorite retort, though I'm ten times brighter than he is. I hear that line come out of his mouth almost every time we are together. I think he's hoping to convince himself.

"C'mon, let's go play tennis." He had dressed for the occasion: white shorts, white tennis shoes, and a white T-shirt. I wore jeans, a sloppy shirt, and street shoes, my usual uniform.

"I'm not going out of the house with this haircut."

Ray sat down in a chair. "What do you mean? We were going to play tennis today."

"Yes."

"Then why aren't you going?"

"Because everyone we see on the courts will probably laugh

at me the same way you did. Most ignorant people laugh at those who look different."

"Don't act so dumb. Come on. Let's go. I love to beat the hell out of you, and this is the last chance I'll have until you come back from Texas."

Sadly true. He beat me in almost every sport where we competed. The only one I could outdo him in was bowling. I'm pretty good at bowling. I used to be in a league, and I have a couple of trophies. However, in basketball, playing one on one, or Around the World, or HORSE, he always beats me. In ping-pong, he pops me. And even in chess, he can outplay me. I don't get that last one, but he's proved his ability over and over.

He loves beating me at chess the most. He claims chess is a game for thinkers and I'm the thinker, and after we play, he runs around saying he beat the thinker. I've stopped playing with him, as he's such a lousy winner.

Ray persisted, and eventually, I relented, changing into my tennis outfit, but only after I made him promise that before I left the car, he'd go into the tennis shop next to the courts to buy me a cap, which I would wear all during the game. "That's crazy stupid," he said. But I held out, and he finally relented.

After he bought the cap and carried it out to the car, where I waited, we went out on a free court and started to volley. I played better than usual. The more pissed I become, the better my game becomes. However, Ray had bought an oversized cap, which kept flying off my head as I ran to return shots. So I'd stop right in the middle of a volley to scoop the cap off the court. Ray really became irritated. We played two sets, which took about an hour each, as I had to constantly chase after my cap. As usual, he ended up beating me, and with the twin issues of the afternoon heat and the oversized cap, we were both pissed at one another by the time we headed back to my place. A dip in the pool cooled us off, though I continued to wear the cap while lounging in the shallow end there. Before Ray left, he promised to return later in the week to say goodbye and have a swim.

The next day, a catalogue arrived from Roxwell Academy. My mother rushed out to the pool holding the paper catalogue in her hand as if she held a precious piece of jewelry. She found me stretched out in a lounge chair, and she sat down on the edge of the chair near my knees. The publication she handed me looked slick, showing smiling boys in their military uniforms in the classroom, at drill, and playing sports. "I think you are going to be very happy there," my Mother concluded after I had thumbed through the catalogue, stopping at various pages to wonder exactly what I had committed to.

"Why do you say that?"

"Well, the place looks so, well, wholesome."

Not the description I would have chosen. Scary would have been more appropriate. I saw a foreign place with strange ideas and customs, full of white Southern boys. How could I possibly fit in?

When I remained silent, Mother continued. "Cal, I do hope you will take the school seriously. The catalogue talks about how they try to balance the lives of their students. If you'll give the place half a chance and not go there with a chip on your shoulder, you will be rewarded in the long run."

"Providing I manage to survive the experience."

Her expression indicated those weren't the words she wanted to hear.

"I will do my best," I promised.

"That's all I ask. I have no doubt that if you apply yourself, you will succeed."

"I'm glad one of us has so much faith in me."

She smiled. "I know you will do your best. I have to get back upstairs. You don't need the car today, do you?"

"No, have fun wherever you are going."

She left me with the school catalogue and my thoughts. This time, I thumbed page after page, trying to glean what the future would hold for me. Several pages dealt with the distinguished graduates of Roxwell Prep. Several army men, most of them lieutenants or higher, had graduated from there, and a number went on to attend college at West Point. Underneath each picture, the caption told the story of the distinguished military man who shared his very positive experience at Roxwell. The pictures reminded me of those signs they have in front of post offices showing a man in a uniform looking proud. "The Marine Corps Builds Men," or "Your Future is in the United States Army." Roxwell builds men. Everyone builds men. This pitch did not impress me.

I continued thumbing through the catalogue, hoping to find a section on people who did not want to be men or at least military men. Was there a place for someone who did not want to be a man's man? I'm not muscular like Keith. I have a small potbelly, but I'm not overweight. I've usually avoided fights, having had only one in my life.

That battle came when I was twelve, and the other guy came after me. A friend and I were tossing a football around in the park when a kid came over and tried to butt in to catch the ball. Neither of us knew this kid. He was shorter than me, but he kept cutting in front of me, trying to catch the ball. But because of my height, I managed to catch the passes instead. This seemed to frustrate him. After two or three misses, he turned red in his face and charged me like a bull. He took a couple of wild swings, and of course, I had to swing back. We rolled around on the ground, and I punched him a couple of times. That was the extent of our encounter. Even though he stalked off defeated, I went home in tears.

After that incident, I learned to avoid fights. Carl tried to teach me how to defend myself. He taught me the proper stance, how to bob and weave, throw a left jab, and even land a 1-2-3. But I never used what he taught me. Fighting seems like nothing more than a release of aggression, and there seem to be many alternative ways to do that without beating someone up.

The catalogue showed a private lake for fishing and swimming. I like fishing and would have gone this week except for the embarrassing haircut. The catalogue also showed photos of a tennis court, a gymnasium for playing basketball, and two swimming pools. Roxwell Academy wasn't only a military school but the Texas version of a country club.

Somehow, this reassured me. With all those features, the place couldn't be too bad. As long as they gave me a decent mix of academic courses, I should be fine.

On Thursday, Ray dropped by for a few minutes to say goodbye. He didn't go swimming, and he seemed uncomfortable and eager to leave.

My mother sometimes gets a certain expression on her face, a guilty look, as if she has done something wrong and regrets her mistake. That's the look she displayed when we sat at the breakfast table Friday morning. She'd made me pancakes. She sat staring at me. "Cal, tomorrow night will be yours. You can choose where you'd like to have dinner, and I'll make a reservation for the three of us. Afterwards, if you want to go to a play or a movie, we'll go with you. It's your choice."

She felt guilty for sure. "Anywhere?"

"Within reason, of course."

What's the reason?"

"Where would you like to eat?"

"Don the Beachcomber?"

"No."

"Chasins?"

"No."

"Romanoffs?"

"No?"

"Pink's hot dog stand?"

"Don't be ridiculous."

"You told me to choose, but you keep knocking my choices down."

"We're not millionaires, Cal."

"But you did say anyplace."

"Within reason."

"How about Steer's?"

"That's okay."

"Can I have a steak?"

"Of course you can. Is there anything you'd like to do afterward?"

"Maybe go to a play. I have to see what's around."

"Fine. You choose what you want to see and make the reservations."

"Okay."

In Los Angeles, finding an interesting play is often a challenge. I'd seen a few good ones in the past year or two. I combed the paper from that morning and chose a play in a small theater in Hollywood. The theme was Southern, and that sounded interesting.

Eager to get started, I dressed early. I wore my only suit, a charcoal one, and a white shirt and black tie. Keith wore a suit that didn't quite fit him, but for some reason, he still looked better in his than I did in mine. We went to Steer's steak house, and I ordered the fillet mignon. The slice of meat turned out to be so tender I could cut pieces off with my fork. The place had a mysterious look, a darkened room with plush booths. I kept my eye open for celebrities. Not that I would have done anything if I'd spotted one, but you can always drop a name like, oh, I had dinner at Steer's, and so-and-so was there. With my baked potato, creamed spinach, and salad, I enjoyed every bite of dinner.

Of course, we lingered too long and had to rush to the theater, only a short drive away. The small space only seated about fifty people with every seat occupied. The stage was at the level of the first row of seats, while each of the other four rows had a slight elevation. The interior looked as if this had once been a storefront.

The story that had attracted my attention presented a touchy theme. The son of a rich southern banker returned to his hometown after attending university at a northern school.

His father gives him a position in his bank. He meets Negro clients who want to borrow money to start businesses or for other reasons, but every time the kid recommends a loan, the loan committee vetoes his proposal. He tries secretly to find ways around what is obviously total racism. There is a terrific scene where the father finds out what he's doing, calls him into his office and explains this is the way things are done here in the South. If he doesn't like the system, he should move back up North. The father even threatens to disinherit him if he doesn't shape up. So, the son agrees to follow bank policy. There is a scene where the father takes him to a rundown business that is months behind in payments to another bank. He uses this as an example of how worthless the Negroes are, how irresponsible, etc. As the boy bends to his father's will, he begins rejecting loans and talking with fellow employees like an "Old boy," complaining about how dangerous and evil Negroes are.

This play gave me a lot of food for thought. As the story unfolded, I kept wondering how I might react when I encountered racism down South. Only a few years earlier, a young Negro child, Emmett Till, had been killed by a gang of whites supposedly for whistling at a white woman. While I sat riveted in my seat throughout the play, Keith took a more relaxed position. Fortunately, he didn't snore.

Sunday, Mother and I spent packing a trunk with what the catalogue said I needed for a year at school. Keith had promised to take the trunk to the railway express for shipping after I left.

Monday morning finally arrived along with a rise in my blood pressure. My mother drove me to the airport. I couldn't sit still in the car. I kept thinking about the future I'd carved for myself. How upset would Mother be if I failed at this as well?

She started her pep talk on the drive to the airport. The monologue, only punctured by a few uh-huhs from me, continued as we entered the terminal, waited in line to check my small bag, and walked together to the gate from where, ticket in hand, I would depart.

Mom looked about 25 years old in her white summer dress and fashionable sun hat.

"You're sure you have everything, Cal?" She asked for the eighth time.

"Uh-huh."

"You'll be good?" Fourth time for that question.

"Of course."

"You'll write and let me know all about it."

"Uh-huh."

"Do you have enough money?"

I could have answered no to the last question each of the five times she asked and possibly accumulated enough cash to have taken a trip to Europe.

"I hope so."

"What I've given you should cover your expenses until you reach the school."

"Okay."

"Don't feel embarrassed if you have to borrow some from your aunt and uncle."

"I won't."

Then, for the first time, I heard the magic words: "You can come home for the Christmas holidays if you like. We'll find a way to work that out."

"Great."

Her next words were drowned out by an announcement over the PA system.

"YOUR ATTENTION PLEASE. FLIGHT 17 IS NOW RECEIVING ALL PASSENGERS AT GATE # SIX."

"I better go," I told her.

"You'll be good?"

"Yes, Mother."

"And you'll write?"

"Of course. I love you."

We hugged, and tears filled her eyes so that a bit of her mascara began to drip onto one cheek. Her sudden sentimentality during the past week surprised me. I sensed something psychological about it. As long as I stayed home, she didn't seem to want me there. But as soon as I prepared to take off, she became a different person, treating me the way I had hoped to be treated all along.

She stood watching as I showed my ticket and walked across the departure area to board the plane. A last wave from the steps and I went aboard.

The stewardess with big brown eyes and short blond hair smiled as I handed her my ticket. She looked very smart dressed in her American Airlines outfit. She wore a baby blue skirt with a matching jacket buttoned over her blouse and a small smart hat in the same color. For an instant, I thought about going to pilot's school. If they all looked like her, I would have an incentive to finish.

She brought me back to my window seat, and a girl around my age stood up in the aisle seat next to mine to let me pass. Her attractive appearance promised to make the journey a pleasant one. As the plane taxied down the runway, then took off, I looked out the window intent on getting a final aerial view of my city.

And what an amazing city I lived in. I could imagine no other city presenting itself so beautifully from the air. The streets looked spread out with empty land between collections of houses, some built in the hills, offering lots of space for the city to grow. Houses dotted the landscape everywhere, many of them with blue swimming pools. With the ocean to the west and the mountains to the east, this Los Angeles represented a paradise…a paradise I had decided to temporarily leave behind.

Once the plane had left the city behind, the mountains and desert loomed ahead, and my attention shifted to my traveling companion. Her mature look suggested she might be a couple of years older than me, a long-haired brunette whose brown eyes were engrossed in a popular fashion magazine. She wore a bright summer dress, white with a pattern that looked very modern.

"Hello," I said. She glanced at me a moment as if trying to size me up before she responded.

"Are you going to Houston?" An admittedly stupid question that just popped out, as the plane did not stop anywhere else along the way. If I'd been smarter, I would have said, "Is Houston your final destination?" She must have found the question equally stupid, as she said, "Uh huh," and then returned to reading her magazine.

Rejected, and embarrassed by my own stupid approach, I picked up a magazine I'd bought and began to thumb through it, though my mind went to Keith as I wondered what he'd do in this situation. Knowing him, he probably would have suggested the two of them talk things over someplace quiet in the back of the plane.

The magazine quickly lost my attention. I turned my head to begin staring at the clouds outside the window, as there wasn't much else to see at 20,000 feet. I tried to make out the curvature of the earth but couldn't see that clearly. Finally, I just stared straight ahead with my arms folded.

A soft female voice interrupted my pout. I looked over and saw the girl had placed her magazine in her lap and stared straight at me. "I didn't mean to be rude," she told me, "but this story engrossed me, and I had to read the ending."

A new energy shot through me. "No problem. My name is Calvin Carter, but everyone calls me Cal."

"HI, Cal. I'm Judy Goodwin."

"Do you live in Houston or LA?" I wanted to know.

"I live in LA. But I'm going to Houston to visit relatives before I fly to New York. Then I'm taking a ship to Europe. I'm going to stay there for a year."

Europe? That sounded so exotic and far away for a kid headed to Texas. "I guess you've graduated from high school then?"

She nodded. "I have. I went to a girl's school called Marlborough. Now, I'm taking a year off to travel before I start college. I plan to go to Stanford."

Marlborough, Stanford. These buzz words signaled mucho

dinero and indicated that this girl would be out of my league. Yet, she acted nice and friendly. "What do you want to study?" I asked.

I loved the way her lips moved when she answered, almost as if she didn't speak at all. "Molecular biology," came the reply. "Stanford is great for the sciences. What are you going to Houston for?"

I'm pretty good at thinking on my feet. "I'm going to visit family too. Just for a couple of weeks. I don't know them very well."

"I hear it's really hot there."

"I've heard that too. That it's humid all day and night, and the heat just drains you."

She didn't act the least bit stuck up, the way so many private school girls act. After a short time, I decided to find out what she thought about my mother's educational choice. "Actually, after I visit my relatives in Houston, I'm going to a military school in Texas for my last year of high school."

Surprise registered across her face. She had high cheekbones that went higher with her look of surprise. "You don't seem the type for that," she said. "I pegged you more for the artistic type."

I may have been in an airplane, but I found myself floating in space. "I got talked into going there. I actually hate the military. But I'm interested in psychology and experiencing the place from that perspective." I felt pleased with the way that sentence emerged.

This led us into a long discussion about President Eisenhower, the military, the stupidity of military schools, and the horrors of war. She proved herself very intelligent with thoughtful opinions, especially for someone so pretty. Too bad she had plans in place for such a great future. If she had stayed in Houston, maybe we could have hated Texas together.

With Judy as company, the trip passed quickly.

"Fasten your seat belts, as we will be landing in ten minutes," came the announcement from the stewardess.

If the rest of my trip could be anywhere as nice as the ride in, I would be extremely lucky.

CHAPTER SEVEN

As the passengers left the plane to walk to the gate, a blast of air from hell greeted us. A short walk in the moist, Humid air made me appreciate the dry desert air of Los Angeles. And once we entered the terminal at Hobby Airport, the air turned as chilly as an iceberg floating near the North Pole.

As I entered the waiting room, I heard a voice with a pronounced Texas accent.

"Cal, Cal," my Aunt called, hidden somewhere in the crowd of people waiting for the deplaning passengers.

"Hi," I yelled back in that direction. All across the room were Texas faces. The scene looked fairly chaotic. People stood in the way as they greeted each other and blocked the paths to the baggage claim area.

My Uncle Sid, who is slightly taller than me and stocky, broke through the crowd, came up, and shook my hand with a grip that would have caused a gorilla to wince. I couldn't remember him very well, as ten years had passed since the two of them last visited California, but he resembled his sister, my mother, except for the moustache and the receding hairline. He had the same broad face, but his skin looked a shade darker than hers. My Aunt, who wore a hat over her curly dyed blond hair, came up from behind to join us. I wouldn't have known her if she had walked past me on the street.

"We just got here and were afraid we came too late," Aunt Esther said. Her warm smile offset her pinched nose and tired blue eyes while her hair curled all across her head below the hat. Little wrinkles showed around both eyes. She had the look of someone who had lived a difficult life and who had definitely seen better days.

"No, I just got off the plane," I reassured her.

"Good, good," my uncle said. His accent sounded so foreign to me, but then I'd been told visiting Texas was like visiting a foreign country. "We'll go with you to get your luggage."

I held up my carry-on bag. "This is all I brought. The rest is being shipped in a trunk to the school."

"Great," my uncle said. "Let's get out of here then."

From the determined way Sid walked, he revealed himself as a no-nonsense man on the move. His steady step kept him about two or three paces ahead of my aunt. I stayed behind with her. I kept thinking this was the same guy who grew up with my mother, knew her as a little girl, and had the same parents. Yet, at first glance, he appeared to be nothing like her.

As we walked across the parking lot, my uncle still in the lead, my aunt asked, "Are you hungry, or can you wait until we get home to eat?"

"I can wait."

I had been here about two minutes, but the heat already encompassed me like a big sky furnace turned on full blast. I didn't understand how anyone in his right mind could live with weather like this. "Is it always this hot?" I asked my aunt.

She looked surprised. "Hot? Today is warm. Yes, summers are like this. You'll get used to the climate. By the way, Cal, that's what your mother said to call you, Cal instead of Calvin. Your uncle Sid and I want you to have a good time before you go off to school. Sid doesn't need the car during the day, and we're often home at night. Your mother says you are a good driver so if you'd like to take the car out to explore Houston or to visit some of your other relatives here, you are welcome to use the car whenever you wish."

The car we arrived at in the parking lot turned out to be a sleek black Buick, the latest model. The thought of driving around town in that car excited me. I regretted not getting Judy's number in Houston. If I'd known I would have had access to a car, I could have possibly taken her out before she left.

My uncle took my small bag to put in the trunk. I opened the rear door to slide into the back seat, sitting in the middle so I could talk to both at once as we drove to their house.

"I told Cal he was welcome to use the car," Esther told Sid.

He started the car, drove to the gate, paid the parking fee, and we headed down the open highway into the city. "You have a driver's license, don't you, boy?" Uncle Sid wanted to know.

"Yes, Sir." Sid's no-nonsense manner made him a good person to practice Southern formality on.

"How is your Mother?"

"She's fine, thank you."

"And your brother?"

"Fine, too, Sir, thanks for asking."

"Glad to hear that," came his deep-throated response. "I know you visited my parents recently in San Mateo. Did they both seem well?"

"Yes, Grandmother's amazing. She works hard all day and still does lots of things."

Sid laughed. "She's always been a doer." His voice grew more serious. "You know when your Mother and I discussed her concerns regarding you, I told her Roxwell was the answer. I know you are going to like being there once you get used to the routine. They have a fine reputation around this part of the state."

So Uncle Sid was the jerk who came up with this stupid idea. She'd failed to mention that little fact.

"I'm sure I will, Sir, if you say so."

"My, isn't he polite?" Aunt Esther said to her husband. "He talks just like a Southern boy."

Oh, Aunt Esther, if you only knew that the words coming out of my mouth don't represent the thoughts going on inside my brain.

"You know your uncle Sidney went to a military college not far from Roxwell," Esther continued, her voice full of respect. "He was a lieutenant in the army during the war."

"Tell you what," Sid popped in. "Maybe one weekend, I'll drive up to the school and get you and take you to a football game at A & M where I went. You like football?"

"Yes, Sir."

"We have a great tradition there. It's called The 12th Man. About 25 years back, our team ran out of players due to injuries during a game. The coach called someone from the press box down to suit up, and that studet stood ready, though he never played. So now we Aggies all stand during the entire game to show we are the 12th man, ready to go on the field in case they need us."

That sounded like the dumbest idea I'd heard in the last 10 years of my life, but I dared not tell him. How could anyone enjoy a game standing up for three hours?

"Yes, Sir, that sounds like going to a game would be great fun."

"Yes, boy, I'll take you around the grounds after the game. You might find you like the military life so much, you'd think about applying to college there. With the draft and all, you might be a lot happier serving your country as an officer."

And I could be really happy jumping into a live volcano, too, I thought. "That's a good idea, Sir, I'll definitely consider it."

We pulled into their driveway, and Sid stopped the car in front of the garage. He turned around to look at me before he got out. "This is a different way of life here, Cal. You might be a bit scared at first, but you'll adjust. Everyone does. One thing good about a military school is routine. Once you know the drill, the place gets easier, but learning the drill takes a while. And this experience will definitely shape you up and make you the kind of man that will make your mother proud."

"No doubt," I agreed. I began to suspect two or three days around my uncle, and I'd be more than happy to go off to the military school.

Aunt Esther had prepared a meal of cold cuts, cole slaw, and potato salad before they left for the airport to pick me up, so she had the table set, and we were ready to eat as soon as we came through the door. Before the meal, they showed me the guest room where I'd be sleeping.

I didn't feel like spending the evening yakking with them, so after dinner, I told them that I felt tired, even though I was still on the earlier Los Angeles time. I spent the rest of the evening in the guest room reading one of the books I'd packed, *Sweet Thursday,* Steinbeck's newest novel. I guess he is my favorite novelist.

Since my mother and father had both been raised in Texas, I had a lot of relatives who lived around the city. The following morning, with a map of Houston spread out on the seat next to me, I drove off to visit the first pair, an aunt and uncle on my father's side I'd never met. As I drove up to their house in the suburbs, the thought struck me. I have no reason on earth to visit these people except we are related by blood.

After a pleasant lunch talking about my new life and avoiding a lot of other subjects, I went off to visit a first cousin who recently had a baby and followed that with a visit to a third cousin who lived near where the Houston Buffs baseball team played. The Buffalos, or Buffs as the locals called them, were a Texas league team. When I visited with my mom a few years earlier, one of my uncles took me to a game. We had to stand for a moment of silence because on that day, Babe Ruth had died.

On the way back to Aunt Esther's house from the third cousin's place, I spotted a frosty stand, which, considering the heat, appealed to me greatly. I parked down the block, and when I approached the stand, I saw two lines of about eight each waiting to be served. I stood at the end of one line when I heard a loud voice in the line next to me.

"Out of the way nigger, you let a white man in." The speaker, overweight and short, had sweat on his reddened face, and he wore a panama hat. He mirrored every racist cliché I'd read about. He addressed an older woman standing at the end of the other line. She silently stepped back so he could move in front of her.

"Hey, fatso, what do you think you're doing? A husky white man in his twenties, who stood in line directly in front of fatso, had turned around to confront the intruder. He did not speak with a Southern drawl.

"Mind your own business," Fatty said, despite being a few inches shorter than the other.

"You are my business," the man told him. "Now get the hell out of here before I shove that hat right through your head."

In a sudden shift, the two ice cream lines formed a circle around the two men. The Negro lady hurried down the street, muttering, "I don't want no trouble."

"Hit him, Fatso," someone in the crowd yelled.

Fatso, who looked as if he was all mouth, stared at the husky guy with fear showing.

"Try anything, fat boy, and sign your death warrant," the husky man told him. He had both fists clenched. His muscular build seemed to totally intimidate his adversary.

Fatso used his mouth as a fist. "Screw you, nigger-lover. Go back to where you came from."

The husky man flattened him with one shot to the jaw. Fatso dropped to the ground with his blubber shaking. I wanted to go up and hug the guy who nailed him.

Suddenly two guys grabbed the victor by the arms, just as Fatso tried to sit up. "Get up, fat boy. Come on, pop him."

The crowd came to life. "Hit him, Fatso," they yelled in unison. Fatso struggled to get on to his feet, and the captive man struggled to get loose, but these guys were huge, like construction workers.

Suddenly Fatso rushed at the man, only to get a kick in the stomach that sent him flying backwards and landing flat on his back once again.

"Get him," someone yelled from the crowd.

All of a sudden, four or five men, and even a couple of women, descended on the guy still being held and started to hit and kick him. The man went down under a flurry of blows. As he lay on the ground, he was kicked by a number of feet.

An old lady next to me kept saying, "Disgusting." I froze, sick to my stomach.

As quick as the melee started, the end came when the crowd dispersed, leaving the man lying in a heap on the ground. I didn't know what to do. I wanted to help him, maybe get him to a hospital, but instead just stood frozen in place until I heard the siren of a police car. Then, I walked at an accelerated pace back to my uncle's car and drove home.

I couldn't shake this incident from my mind. All the way home, I felt lousy for not stepping in, even though I would have had my ass kicked. Whenever there is violence, I freeze. I'm not sure why. After Carl taught me to box, I'm sure I can defend myself. The problem is fighting seems so stupid. This guy acted for the right reasons, but he attacked a guy who obviously couldn't take care of himself.

That night, I had nightmarish kinds of dreams that caused me to wake up in a cold sweat.

I sat up in bed and read for a while, then managed to go back to sleep.

The next morning, when I came down to breakfast, Uncle Sid had his nose buried behind the morning paper. Aunt Esther began frying some eggs. She served me a cup of coffee. I asked my uncle for the sports section.

He peered over his paper. "Before I give you that, Cal, I want to read you something that might be of help to you. "

"Okay, but I wouldn't mind reading the piece myself."

He handed me the front section of the *Houston Chronicle*. Much to my surprise, he'd already circled the article with a pen.

TROUBLEMAKER JAILED

Steve Macklin, 23, of Minneapolis, Minnesota, was jailed late yesterday afternoon after violently attacking one of our local citizens in a dispute at a frosty stand near downtown Houston. Macklin, an unemployed construction worker, was held at city jail in lieu of $500 bail. Gerald L. K. Larson, a Houston businessman, filed the complaint and gave this version of the incident. "I was standing in line waiting to buy a frosty when Macklin pushed his way in front of me. When I asked him to get in the back of the line, he picked a fight. He used abusive language, and I remained still, not wanting to cause trouble. Then he suddenly attacked me, hitting and kicking and knocking me over. Fortunately, some of the others in line came to my aid and held him off."

Macklin was taken to the hospital to have his cuts and bruises attended before being brought to the jail. He will appear before Judge Smith tomorrow to answer the charge of assault.

A wave of nausea came over me as I put the paper down.

"Let me tell you why I wanted you to read that," Uncle Sid said, in an accent I'd already begun to hate. "You can't go pushing your weight around down here."

"All I wish is that I had $500 bucks to bail the guy out," I told my uncle. "I saw this happen, Uncle Sid. This didn't happen like the story says at all. The whole story is a lie."

"That's not what matters," my uncle replied, a sharp tone to his words. "I let you read the story so you can see what happens when someone from out of state starts trouble here. So you were there. You know that people around here don't take kindly to strangers."

"Yes, Sir. I don't plan to start any trouble." He didn't ask, and I didn't tell him the true story. I'm sure he wouldn't have understood.

Aunt Esther brought me a plate with two fried eggs and toast. I had no stomach for food.

"You see, Sid," she said, rubbing my hair. "The boy was there, and he didn't do a thing. He's smart. I can tell. We won't have to worry about him getting in trouble."

The rest of the week went by slowly, punctuated by visits with relatives. These were my mother's relatives, most of them, and they were all Jewish like her. Despite our Jewish history, they were prejudiced like most Texans. I couldn't understand how Jews could look down on another race when, only ten years ago, their own relatives had been burned up in ovens by the Germans during the war.

My mistake, I realized later, was to expect these relatives to think like me, especially since my own mother and brother weren't anything like me.

Being different, that's a lonely feeling. That feeling lingered with me during the week. My friends, my family, no one seemed to be the way I saw myself, as an outsider, a reader, a seeker of new experiences. Nobody wants to be alone in this world, yet, somehow, we all are.

The last night before my aunt would drive me to Roxwell, I asked to borrow the car.

"Don't do anything foolish," my uncle said as he handed me the keys.

"No, Sir." With Uncle Sid, I felt as if I'd already started military school.

Even as a kid, I loved amusement parks. We used to go to the one out at Ocean Park, the place I wrote about. Any time a carnival came to town, I wanted to be there. So when I read about the local amusement park, I decided to pay a visit on my last night in the real world. I still had most of the money my mother had given me, more than enough to go on all the rides I wanted.

A dirt lot next to the entrance served as a parking lot. I parked the car in the field lined with rows of cars, a lot of them old junk heaps. Inside, a flood of bright lights exposed the attractions, games of chance, and lots of rides, drawing people like moths to a flame. I always give carnival games a shot. I tried to knock over the milk bottles. Pitch a dime and win a ham. Make five baskets in two minutes. At home, I'd watched a program on television that explained how all these carnival games were rigged, which made any of them almost impossible to win. So I knew these games were rackets, but I didn't care. Tonight was my last night of freedom before my life would change, and this evening, I would do whatever I wanted.

As I walked from game to game, little kids ran loose everywhere, some dragging their parents or older sisters or brothers from ride to ride and to the wagons selling cotton candy and other junk. All these people somehow made me feel more alive. Still, they were all white as sheets. I wondered what the black people who lived here did for fun.

Maybe they had their own carnival.

Lines for some rides were long, but I didn't mind the wait. Lots of cute girls to look at, most laughing together in groups of two or three, kids eating ice cream, and the cacophony of sounds cranked out from the games and the corny music from the rides. I rode on the whip, the loop-de-loop, the Ferris wheel, and then located the end of a long line to ride the roller coaster. This wasn't like the giant one we'd had at the beach; less intimidating but still fun. A girl stood directly in front of me. She looked to be sixteen or so with a long blond ponytail down her back. She wore black Capri pants and a black sweater. I wanted to talk to her, but I hesitated, sure her boyfriend would show up at any moment. He'd probably gone off to buy a snack.

To my surprise, she turned around. In an accent that dripped sugar, she asked, "Do ya'all mind if ah ride on the roller coaster with you? That old roller coaster just scares the dickens out of me."

I pointed to myself. "You want to ride with me?"

"If ya'all don't mind."

"Sure. No problem. My pleasure."

I moved up next to her in line.

"Mah name's Kitty, like Kitty Kat. Who are you?"

"Cal's my name. " I wanted to say more, but the shock proved too much. "Did you come here alone?"

"My Daddy let me come. We just moved to town, and I've been so bored. So he let me come here tonight. He's going to meet me at 11:30."

"Oh. What part of the South did you move from?"

"Well, aren't you the clever one? We came from Mobile. How'd you know?"

"Just a wild guess," I answered.

"Oh. Do you live in Houston, Cal?"

"No. I'm from Hollywood, California." Now, technically, Brentwood is part of Los Angeles, but whenever a stranger asks, I always say Hollywood. That word sounds so much more glamorous, and the name is sure to catch the person's attention.

"I declare, Hollywood. I never met anyone from there before. That's so exciting. I read all the fan magazines. Have you ever met any real movie stars? What's it like there? Do y'all just see movie stars walking along the street?"

"Whoa, there, cowgirl. One question at a time."

As we moved toward the ticket line, I answered each of her questions as much as possible. I purchased two tickets. Kitty tried to pay for hers, but I insisted. When we got into the car, she pressed up against me and held onto the crossbar with a fierce grip. She wouldn't let go during the entire ride, and when we stumbled out, she walked the first few steps a little bit like a drunk.

For one brief evening, we had found each other. I took her on several other rides, paying for her tickets, buying cokes, and even throwing rings at coke bottles, trying to win her a teddy bear. In between rides, I told her stories of Hollywood, a few embellished, but they seemed to amaze her. In return, she hung on my arm and smiled a lot.

When 11:15 came, we parted. I kissed her cheek and told her how much I had enjoyed her company. I hadn't tried to make any time with her. What would have been the point? I would never see her again. I felt wonderful just having her company for most of the evening.

I realize that it's unusual to just enjoy being with someone without even getting to first base. If I had kissed her on the lips, or French kissed or made out, or any of that, the evening would have been ruined for me. Don't ask me to explain why.

The next morning, right after breakfast, Esther prepared to drive me to the school in the big Buick. Why she chose to drive rather than my uncle nobody explained. I had no problem with the decision. Of the two, she won hands down as the easiest to be with. Before we left, my uncle shook my hand in the proper manner; that is man to man. "Don't let us down, Cal," Uncle Sid said, reinforcing the warning with his most solemn expression.

The good soldier replied, "I'll do my best, Sir. Thanks for everything."

Aunt Esther kindly let me drive a hundred miles to the school in Cullen, Texas. I drove slowly, not out of fear or concern of an accident, but to savor every last minute of freedom. Neither of us spoke throughout the trip. I was on another trip, one all my own, an anxiety trip about what the future would hold.

After a stop at a gas station for directions, we drove the five or six blocks from the town center to the gated walls with the prominent sign that read, ROXWELL MILITARY ACADEMY. We parked near the reception center. A new segment of my life had finally arrived. That new life would begin here and now.

CHAPTER EIGHT

My aunt walked me inside the main building that held the administrative offices. The white walls and wooden trim looked about as boring as one would expect from a military mindset that believed in wearing khaki for a color.

In the office, I filled out an enrollment card. An old lady told me to go to the Dean's office down the hall with the card, and she had my aunt sign a form as my legal guardian in the event I got shot during military training exercises or someone threw me out of a window. Before visiting the dean, I walked my aunt to the car and gave her a kiss on the cheek. She'd been as nice as anyone could ask, cooking, giving me access to the car, and not bugging me the way her husband did. Before she entered the car, she promised my Uncle "would visit in a month or so."

"No need to rush," I told her, as he would probably follow through on his desire to take me to one of those "12th man" games he'd mentioned. As she drove the Buick out through the gate, my head drooped. I felt more alone than at any time in my entire life.

Dean Cromwell (I learned later his nickname given by the cadets was Crommy) occupied a drab but spacious office down the hall. Like a true dean, he looked immersed in some papers when I knocked on the window of the closed door and responded to his invitation to come inside and sit down. He took my enrollment card and studied the card carefully before speaking. He sat with a military bearing, head straight up, his shoulders back, and an intense expression on his thin cheeks. Above his lip, the small moustache he'd carefully nourished appeared to have been dyed, as did his black thinning hair, which clung to the top of his mostly bald head in carefully combed strands. Dressed in what I'd call a dark suit, white shirt, and bow tie, he appeared the stereotype of an actor playing a dean in a movie, one you'd see in a film about teenagers, a real dean's dean. With his penetrating blue eyes, he studied me after he put down the enrollment card.

"So Calvin Carter, tell me why you wanted to come to Roxwell Academy all the way from Hollywood." His deep voice, clipping each word, resonated through the room.

The question threw me off. "Actually, my mother wanted me to come. She thought the school would help me gain some direction."

"Are you in need of direction?" He asked.

I shifted around in my chair, unprepared for the third degree. "Sure, I guess so. I'm not sure what I want to do in the future."

"You'll have an opportunity to find out here, Carter. You're a long way from Hollywood, but we've had cadets come to Roxwell from all over the country and from Latin America as well. Cadets, once they adjust to the order and discipline so essential to a military-based academy, find they like being here. We are all quite proud of Roxwell Academy and what the program accomplishes for the cadet corps."

"I'm looking forward to the experience," I said, hoping to get off on the right foot.

He cracked a brief smile. "Glad to hear that, Carter. Attitude is important. You can go a long way in life if you maintain the correct attitude."

He paused to look through his files for my school program. To my surprise, he'd apparently hit the nail on the head with his comment on the importance of attitude. Maybe attitude defined my problems in general.

"Here is your copy of your classroom program for the first semester of the 12th grade. Look the classes over and let me know if you have any questions." I stood up and went to his desk, where he handed me a schedule card.

Once I returned to my seat, a quick perusal of the classes dropped my heart into my lower intestines. Geometry, Advanced Algebra, Chemistry, Military Science and Tactics, English, and study hall filled out my dance card, leaving me doing the Texas two-step. I turned the sheet over to make sure a mix-up in names hadn't occurred.

My mouth screwed up as I held up the sheet listing my classes. "There must be some mistake, Sir. I'm not a math or science major. I flunked geometry. And I haven't had the first part of algebra since I took the course a few years ago in junior high."

The dean shook his head. "No, there's no mistake, Carter. We received your high school transcript and read through the courses you've previously taken. You need to pass geometry in order to graduate high school. If you want to graduate from Roxwell at the end of the year, these are courses necessary to take. Math and science are very important if you plan to apply to one of the military colleges like Texas A & M, Annapolis, or West Point."

"I'm sure that's true, Sir, but I have no plans to go to a military college."

Like a good soldier, the Dean dug into his position. "I'm sorry. But these are the courses you will need to graduate from here no matter where you choose to go to college."

In my mind, I had already flunked out five minutes after arriving.

Dean Cromwell sat forward at his desk and clasped his hands. "Now, I need to explain additional information about the school program. Classes begin at 8:00 each morning and continue until 11:00. We then drill for an hour on the drill field, and then we have lunch. The afternoon academic session is from 13:30, that's military time, until 16:00. School starts each week on Tuesday and runs through Saturday, except for this coming Monday afternoon when the semester begins. On this first Monday only, you will attend your afternoon classes. After this orientation week, Monday mornings will be spent marching on the drill field, and after lunch each Monday afternoon, you will be free until dinner roll call. Needless to say, Sunday mornings are reserved for church. By the way, which church do you attend? We have almost all denominations here in town."

"None," I informed him.

He blinked a couple of times as if my words surprised him. "Well, you are required to attend church here. Your duty is to your country and to God. What religion do you follow?"

"None," I answered after a moment's hesitation.

Visibly caught off-guard, he asked, "You do believe in God,

don't you?" His expression told me he had already answered his own question.

Once again, I hesitated. I'm smart enough to realize that we were beginning badly. I guess I could have tried to lie, but I'd come this far.

"Nooo, not really." The words barely broke any barrier of sound.

"That means you are an atheist. We have no churches for atheists here." The muscles in his face tightened, and his voice shifted. "When I was your age, my parents taught me to respect the Lord. Do you live in a heathen home?"

Hmm. He raised issues I'd never thought about.

"What exactly is a heathen home?" I asked.

"Do your people attend church?"

"No. But maybe they believe in God. I don't know. We don't talk about religion at home."

He'd surrendered that quality of control he possessed when I entered the room. Outflanked by a student, his cheeks had reddened, and his breath shortened. He looked like he might throw a tantrum right there behind his desk. He tapped his fingers against the desk, the steady tattoo somehow soothing him as he struggled to gain control, remaining silent until the flush in his cheeks dissipated.

"What were your ancestors originally?" He asked.

"Polish and Russian, I think."

"No, I mean, what religion did they practice?"

"My mother's family is Jewish. I don't know exactly what my Dad's was. He died when I was still little."

"Then I will assign you to attend a synagogue in town."

"Okay," I said. That didn't matter much. "There's no way I could just skip the whole thing?"

His voice tightened. "No, I'm afraid that's not allowed. Though I suspect in your case, this will serve no useful purpose, you are required to attend some form of worship. Have you ever been to a church or synagogue?"

"Oh, sure. I've been to a lot of different types of churches: Catholic, Methodist, Jewish, Mormon, and I even had a Japanese classmate who took me to a Buddhist temple."

"And none of those whetted your curiosity to learn more about our creator?"

Now, I really hesitated before blurting out. "Well, to be honest, Darwin's ideas about evolution make a lot more sense to me."

His left eye twitched. "Choose one," he said, moving the conversation forward.

"Do you have any Eastern religions here?"

"This is Texas, not Tokyo."

"Then I guess I'll settle for the Synagogue."

"You're sure? This is a Christian country we live in. A Church service would certainly put you more in step with your fellow cadets."

"A puritanical country," I muttered to myself, but a little too loud.

"What?"

"Sorry, I was just thinking out loud. Since my mother's family is Jewish, maybe I'll learn something if I go to Synagogue."

He wanted to end the conversation, but he found difficulty letting go.

"Well, of course, you can choose, but I don't think you'll learn much from the Hebrew religion."

I wanted to respond, "I wouldn't get much out of any of them." But I kept my mouth zipped. I'd put my foot far enough down my throat to choke.

"Yes, that's my choice."

"All right. Since there are only five of you Jews on campus, and you are the oldest, you will be in charge of taking them into town each Friday night for services."

"What do I have to do?"

"You will take them all to the Synagogue for the start of the service, and after the service ends, you are responsible for making sure they all return to the school. Now, let's move on. I don't have all day. You'll wake up at 6:15 to the bugle's call, then at 7:00, line up for formation before breakfast. School formation starts at 8:00, drill at 11:00, lunch and mail call at noon, and a free half hour after lunch. At 13:15, you line up for formation and go to school until 16:00, as I mentioned before. Dinner formation is at 18:00 hours. Free time until 19:30, and then study period until 22:00 hours. Lights go out at 22:30. No smoking is allowed on the campus. Of course, no alcohol or drugs are allowed. Any questions?"

"There doesn't sound like there's much free time"

"Idle hands are the Devil's workshop," the Dean informed me by clarifying his most serious biblical philosophy.

"Yes, Sir."

"One of the functions of a military school is to teach the cadets order and discipline. Nothing accomplishes that goal more effectively than a rigid schedule. We follow this same schedule all through the year. You will see in future years the importance of organization and discipline."

"You kept mentioning a formation; what is that?"

The Dean's frustration returned. "A formation is when the entire school lines up by companies and squads. Then, the role is called, and each person answers present. You'll learn more about these terms on Monday morning when squads are assigned. Your uniform will be issued later today, so before you proceed to your room, drop into the tailor shop for measurements. Any further questions?"

About a million swamed around my brain, but I shook my head no.

The Dean handed me a sheet of paper. "All right. There is a boy waiting in the hallway. He will take you to the tailor shop and then to your room, where you can unpack."

"All right, thank you, Sir."

He dismissed me with a wave while he muttered, "You're welcome."

The boy assigned to take care of me looked to be about my height, and he sported a piggy face anyone would love to punch. He had loitered in the hallway waiting, then gave me the once over as I left the office. "You're supposed to take me to the tailor and my room," I told him, handing him a slip with the room number.

"Okay, let's go."

He led me through the building and out onto the grounds. He waddled like he'd swallowed a bit too much barbecue. But he was all I had. "What's it like here?"

His small piggy eyes regarded me with the contempt he obviously reserved for anyone new. "Oh, sure 'nough, you gonna like it here. Just keep your mouth shut and do what you told."

He waited outside the tailor shop while I went in to get measurements for my dress uniform. They told me to come back in an hour to get my issue of day-to-day uniforms. Then we proceeded to a rather beat-up wood frame two-story house with peeling paint and outside stairs that led to a second floor. "This here's McFadden house," Pig Face told me. "You'll be livin' here."

We walked up the rickety stairway that led to a second-floor landing. A door led into a hallway. There were four rooms on the floor, and my guide opened the door to my room. "Want some advice?" He asked, just before leaving.

"What's that?"

"Ya'll better keep your door locked at night, or niggers'll come in and beat ya'll to death with a stick."

"Oh," I said, keeping a straight face. "How many times a year does that occur?"

The unexpected response caused his narrow eyes to widen. He turned around and marched out of the room. As soon as he left, I shut the door and flopped down on the bed. "Cal," I told myself, "You have created a big mess to start with." That dean would be no friend. Pig Face might have friends. Religion just wasn't a topic of discussion in LA because nobody I knew cared what religion anyone practiced or didn't, but obviously, here they saw the God business differently.

Then I spotted my trunk shipped from home placed on the floor at the foot of my bed. Evidently, someone had delivered the trunk to my room before my arrival. For a moment, the sight comforted me. A little bit of LA lay within: Sheets, pillowcases, towels, underwear, a raincoat, and books I'd packed to have during my time here. I opened the trunk and spent a half hour organizing the contents, putting sheets on the thin single bed mattress, covering the pillow, placing the towels, extra sheets, and other items in a drawer, lining up the books in a small area designed for books and other items in a nightstand at the head of my bed.

That task completed, I stood staring out through the window of my room. At home my room looked out on the apartment building next door. Now, my backyard consisted of a field about the size of a football field that separated McFadden House from a small parking lot next to a high wall that surrounded the school property. The room itself, as I anticipated, lacked any character. Outside, the air felt like the inside of a steam bath, while inside the room, the air felt cooler but retained an odor from last year's residents and needed an airing out. I turned on the ceiling fan and pulled open the window, letting the afternoon heat sink in along with fresh air. I began a careful examination of my new home. Twin beds, one on each side of the entry door, probably meant a roommate. Two dressers, three drawers high, stood at the foot of each bed, and each bed had a nightstand in front. No decorations cluttered the walls. A few cracks showed across the ceiling. A throw rug separated the two sides of the room, leaving just enough space in one corner for a single desk opposite a closet that occupied all the space on the opposite side. Obviously, the roommates had to fight over desk time.

Though my aunt and I had stopped for lunch along the way, pangs of hunger began to take over. I decided to try to find the cafeteria to see if I could get a bite. Just as I reached the outside landing, I spotted a guy with suitcases about to ascend the stairs. I suspected this could be my new roommate and waited on the landing at the top of the stairs. When this kid, lugging two suitcases, hit the top landing with a dull thud, I opened the door so he could enter the hallway. Inside went a string bean over six feet tall with an acne-scarred face and a haircut even worse than my own.

He passed me without a word or greeting. Once inside, he checked the numbers on each door. Finally, and much to my relief, he stood in front of the room opposite my own, dropped the suitcases, and checked a paper he had pulled from his pocket two or three times to make sure he had the correct room. The door to his room was closed and locked. He moved his head close to the lock to examine the keyhole. Thick, horn-rimmed glasses indicated he couldn't see well. I remained in the hallway beside the screen door that led to the landing, but he appeared not to notice my existence.

He fumbled with the key that would unlock the door to his room.

"Hi," I said, causing him to jerk his head around.

"Hello." He turned his attention back to forcing the key to turn in the lock.

"Do you need help bringing your junk up?" I asked.

He finally succeeded in opening the door to his room. He picked up both suitcases and started through the doorway, only to bang his head at the very top of the entrance. He let out a yelp and dropped the suitcases.

"You all right?" I asked, coming up to the open doorway, where I saw a room shaped in an identical way to my own but facing towards the parade ground area.

"Mah glasses, mah glasses," he moaned as he squirmed around in a fit of panic. "Ah can't see nothin' without mah glasses." He entered the room walking something like Frankenstein's monster with his arms extended in front of him.

I stepped inside and quickly located the glasses on the floor. "They didn't even break," I said as I handed them to him. With an expert motion, he put them back on.

The lenses looked thick, but beneath them, he blinked about fifteen times in a row. "Kind of you," he said. "I'm blind without mah glasses."

"What's your name?" I asked.

"Roland Grooper."

"Roland, what?"

"Grooper. That's G-R-O-O-P-E-R. Like a grouper fish, only spelled different. What's your name?"

"Carter. Cal Carter."

"Glad to get to know you, Cal."

His hand jumped out at me, and I shook the sweaty palm. His dead fish grip made me feel real sorry for him. On top of being one of the ugliest guys I'd encountered in recent years, he projected all kinds of problems and complexes. No doubt, everyone called him Gooper, or Grouper Fish, or some other disgusting name. Guys like him, unless they are born rich or have a high IQ, don't have much chance in this world. Roland might be from a rich family, but that would have been the only thing he had going for him.

"Do you have a nickname, Roland?"

He hesitated for a moment as if trying to decide. "No nickname. What was it you said your name was again?"

"Cal."

"Oh yeah."

"Should I call you Roland then?"

"That's what my mama calls me."

"If Roland's good enough for your mama, the name's good enough for me."

"Nice to meet you, Hal."

"Cal."

"Cal."

"I'm going over to see if I can rustle up some grub," I told him. "Want to come?"

"My mama packed a lunch for me. I'm gonna stay here and eat mah sandwich."

I told Roland goodbye, wondering how he would ever survive through the year. He seemed to have the kind of personality that tended to become a scapegoat. I'd read a bit about scapegoats, and Roland filled the bill. He obviously was very close to his mother, who may have been too protective, which may have led to an Oedipus complex. With my thirty-second personality analysis completed, I left the room.

Taking the outside stairs two at a time, I found my way to the mess hall, as they called the dining room, and learned that they didn't serve food all day long. I was pointed toward a hamburger stand open long hours on the grounds. Frenchy's served as a hangout for the cadets who gathered there when they had time between meals or at night. A small stand with a counter and a couple of outside tables, the place served up a decent hamburger, fries, and a coke. As I ate, I tried to decide what to do about Roland.

He would obviously be the subject of bullying without his mother around to take care of him. I wondered why she'd sent him to a place like this. He didn't seem like the type that needed discipline. Maybe she thought the same way as my mom did, that a military school would make a man out of him. From what I'd briefly observed, his mom had faulty reasoning. Roland would always need protection from the world. Someone would have to fight his battles for him. I could fight verbally, but I would draw the line at becoming physical to protect him. Verbal protection seemed like an acceptable trade-off.

I finished my late lunch and afterwards wandered back across the campus to the tailor shop, where I picked up my day-to-day uniforms. They told me my dress uniform would be ready in about a month. Back in my room, I unloaded the box that contained boots, shoes, four pairs of khaki pants, four khaki shirts, two ties, fifteen pairs of socks, and a pair of fatigues that looked like khaki overalls. I didn't know what to do with all this stuff, so I dumped the whole lot on the bed before I placed the socks and shirts next to my underwear and towels in one dresser drawer, and I put the pants and shirts in another drawer, which finished off the space in my dresser. The shoes and boots I placed neatly side-by-side on the closet floor. I stretched out on the now-empty bed to contemplate my plight. This place seemed crazy. A nap before dinner became the answer. I had just begun to doze off when a knock on the door caused me to jump up.

"Who is it?" I called out.

Two guys walked in. Both appeared overweight and around the same size. They each wore khaki pants and a sports shirt.

Why did everyone in Texas look like Porky Pig?

"You're supposed to jump to your feet, Freshy," one of them said.

"Why should I?"

"Because you are a freshman, a freshy," came the distinctive Texan inflection.

I shook my head. "I'm a senior in high school."

"Grades got nothin' to do with it," the same overweight one told me. "Any first-year man is a freshy here whether he's in the seventh grade or college. Don't matter a lick. What's your name, Freshy?"

"Cal Carter, what's yours?"

"Up on your feet, Carter. And you call me Sir. All freshys call everyone Sir, unless it's another freshy, like Tommy Allen here. I'm Gibbons, and Tommy and I come from San Antone. Where are you from?"

"Hollywood."

Gibbons whistled through his teeth. "Son of a gun. Whatcha think, Allen? We got us a real live Hollywood boy."

"Great," Allen said with unbridled enthusiasm. "Do you know any movie stars?"

"Oh, three or four," I answered.

"How come you're still in your civvies, Carter?" Gibbons asked.

"My what?"

"Civvies, civilian clothes. You can't go off to dinner dressed like that. Since school ain't started yet, you can just wear a shirt and khakis like we got on."

"Oh, yeah, I just got all my clothes and junk," I said, acting as if I knew all about the dress code. "I haven't had time to change yet."

Gibbons glared as if the word junk was offensive to someone who called himself Sir.

"C'mon, let's go," Gibbons told Allen, grabbing his arm to yank him toward the door. "We're in the next room over. Make sure you knock before you come in."

"Yes, Sir," I replied, putting an inflection on the second word and sealing the sarcasm with a smile.

"One more thing, Carter. Do you know who that funny-looking guy is across the hall?"

"Roland Grooper."

Gibbons's little beady eyes lit up. "C'mon Allen, we got ourselves a big Goober."

They left, and I tried once more to sleep. Through the door, I could hear Gibbons already giving Grooper a hard time. I hadn't expected that to happen so fast, but obviously, Gibbons feasted on the vulnerable.

I couldn't sleep, pulled out a book, and read for an hour. I dressed in a pair of khaki pants and a shirt, and those boring looking brown shoes they issued us, which squeaked and squashed my feet during my walk across campus to the mess hall.

A few other arrivals were spread in small groups around the cavernous room eating dinner. Food arrived cafeteria style. I took a tray and went along the line, selecting what looked like the best of a bad lot. I found the farthest corner in the room where I could sit by myself, as far from all Roxwell cadets as possible.

After dinner, I returned to my room and spent a quiet evening reading. Nobody else came in, nobody bothered me, and at about 10:30, I turned off my lights and fell into an uneasy sleep, knowing this experience of mine would inevitably get worse before it got better if that ever happened.

CHAPTER NINE

I woke the next morning only to find myself trapped like *Alice in Wonderland,* in the wrong room, in the wrong world. At first, I thought I'd awakened at home, though the room had a different look than my room at home. Just prior to waking, Ray and I had been cruising the "Boulevard" in a cool military jeep, and we had picked up two beautiful girls. They told us they were starlets making a movie, and offered to get us parts in the film. But Ray and I told them we were rich and didn't need to act. We told them we owned a racetrack and a stable of horses. I remember the blond-haired girl sitting beside me and telling me I was her kind of man as she gently stroked my face.

Imagine, waking to my room in Roxwell after a dream like that.

I dragged myself up from bed, went to the communal bathroom to wash up, and then dressed in the same clothes I'd worn the previous night. We still had two more days before school officially began. I stared at my crew-cut-khaki-pants-self in the mirror. I didn't resemble anyone I knew, less so me.

I knocked on Grooper's door to ask if he wanted to join me for breakfast. I waited a few minutes while he finished dressing. He came out in full uniform, wearing a poorly tied and unnecessary tie. His acne jumped out when surrounded by a sea of khaki. We walked across the center drill field and crossed in front of the offices until we reached the mess hall. I chose warm cereal and pancakes. My aunt had made me pancakes in southern style, which were delicious. I anticipated these would be the same until I learned the syrup I'd just poured all over them turned out to be molasses, a mixture so thick the pancakes tasted like glue. I settled for cereal and coffee.

Grooper and I returned to our rooms, walking back with Gibbons and Allen. After we walked upstairs, both cadets entered Grooper's room behind him. After hesitating in the hall for a moment, I followed them in.

Gibbons couldn't wait. "Hey, Goober, did you ever date a girl?"

"Uhh, once at our senior dance."

"Boy, that must have been exciting. Did you screw her?"

"Uhh, I'm not sure what you all mean, Gibbons."

"Mr. Gibbons," Gibbons reminded Grooper, as he sat down on the freshy's bed.

"Mr. Gibbons."

"Ya don't know what screwin' a girl is, Goober? What kind of warped life have you led?"

Grooper pondered an answer.

"I don't know," he finally said.

"Now listen here, Goober," Gibbons said, his voice rising with excitement. "A girl's got a pussy and you've got a dick. When you bring them together, the fun begins." He broke out in a big laugh, and like his faithful parrot, Allen laughed as well.

"If my mama heard me talk like that, she'd wash my mouth out with soap," Grooper informed them. This brought on more laughter.

"Guess we're going to have to educate old Goober here," Allen said. He spotted a framed photo of a woman on Grooper's desk. He picked the frame up and asked Grooper if he liked older women and if that was his girl friend whose picture filled the frame.

"That's my mama," Grooper informed them, a nervous tone creeping into the words.

"Boy, she is ugly," Allen said to Gibbons.

Gibbons grabbed the frame from Allen and examined the image.

"She sure is one ugly woman," Gibbons agreed, tossing the frame back to Allen like a football.

"Hey, fellas, don't do that," Grooper pleaded.

"Sure enough, that woman has a face like one of them army mules."

Allen put the picture down. "If my mama looked like that, I'd have drowned her in a creek a long time ago."

I'd had enough, as Grooper's expression indicated he might burst into tears at any moment.

"You guys have had your fun. Why don't you lay off?"

"Why don't you butt out, Freshy?" Gibbons fired back.

"I don't want to."

"Well, I want you to, Hollywood."

"Then get some sense in your head and get out of his room."

"Hold your tongue, boy," Gibbons said. He had on his khaki school shirt, allowing him to flash the sergeant's stripes so proudly displayed on his arm.

"Too slippery," I replied.

That drew a blank.

"You are a freshy. You gotta respect me."

"You've got to learn to respect others."

"We're just having fun. Why don't you get lost?"

"You guys have a room. Why don't you go there?" I insisted. My voice didn't crack, but inside my stomach did a flip-flop.

Gibbons moved in closer to me. "Don't you give me no trouble, you hear, Freshy? I've got lots of friends coming back and I'll make you pay."

"Guys like you always claim to have friends."

"You're a snot, Carter."

I turned to leave with a warning, "Keep that crap up, SIR, and I promise your bullying will come back and bite you in the ass."

"Careful, boy. You skatin' on thin ice here."

A day at the school and already on thin ice in Texas, not exactly where I wanted to skate. Gibbons suddenly turned his attention back to Grooper, who seemed to be attempting to shrink into the wall to be less noticed.

"You a Texan, Goober?"

"Yes."

"Hard to believe, ain't it Allen? All the Texans I know have some brains."

"Yeah, all of them," Allen agreed.

A powerful voice boomed words from the doorway, the deep-throated sound swallowing the room with a display of power.

"You are about the dumbest Texan I ever met, Gibbons," the voice said.

Gibbons jerked around, his expression indicating the voice sounded familiar. His demeanor changed from bully to frightened sergeant in an instant. "I thought you said you wasn't coming back, Thompson."

The presence filled the doorway, just as the voice filled the room. "I had to come back, Gibbons, just to save this place from your sorry ass stupidity. Now, get the hell out of here before I do to you what I've done before. And take your little pudgy pal with you."

He pointed a finger at Tommy Allen. Tommy came forward to introduce himself, but Thompson waved him away, and he backed off at once. Thompson stood aside to let Tommy and Gibbons out of the room. They had to squeeze through the doorway because Thompson barely gave them any room to pass.

I exhaled in relief.

At first glance, this Thompson had everything going for him. Back in LA, he could pass for the high school hero, star quarterback of the team, student body president, movie star in training. He stood about six feet two with wide shoulders and the kind of chiseled jaw and cheeks that would turn a girl's eye in an instant. Unlike me, he had retained his full head of hair. Blond and wavy, he wore the hair not too long, probably to conform to some school regulation. Muscles bulged beneath what looked like an elegant, silk, short sleeve sport shirt. His deep-set blue eyes surveyed the two of us. His brown complexion made me wonder if he was Latin, but with a last name like Thompson, I figured he just had a great tan. He entered the room, leaving his suitcases in the hallway.

"Larry Thompson," he said, extending his hand first to me, then to Grooper.

"Cal Carter." Grooper remained silent, apparently dumbstruck by the events that had just unfolded. I introduced him as well.

"Glad to meet you fellows. Don't let that jerk Gibbons get under your skin. He's all mouth. He'll probably try to pull rank and push you around, but don't pay any attention to his crap and he'll soon stop. He's been here forever probably because his parents can't stand to have him around."

"Thanks for the advice," I said. I couldn't figure out the accent, which didn't sound Southern or anything else, though his words came out clearly. "Are you from around here?"

He laughed. "No, thank God for that. I grew up in Venezuela."

"You don't look Spanish," I said.

That drew a laugh. "No my father runs an oil company down there. I went to English language schools growing up."

After a moment's pause, Roland asked, "Are you going to be my roommate?"

Larry shook his head. "I'm in the room across the hall from you."

"You mean that one?" I asked, pointing to my own.

"That's the one."

I almost jumped in joy. "Great, welcome aboard, roomy. Do you need any help bringing your stuff up?"

"Sure," he said. He deposited his suitcases in our room. As I followed him down the outside stairs, he looked back and said, "I'm glad we're roomies. I think we'll do fine."

"I hope so. I don't know what I'm doing here."

We walked around the house to the back and across the field to where Larry's car was parked in the small lot. As we walked, he informed me, "The place takes a while to get used to, but once you catch on to the routine, you'll be fine." We reached the small lot beside the wall that surrounds the school. The sign read *FOR FACULTY ONLY*. Among the few cars parked there, his car stood out the way Marilyn Monroe would stand out if she were to visit an old age home. This black Ferrari 250 convertible looked like a million dollars, or at least $20,000.

All I could do was let out a whistle.

"She's a beaut, isn't she?" Larry agreed. "My Dad spotted the car at the Paris Auto show and ordered one for me as a gift for returning here for another year. They shipped the car to Houston for me to pick up after I flew into Hobby this morning. I'll take you out for a spin later, and you can see it for yourself."

He didn't have much stuff to carry to our room. The car trunk didn't hold much, but he had a record player, a typewriter, and a closed box. I carried the box, and he took the rest. This guy traveled strictly first class.

Even the LA crowd would be impressed by my new roomy. On the way up the stairs, I tried to find out more about him.

"What year are you?"

"I'm a senior. I graduate in June. The car was actually supposed to be a graduation present, but he let me take delivery a year early. What about you?"

"I'm a senior too."

"Wow, that's tough. You're doing your last year here as a freshy."

I put the box down on the nightstand next to Larry's bed. I flopped down on my bed, wondering about the contents of the box and the suitcases. I soon found out he'd brought records for the record player and some personal photos and toiletries. His organising style as he emptied the box made me aware that he was a neat freak. I knew I'd have to stretch myself so as not to fall back to my usual messy habits. I sensed I could learn a lot of the right things from this guy.

Larry first set up his record player, took an album from the collection he'd placed in a neat row close by, and put a cool sound on the turnstyle. The cover said *Blue Moods* by someone named Miles Davis.

"This album just came out," Larry informed me, settling down on his bed to enjoy the sounds. "I picked up the record player and records in Houston. I thought listening to music would help with all the down time we've got here."

That sentence threw me. With the classes I'd been given, I couldn't imagine any down time. I secretly hoped that on top of all his other qualities, Larry, for my sake, would prove to be some kind of math and science genius.

The music had a great vibe. "Those are cool sounds. I mostly like popular and classical, but this is great."

He sat up to face me. "Where are you from, Cal?"

"Cal, California," I said. "Actually, Hollywood." I paused, waiting for the anticipated response.

"I hear that's quite a place," Larry said.

"Yes, that's for sure."

He nodded but didn't say a word about movie stars.

With the music playing loudly, Larry stood up and began to empty the contents of a pair of amazing alligator suitcases. He opened the first one on his bed. Everything inside had a place, had been folded neatly, and he worked diligently taking hangers out to organize and hang his military clothes, which he appeared to have brought back with him. He hung the dress clothes and shirts and then placed the underwear and socks in his dresser drawers. Once he'd emptied the first suitcase, he slid that one under his bed and opened the second. I hoped to see better results than the school clothes he'd unpacked in the first suitcase. To waste such a gorgeous suitcase on crap like those school clothes seemed a crime to me. Ah yes, the open suitcase revealed I had no cause for concern. A suitcase full of classy-looking clothes appeared. He filled the closet with a couple of suits, then the drawers with several sports shirts, dress shirts, ties, cufflinks, and the whole works. Every item he owned showed an elegance of style. Luckily, rooming with a slob like me, Larry had the closet mostly to himself. In LA, I'd known people with bigger houses or more money in the family, but they never made me feel poor like Larry did. While he seemed like a great guy, he enlarged my inferiority complex, an issue that had screwed me up enough already. Curious, I asked, "Those are beautiful clothes, but what will you do with them here?"

"Well, we get holidays and extra time off at Thanksgiving and Christmas. The last thing I want to do is run around Texas in a military school uniform if you catch my drift."

I caught his drift, with thoughts about my two meager pairs of civilian pants and the few shirts I had packed to bring to Texas with me.

"When do you get time away from here?" I wanted to know. Already, my thoughts had moved ahead to vacations at Thanksgiving and Christmas.

"You're allowed one weekend off a month if you have relatives living nearby to visit. Then there are the holidays I mentioned. By the time Thanksgiving comes around, you'll be looking forward to that day, believe me."

"I'm ready for that turkey now," I said with a laugh.

"That's the way I felt when I came here a couple of years ago. But once you get the routine down, you'll relax. The place isn't that difficult if you follow the rules, or avoid them carefully. Put on your cap, school shirt and tie, and we'll head into town for a while."

So you had to wear your uniform in town, bad news. "We have to dress in uniform anytime we go into town?"

"Once classes start, you have to wear a tie and cap every time you leave your room."

"Seriously?"

"Afraid so. And that Texas sun will beat you down. Air conditioning is the only thing that keeps you sane."

"You mean you dress with a tie and all to go to classes?"

"Classes, dinner, inspections, drills. Everyone dresses the same. I'm going to change. As soon as we're ready, we can get a pass so we can go into town for a while."

I stood in front of the wall mirror, trying to tie my tie. The first time, the back section hung way below the front section. The second time the two came closer. With the black tie, the uniform and the brown shoes, I almost resembled a military man, though that wasn't the way I felt. "Can I borrow a cap? I think they forgot to issue me one."

Larry tossed me one of his, which I proceeded to put on backwards. "Here, look," he said, coming to help, for my frustration was apparent in the mirror. He showed me how to peak my cap properly. "We have to go over to the special requests office to get a pass. A pass is needed anytime you leave the grounds at an unauthorized time.'"

"Let's cut out," I said.

We crossed the drill field and headed inside the administration building, only to find the Special Requests office closed.

"Probably closed because school isn't officially open until Monday," Larry guessed.

"What now?"

"We go into town anyway. They can get on my case, but you can claim you didn't know you needed a pass. Since school hasn't started, we'll be okay."

For the first time in my life, I found myself in the passenger seat of a Ferrari convertible. Larry started the car up and the engine roared like a locomotive. We headed into the town of Cullen, Texas, with a population of 12,618 as per the 1950 census. Larry covered the quarter-mile distance in a split second or less. The car could have left the ground and flown into town. That wouldn't have been a surprise. He parked in front of a drugstore that advertised a soda fountain inside. As we were the only occupants sitting on the stools in the middle of the afternoon, we ordered cokes and played records on the jukebox. We didn't know what to do.

"Is this town always so dead?" I asked.

"If you want to see the place jump, wait until tonight. Saturday night is when the cotton pickers hit town. We're allowed to go into town then, but we are required to take taxis to and from wherever we are headed. Last year, a couple of guys got stabbed the first week of school. You know, in a small town like this, they don't have many cops, just enough to keep order and hand out tickets during the week. Well, when the cotton pickers show up on Saturday night and get liquored up, the town blows wide open. It's every man for himself."

"Can't you drive your car in?"

"They stopped that three years ago. Two cadets drove into town on a Saturday night to go to a movie. They do have one theater here. During the movie, they had a problem with some guys sitting behind them. When the picture ended, the guys followed them out. As they started their car to leave, one of those jokers tossed a brick through the front window. Both cadets were cut up badly. One lost a lot of blood and almost died. Now, the school doesn't allow cadets to keep cars during the school year."

Larry confused me. "But you have a car?"

"Yeah, and the day school starts, I'll park my beauty in a garage I've rented here in town. I'll leave the car there to use whenever I feel the need. What they don't know won't hurt them."

"When my aunt drove me here, we both noticed what a nice-looking little town this appeared to be. The school bulletin called Cullen an 'industrious little town,' filled with various churches and white picket fences. From what you have told me, there's a whole different side to the place."

"The only thing Cullen is known for is race riots. Don't believe what they tell you in the Roxwell BS book."

"Like?"

"Like you read the school catalogue, and you think you're headed to a resort. That's not anywhere near the truth. They talk a great game. The lake they write about, claiming you can fish and row their boats around, has been dried up for years; if someone mentions that, they say they must update the catalogue, but they never do. The only open water around the school is the cesspool."

"And the swimming pool?" I cut in.

"Great if you like swimming in green slime."

I began to wonder at my stupidity. We were all taken in, and I agreed to go without seeing the place. I told that to Larry.

"Most of the kids who go here are Texas kids, so they come to visit before they sign up. They see that the catalogue is full of crap, but their parents still sign them up. Every year, the place almost fills up. The school must have some of the best salesmen in Texas."

"But you came back, though you don't like the place. What do you plan to do after you graduate?"

Before he answered, he called for a refill on our cokes and ordered a sandwich. As a growing boy, I followed suit.

"I'm not sure. We own a big ranch in Venezuela. I might learn how to run that. I might travel around Europe for a while. My Dad wants me to go into the oil business. What about you?"

That same question had been bugging me through all the summer. "I don't know. I love learning, though. I want to go to college. Then, I'm not sure. Maybe do something to help people."

He gave me a look, like why would you care? I'd seen that reaction from others before.

Just like that, the focus of the afternoon shifted. A girl came in and sat down on a stool next to me, though all the other counter stools remained empty. She'd permed her brown hair and wore a fluffy, tight, white blouse whose cut best showed off her endowments. She wore black pants and sandals. The heavy makeup around her blue eyes gave her a somewhat hardened look, and she smiled in our direction just as she ordered a cup of coffee.

Before I could even think of a word to get out, Larry had shifted to the stool on the girl's other side. He began a low-range conversation that made the words difficult to hear, but from her body language and occasional laughter, she enjoyed hearing whatever words flowed from his mouth. I did catch the word Ferrari in the conversation. Larry laid his pitch on as smooth as the butter I spread across my morning toast. Within a couple of minutes, they both stood up.

"Cal, can you find your way back? I'm going to take Jill here for a spin in the car and I may be gone a while. See you later."

As they exited the drugstore, he winked at me just as the counter girl handed me a bill for the cokes and sandwiches.

On the walk back to the school, my blood boiled. When I reached the room, I slammed the door shut and stretched out across the bed. Watching that guy operate after I froze up filled me with anger. Why did flirting come so easy to some people and so hard to others, that is to me? I thought of Keith. I recalled the only chance I'd ever had for sex. Four of us members from my high school club drove down to TJ to spend the night partying. One of the guys had a brother in San Diego with whom we could stay, so we didn't have to drive all the way back home to LA. First, we went drinking in a bar filled with music and Bar girls. A guy picked up on us and took us to a whorehouse a couple of blocks off the main street. I'd never seen anything like this dump. The building, made of wood, had a ramshackle appearance as if the place might collapse at any moment. Past the small entry area, beds had been placed in long rows on each side of a walkway, each bed with only a mattress and each separated from the next by curtains. We stood in the front reception area, waiting until four girls appeared to escort each one of us back to a bed.

I think the price they charged was two dollars. When my turn came, a slightly overweight girl took my hand to lead me back to her bed. She looked a few years older than me with her dark hair and sad brown eyes. She reminded me of all those sad songs I'd heard in Spanish but couldn't understand. At the bed, she asked for the two dollars in Spanish, holding up two fingers for emphasis. Then she closed the curtains. All around were the sounds of lovemaking. I stood at the foot of the bed as she pulled her dress over her head. Flab from her stomach hung down over her brown skin. Never before had I seen a naked girl in the flesh. Never had I imagined such a repulsive environment. I stared at the mattress with only a stained sheet covering. Instead of wanting sex, I wanted to throw up. I stood there with my pants half down, and then I pulled them back up. I retreated up the walkway between the rows of beds and rushed straight out the front door to the night and fresh air. I didn't say a word to my friends; I just listened to them brag about their paid conquests, as if each one had turned into Don Juan.

Now, lying on the bed thinking about Larry's smooth moves, all those paralyzing moments of indecision and fear returned. My shoulders ached, and I wanted to puke. I'd only known the guy a couple of hours, but clearly, Larry made life look so easy. He didn't hesitate. He didn't question himself. Keith acted the same way. No thought, just actions.

I know I'm not ugly. That girl sat down next to me, not Larry. I'm no Goober. That thought led to an impulse; I wanted to jump right out our second story window. But who would care? My mother would weep some tears but still have her pride and joy, Keith. My uncle would say, "Maybe military school wasn't right for the kid after all." Larry wouldn't give my death a second thought. Keith would attend the funeral, but would he really care? He saw me as a loser. Besides, with my luck, I'd jump and just break an ankle.

I'd waded through this issue numerous times, my feelings bursting over me like a sudden afternoon drenching. What brought me to this point? Am I always going to be this way? What if I took my razor and cut my wrists or my throat? What would Roxwell say when they found me lying in a pool of blood? Why, they'd ask, why did he do himself in? Not that they'd really care. They'd just be curious why young

Calvin Carter, with his whole life before him, would want to commit suicide. Then, again, maybe that's happened at the school more than once, and they would just write me off as another loser who couldn't handle the pressure. They probably already have some bullshit story made up for kids who do themselves in. I suspect that probably happens at least once or twice every year. Schools, all institutions, just want to cover their asses.

Nobody would know or understand the real reasons Cal Carter, a Hollywood boy, spent his whole life living outside the day-to-day world, viewing events through an imaginary plate glass window, never really becoming a part of his surroundings. He'd watched the passing parade, people marching like a troop of lemmings headed to certain death.

That made me laugh. I began to feel better.

I'd answered my own question. My job consisted of standing at that window that separated me from the world to watch life march by, never good enough, clever enough, smart enough, mean enough, to join the parade. Keith had brought up these feelings often, and now Larry did the same. But he seemed nicer than Keith.

As an odd creature, an outsider. I had labored to be an insider instead of accepting myself as I am. All these thoughts shot through my mind like bullets and gave me new energy. I sat up on the edge of the bed. For better or worse, in the future, I would remain true to myself and the consequences be damned.

Dealing with this crisis in my head made me feel better. I just had to be patient. With patience, my time would come.

I flipped on the radio and stretched out across my bed to listen. The only station without static came from Cullen, and they played one hick country song after the next. What a waste. I sat up, thinking perhaps to try Larry's record player. Maybe that would piss him off. I didn't know him well enough yet to take the risk. It was time to start one of the new books that arrived in the trunk. Books are great if you want to lose yourself, and living here, I would need to lose myself in order to survive.

When Larry walked in, I remained still sprawled across the bed, staring up at the ceiling.

"Hey, how come you didn't wait there?" He asked.

"You said to find my way back. I thought you might be a long time. Sitting at the counter myself seemed boring. Anyway, I liked walking back. How was the doll?"

"Really sharp. Lucky she walked in. She's just come to live here from Houston, moved with her parents, and doesn't know anyone yet. In her last year of high school."

"You couldn't have gone to her place."

A big smile crossed his face. He sat down on his bed across from me. "Wanna bet? Her parents are back in Houston until Monday, finishing up some stuff. I'm going back over there tomorrow. I asked if she had a friend for you, but she really doesn't know anyone yet."

His words relaxed me. "Sounds like you've got a cool deal going. Well, this is Saturday night. Is there anything to do? Should we hit a movie?"

"Why don't we take a spin? We could drive to Stinson. Since school hasn't officially opened, we can sneak off in our civvies after dark. Then we can take in a movie or mess around there. Stinson's a lot bigger, and there are fewer cotton pickers in town."

Was I ever up for doing something fun, anything fun.

Dressed in sports shirts and slacks, we drove to Stinson in about 40 seconds in his Ferrari. Never in my life had I felt the power of a car until I rode at speeds over a hundred miles an hour. With the top down, I feared my head would blow off and go flying down the road. Larry drove like a maniac, but a really skilled one.

As Larry said, Stinson proved to be much larger than Cullen, hosting three different movie theaters. We chose one and grabbed a bite before the next feature, a western, began. The second film made me homesick. This is what is known as a B picture that a theater tacks on to a double bill after the feature, a cheapie; this one told a story of teenagers running around LA doing bad things. As I saw streets I'd driven on, places I'd visited at one time or another, a wave of nostalgia came over me. Again, I questioned why the hell I'd agreed to come here. I couldn't stop thinking about the consequences of my decision.

Afterwards, we found a drive-in open, parked the car in a space and had a carhop bring us coffee and hamburgers. The girls on one side kept checking out the car. The guys on the other side played country music so loud you couldn't hear yourself think…that worked okay for me. Larry made a feeble effort to hustle the two girls, but he didn't have his heart in his banter, and I wasn't much help.

On the way home, I timed our trip back to Cullen. We made thirty miles in 18 minutes with no ticket. He parked the car in the special lot, and we quietly made our way back, though the damn stairs creaked as we crept up to the second-floor landing.

"We gotta oil them damn stairs," Larry joked as we opened the door to our room. We were in bed by one.

Sunday, I spent most of the day applying indelible ink to my uniforms. This tedious job took a long time. Larry showed me how to mark each item and where to apply it before he took off to see his new best girl, Carol. After I finished marking all my clothes and ate lunch, I stretched out on the bed, wondering about the start of school, how I'd survive my classes, and what the teachers were like in a military school. Monday would undoubtedly be the beginning of the rest of my life.

That night, we had a bull session with Larry, me, Grooper, and his new roommate, Charlie Harris. He had arrived during the day. Charlie seemed a quiet guy with short brown hair and a face soft as a teddy bear. He came from Houston and had returned to Roxwell for his junior year. After an hour of meaningless chatter, I headed to bed, knowing we had to get up at 6:30 for a roll call and breakfast before the day began.

That night, sleep became evasive, like a thief I couldn't catch.

CHAPTER TEN

"Right faaaace. Forward, marrrrch." The Cadet Major's sonorous voice boomed across the open space like the beginning credits of a horror film. Facing him were two hundred cadets, uniforms drenched, reddened faces eaten by the Texas sun, producing perspiration like a waterfall of tears. The Cadet Major's voice sliced the thick morning air as we marched toward the drill field. "Keep in step. A left…a left…a left right left."

I tried my best to keep up. If I lagged for even an instant, good old Sergeant Gibbons, marching directly behind me, stepped on my shoe, causing me to lurch forward. My soaked shirt stuck to my wet skin. I have always sweated easier than others, and today the liquid poured down my body like a heavy rain.

"Division halt, one-two."

Two hundred cadets halted, but possibly only one had the back of his shoe stepped on at that moment. I lurched forward as we all turned on command to face the temporary platform, where a tall man in an officer's uniform stared down at rows of cadets lined up in a shoddy formation.

"Good day, gentlemen. My name is Major Peters, and I am the representative officer for the United States Army here at Roxwell. First, let me offer a word for you returning cadets. I have enjoyed the association we have developed over the past year, which, as you know, was my first in service here. I hope this relationship will continue to make this year profitable for all of us. And now, I offer this word to you, new cadets. Like you, I had to find my way here only a year ago. A new situation always includes some difficulty, but for a military man overcoming difficulty is what makes for a better officer. I would like to offer each of you a piece of advice. If you want to succeed at Roxwell, treat the experience seriously and do as you are told. Have respect for your superiors whether they are your cadet officers, teachers, or the administration. If you follow this course, life here at Roxwell will soon become rewarding for you. You will have the opportunity to watch yourself grow from boys to men. Remember, a man is someone who can take orders as well as give them. Unfortunately, and I saw this last year, there are always those few who rebel against authority, who do not take Roxwell seriously, or think they know more than others. To those few, I address the next part of my talk. Your rebellion will not work here. Do not bother to try. I saw a few who failed last year, but I would be pleased to see no one fail this year. If you accept the situation ahead, even if you did not choose to be here, you will make the best of your experience. If you cannot do that, I advise you to get out now before the going gets rough, for you will experience some rough moments in your first year at Roxwell. I will now turn the platform over to Mr. Roxwell. He will read out the list of promotions for this year. And thank you for your kind attention."

As Roxwell stepped to the podium, I silently laughed at the "kind attention" we all had given him, as if we had a choice.

"May I have your attention, please?" Asked Mr. Roxwell, though there wasn't a peep out of anyone in attendance. Mr.

Roxwell started with the meaningless task of reading off promotions, our great leaders for this year. He stood on the podium tall and firm, with shoulders erect. He had an expression that telegraphed and harbored no nonsense. Somehow, and I couldn't begin to tell you why at the time, I sensed in that man a gentleness that he kept hidden beneath the stern façade he showed the cadets. He started by naming the cadet captains, then worked his way down to the corporals and various squad leaders over what felt like an eternity. As each cadet heard his name called, he took a step forward, and moved to his assigned place. For a moment, I fantasized that he would call my name. "Cadet Carter, step forward. You are appointed a company captain." Ridiculous. Why would I even care? Still, as the admiring cadets looked on, I pictured myself stepping forward to applause. As I accepted the appointment, I would concurrently be thinking how stupid the whole military system was. That appealed to my sense of irony.

Roxwell's tone shifted after finishing the list of promotions. He turned his attention to those of us who would be the followers. "Gentlemen, when you marched out here, you were arranged according to height. The purpose behind this was to assign you a company by height. The tallest cadets will make company A, the next group, Company B, and the remainder of cadets make up companies C and D. In addition, there will be a band company built on your ability to play an instrument rather than your height."

If he meant to draw a laugh with that line, he failed. "Any cadet who plays a musical instrument, and is not currently in the band company, step forward." A few cadets took a step.

"You cadets fall out and report to Lieutenant McDonald directly behind this speaker's platform, please."

The cadets hesitated.

"Now, please," Roxwell commanded.

For the first time in my life, I wished I played the tuba, trombone, or any instrument that would have put me in the band. They undoubtedly would have more fun goofing around than the rest of us.

I watched the lucky musical cadets disappear behind the speaker's platform. "As for the rest of you men, stay in place until you are assigned to a company. That's all for now and may I wish you luck in the forthcoming year. Thank you."

Mr. Roxwell left the speaker's stand to polite applause. The newly chosen officers conferred for a while and then divided the groups. I ended up in C company because I was about average height at five-nine. C company was then divided into two platoons, each containing five squads. Five men composed a squad. Once divided, a brand new cadet lieutenant marched us back over to where we'd begun this bit of theater, directly under the flagpole, where we pledged our allegiance each morning to god and country.

The lieutenant and his sergeant went about lining up squads in an orderly fashion. When they were satisfied, the lieutenant barked, "All right, you men, take a good look at where you are standing. Study the man behind you and in front of you, the one to your left and right. At every formation, you will be lined up beside them, in front of them and behind them. Memorize their faces. You will be standing in this same formation all year long. Learn your squad number. You are in Company C, either first or second platoon. You are either in squad one, two, three, four, or five. And in that squad you are either the first, second, third, fourth, or fifth man. Have your mail sent care of C Company and your platoon. That's all for now. The next formation will be at noon. Dismisssssed."

All I wanted to do was head for my room, take off my soaking shirt and towel myself off. Instead, I found Larry. "How come you weren't promoted?" I asked him.

Unlike me, his shirt only showed a small amount of moisture over his chest and no sweat on his face. "I didn't stay through the whole year last year."

"I didn't know that. How long were you here?"

"Six months. Come on. Let's go over and get a coke. I'm beat and we've only got fifteen minutes until lunch formation."

"Sounds good," I said, sweaty shirt forgotten.

We went to the room that housed the coke machine and waited in line for a few minutes until we could buy our cokes. We joined two other guys at a table and talked about nothing. The trend in this school seemed to be that everyone liked to shoot the breeze about nothing. I couldn't help thinking…was that my future? To spend the rest of my life discussing nothing with people who had nothing to talk about.

Then the mighty bugle sounded, and we hurried off to formation. In a panic, I ran around trying to find the faces in front and back of me, the guys to each side. A couple of wrong turns, a right one, and there I stood in my correct place in line, surrounded by cadet left side, cadet right side, cadet in front, and the cadet behind.

"This is your meal formation," the lieutenant shouted out. "You will line up every day prior to breakfast, lunch and dinner. There's already some mail that has arrived, and you all come up and get your letter when I call your name. Jackson, Robinson." He paused. "Robinson, is he in this company?"

Silence.

"No Robinson. Okay, Stone, Pendergast, Carter, Arnold and Bender."

I broke formation to retrieve the letter, which, to my surprise, came from Ray. As I returned, I tucked the letter into my rear pocket, planning to enjoy the contents later in the quiet of my room. Touching the envelope brought memories of home: cool breezes, fun nights, lazy days.

In step, or mostly in step, we marched by squad and squadron into the mess hall, peeling off into circular tables where we sat down with our squad. As we took our food squad by squad, and ate our lunch, the Dean stood up in front of a mike and made a few personal announcements: Curfew times, 13:30 formation, and to consult our schedule to make sure we attended all our afternoon classes. 12:30 arrived. Dismissed. Everyone stood up at once, and the noise of a couple hundred cadets rushing out the door surprised me. With only an hour before the next formation, I hurried back to my room, flopped down on the bed, and pulled the slightly bowed envelope from my back pocket.

Inside the envelope, Ray had sent a clipping from the local LA Times: the race results. I examined the folded paper closely, recognizing the names of horses I'd seen run and a couple I'd even bet on. Ray had circled the names of several of the horses. I put the clipping down to read the letter.

A lot of chatter filled Ray's letter, similar to the chatter heard here at school. He wrote that Bob was doing this, Joe had dropped out and decided not to go to college, and Mike got busted for being drunk in public, just typical of what Ray would write about. He talked about a girl he was dating, how he'd started back to school, and how a few people asked about me. He told me he'd gone to the track, but the afternoon wasn't the same. The horses he'd circled were the ones he'd bet on. I noticed they'd all run out of the money.

I tucked the letter and the clipping back into the envelope and placed the contents in my nightstand drawer. As this letter became my first contact from home, I'd pull the envelope out over the next few days to read Ray's words again, three or four times. With the letter safe, I turned to my class schedule written in my notebook, which read like a doomsday book: Chemistry and English, with a fifteen-minute break between the two classes. That afternoon schedule appeared to be the best part of my day, for Chemistry alternated with study hall. No doubt I'd flunk chemistry. Maybe I'd be here until I turned thirty, trying to pass a bunch of courses I hated.

Larry had come in while I tried to figure out where to go for those classes, and instantly passed out on his bed. As the hour for assembling approached, I woke him up, and we rushed off to formation. This time I located my place in line easier.

Standing with a notebook in one hand and my class schedule in the other, I morphed into Calvin Carter, a Student Cadet. The Lieutenant barked out the information to all us dummies. We would be marching through the various buildings that housed the classrooms. When we reached our first designated class of the afternoon, we should drop out of the line and enter the classroom. A freshy made the mistake of asking if we would line up like this before each class, which drew a sarcastic laugh from the Lieutenant in charge. "Sure, Cadet, feel free to do that. But don't expect to have any company." The cadets roared, and the questioner turned a bright red.

Off we marched to class after learning our next formation would be before dinner at six o'clock. "No talking in line now. One, two, one, two, left right left."

We entered the first building, the building my class was scheduled in, and marched down the hallway, cadets dropping off as we passed various classrooms. When I spotted room 17, I dropped out of the line and entered the front door of the dreaded chemistry class, which inside the room felt like a visit to Dante's inferno. If the classroom had been a degree hotter, the entire place might have exploded from chemical combustion. Fresh sweat sprang out beneath my already stained uniform as I located a seat far from the front of the class, sitting down in one of those old-fashioned chairs with an attached wooden pallet for writing on. The cadet to my left looked as terrified as I felt.

The instructor, a no-nonsense type with hollow cheeks and a

gray moustache, entered the room. He wore a white shirt, a tie, and a pair of slacks. His gray hair appeared to have been lawn-mowed across the top. He called role out of a book before he passed out our chemistry books. This may have been orientation week, but there was no orientation. No formalities, no niceties, just let's get to work and learn this chemistry. Back home, at my old school, classes sometimes took a week to get into any kind of serious rhythm, and sometimes the entire semester passed without a serious moment.

This guy attacked chemical formulas with a passion usually reserved for gamblers. From the moment he started explaining that first compound, I felt lost from his initial words. Chemistry was for people interested in chemicals. I tried to concentrate on what he explained, but within a few minutes, my mind dived into the swimming pool in our apartment building at home, recalled girls in sexy bathing suits, rode around in souped-up cars, and ate a burger and a silver goblet at Bob's Big Boy. After filling a blackboard with an hour and fifteen minutes of non-stop confusion, he handed out a three-page homework assignment and dismissed the class.

The guy who had been sitting next to me shook his head as we left the class together. "I don't get any of this," he said.

"You've got some company, namely me."

"All those formulas and stuff. They don't make sense."

"None of this does." We turned to go in different directions. "Well, we'll see you," I muttered, a stock phrase of mine. The next class, room 26, was English. At least this instructor had a fan going, and the room felt reasonably pleasant. We sat quietly for a few minutes before a bell ran, and the instructor entered: a short bald-headed man with a big nose who looked as if he wanted to be somewhere else, anywhere else, instead of trying to teach English to a bunch of boneheads wearing uniforms. As he outlined the expectations for the semester, my heart sank. I had anticipated that this class would offer a respite, literature, poetry, and provocative discussions. Instead, in a voice that lulled one to sleep, he droned on about outlines and the textbook and papers that would be due. When he finally passed out the textbook, I wondered if the John Birch society had assembled the contents. At first glance, each essay highlighted or glorified patriotic acts to emphasize America's greatness. If some foreigner arrived here, and he only had this textbook to help him understand the country, he'd think we were the most flawless country in the world. How ironic to be here in the land of slaves and whips, among secessionists who had lost the Civil War, and then to receive a textbook about how great America is. When the class ended, the one highlight was the sound of that bell that finally ended our misery.

Next came an hour of study hall, a class that ordinarily alternated with chemistry, but on this first day of orientation, we were expected to attend an hour class at 16:00 hours. Entering the room, I spotted Gibbon's sidekick, Allen, sitting by himself and decided to join him.

Hi, Allen, what's happening?" I asked, as I plopped down into the desk chair next to him.

"Oh, nothin' much. I just finished a class in military science. Man, that's really bad."

"Sounds like it would be. What made you decide to come here?"

Allen scratched his nose as he contemplated such a deep question. "Oh, I don't know. Guess I came along because Gibbons wanted me to, and my Pa thought Roxwell might shape me up, or something like that. I think Gibbons was missin' having one of his San Antone boys around."

I nodded understanding. I'd been a lot happier if my pal Ray had come along to share the misery. Allen, by himself, didn't seem like such a bad guy. A little slow, perhaps, but okay.

The instructor arrived. Like the others, he looked like a man bored with life and himself. He sat down and laid out the rules. No talking in the study hall. He said we'd get a slip if he heard any of us talking, and three slips would bring a demerit. That sounded like no big deal, as I had no idea what a demerit meant at that time.

The first English exercises we'd been given in our workbook were a breeze. I finished them up in about ten minutes, then bored with this boring study hall, laid my head down on my desk and tried to sleep. Perhaps they gave demerits for sleeping. But I couldn't sleep, and as far as I know, I didn't receive a demerit.

Back in our room, Larry was sitting at the desk working on something when I barged in. "Hey, Lar, what the hell is a demerit?"

That brought a squeal you might call a laugh as he turned to face me. "So. You've never heard about the famous Roxwell demerit system?" I shook my head in response.

"What do you say I explain as we go to Frenchy's for a hamburger?" This suggestion came just an hour before we would line up for dinner.

On our way across campus, Larry explained the system. "There are a number of different ways to get demerits. But for every demerit you get, you have to do an hour of marching with your rifle."

"I don't have a rifle."

"Not yet, but you will. They'll issue you one sometime this week, an M-1 like the ones they use in the regular army."

This made no sense. "For God's sake, when is there time to march? They've got you going day and night here."

"You know, we only go to school Tuesday through Saturday starting next week. Monday mornings are spent drilling on the parade field. Afterwards, there's lunch and then the afternoon is free. You screw up, you march on Monday afternoon."

"You're messing with me, aren't you?"

We reached Frenchy's and ordered hamburgers and cokes before he answered. "I wish I was. Monday afternoon is the only day you are free to do what you want. I mean, there's Sunday after church, but there isn't anything open. You've got five hours between the end of lunch and dinner formation on Monday, and if you screw up enough, you can march the whole afternoon."

"There's got to be a limit on how many demerits you can get."

"Bullshit." This was the first time I'd heard him swear. "No limit. For different infractions, you get different demerits. The most you can get at one time is forty. That's if you go AWOL and get caught. Each of the others depends on the seriousness of the offense. Watch out. Certain officers will pop them on you just because they don't like the way you look."

"Jeez," I said, then didn't know what else to say. I had no idea of any of this. "But do people really go AWOL from here?"

Frenchy, wearing his funny chef's hat, brought out two plates, each with hamburgers and fries, and Larry consumed a large bite of his sandwich before he replied. "Sure, lots of guys take off during the year. This is how that works. You're in a company. That company competes with every other company every year to win the Giles cup. That's a big deal. The company that has the lowest demerits at the end of the year wins it. So if someone gets caught going AWOL, he and the company get forty demerits. He has to do forty hours of marching, that's about ten weeks of four-hour marches on Monday afternoons, and on top of that, the company usually beats his ass for causing them so many demerits. But if you AWOL, and you don't get caught, and you don't return, the company doesn't get any demerits. So if you decide to take off, you better make sure you are gone if you know what's good for you. That's why everything is a game here. Last year, a kid took off. He was so scared he'd get caught and brought back, he hitched all the way to New Orleans and stowed away on a boat going to Africa."

Larry had planted a seed. "So, did he make it?"

"Yes, as a matter of fact, from what I heard, he's still over there."

"Who told you?"

"His brother still goes here."

"What about your leaving? Did you get demerits?"

By now, he had polished off half his burger. He shook his head. "Approved withdrawal doesn't count against anything," he explained.

Fatigue grabbed me, and in an instant, my body drained, making me as weak as a baby. All I wanted to do was hit the sack. "We better go back. I'm bushed."

We finished our food and drinks, paid up, and side by side, headed back to the room. My shirt had now sustained a couple of soakings and drying outs since I'd dressed early in the morning, and the walk back across campus in the late afternoon steam bath brought out a third layer of moisture. As soon as we reached the room, I removed my tie and shirt and stretched out on the bed.

"Better put a clean shirt on," came a voice. I thought my dream had spoken. My watch said no, you have ten minutes before formation. I hurriedly put on a clean shirt and tied the tie. Larry and I rushed off to formation.

On the way, I glanced at my roommate and wondered what made Larry so attractive as a friend. Aside from the fact that he had his act together, stood for the right things, and owned a Ferrari, what made me feel so comfortable with him? We didn't share any common intellectual interests. He didn't seem to care about literature or art. He didn't seem particularly brilliant. The bottom line was that his closeness gave me a sense of calm, and that all would be right. Ray had given me somewhat the same secure feeling. So many similar guys would bore me, but not those two.

I didn't have time to resolve this because dinner formation became my priority. We lined up and marched to the dining hall for dinner. For our first official day, they served a real Southern treat: pork chops and yams. Much to my amazement, despite eating the hamburger, I still had an appetite. At least the food tasted great. Dean Crommy, my favorite person, stood up to make a few announcements as we were eating dessert.

"There will be no study hall tonight. Tomorrow night, there will be a study hall for men with last names beginning with the letters A and B. Look for daily posts regarding night study hall. If you are assigned to the night study hall, you will report to the study hall directly within thirty minutes after dinner ends. That should give you time to go back to get your books. As for the rest of you, demerits are now in effect. We will begin with the regular nightly program. You are free until 19:30, when you return to your room for study hours. Anyone caught outside his room without a pass will be issued demerits. Lights go out at 21:30. Any questions?"

The Dean made a quick survey of the room and sat down. Dinner was dismissed. I met Larry outside the mess hall. We returned to our room and stretched out after Larry put on a record. A minute later, Gibbons appeared.

"Don't you knock?" Larry asked.

"I forgot. I wanted to see if you fellows were up for a poker game. Allen, I, and Dugan from downstairs are lookin' to start a game."

Larry and I traded glances. Poker sure beat studying chemistry. "I'm in," I told Gibbons. "How about you, Larry?"

A wry smile crossed my roomie's lips. "Well, I guess I could take some money from a Gibbons ape."

We laughed while Gibbons held his tongue.

"Where's the game?" Larry asked.

"In Goober's room. But Goober ain't playin' cause he don't know how, and his roommate is downstairs doing something."

Gibbons left to bring the others while Larry and I walked across the hall. I hadn't played poker for a while, but I used to play almost every weekend with Ray and some of the guys from our club.

In Grooper's room, the players exchanged Texas "howdy's" before we settled down on the floor between the two beds to play in earnest. Five of us played, while a few cadets I didn't know acted as kibitzers. Stakes were nickels, dimes, and quarters, and we used different colored chips that Gibbons had brought. Despite the rule against smoking, the players all sat cross-legged in a circle with cigarettes dangling from their lips, reminding me of the dice games we played behind the bleachers in high school. Roland appeared totally disconnected, sitting on his bed, unable to follow a game he didn't know. He kept waving his hand in front of his face, trying to push away the smoke that began to hang over the room like a layer of LA smog, even with the window open. We played steadily until the clock struck 7:30, that is 19:30 military time when Roland tried to put his foot down.

"Hey, uh, fellas, it's time to start studying. Can't you go to another room to play?"

"Goober, can't you just keep your mouth shut?" Gibbons asked. He must have had a hot hand because he bet the limit even before any of us drew our cards in a five-card draw.

Grooper looked around, seeking support, but none came. Even his roommate, Charles Hammer, had returned to the room and was sitting on his own bed following the game. Roland picked up a book and started to read, then glanced in my direction.

"Cal, don't you all have to study now?"

"Forget it, Roland. This beats studying any day." I hesitated before I turned to Larry. "Say, Lar, can't we get demerits if someone catches people smoking and playing poker like this?"

"Sure, but they have to catch us first. And we can always hear someone on those creaky stairs. And if another cadet is coming, he calls out 'rest', so you know you can go on with whatever you are doing."

Roland had opened a book, but he couldn't concentrate. He had begun to cough from the smoke.

Since Larry and I were both winning, Gibbons figured everything was palsy-walsy between Larry and him. He stood up during a break, spotted an open drawer filled with underwear and pulled out a pair of white boxer shorts with blue polka dots. He pointed them at Roland. "These yours, Goober?"

Roland looked up, and saw the underwear, and his eyes narrowed.

"They kind of look like a flag," Gibbons babbled on. "Think I'll wave them out the window so everyone can see what pretty underwear you wear, Goober. You like that idea, Goober?"

I glanced at Larry. Without a word, I understood he thought the time had come for Roland to stand up for himself.

"Don't do that, Gibbons."

"Mr. Gibbons, Freshy."

"Please, Mr. Gibbons, don't do that."

"Any why not?" Gibbons asked. He walked over to the window, which overlooked the empty marching field. Grooper's roommate was following Gibbons with his eyes. He appeared ready to step in if the situation grew out of hand. The baiting seemed so stupid, as nobody would see a damn thing if Gibbons waved those boxers around all night.

The moment Gibbons pretended to move the boxers toward the window, Roland jumped up and moved towards him. He stood about a head above his adversary. He made a wild grab at his underwear, but Gibbons kept moving the pair of shorts out of reach.

"Give them to me," Roland demanded.

Gibbons gave him a shove instead. Then he waved the boxers out the window with one hand.

That's when Roland lost what little cool he had and snapped. He took a wild swing at Gibbons and, much to the surprise of all assembled, landed a clenched fist smack on Gibbon's mouth. Off balance, Gibbons tumbled back against a dresser and dropped to the floor, somehow depositing the disputed boxers out the window where they floated like a parachute to the ground. Roland ran out of the room in pursuit, and we next heard the clattering of his shoes against the rickety outside stairs as he retrieved his beloved shorts from the ground below.

Gibbons stood up slowly, rubbing his mouth with one hand and the back of his head with the other. He had a dazed expression, like someone who had accidentally bounced into a wall he hadn't seen. As he regained what senses he had, his fists tightened.

The entire room had broken into laughter at the unexpected ending to the confrontation. Larry and I, both seeing Gibbons's intent, jumped up just as Roland entered the room, cradling his shorts. Gibbons started moving toward him, freezing when Larry and Charles stepped in his path.

"Lay a finger on him, Gibbons, and I'll flatten you."

"Me too," I added. Charles just stared.

When Gibbons spoke, his voice assumed a little boy whine. "Wal, he hit me."

The room erupted in new laughter, and a humiliated Gibbons stalked out the door, followed by his loyal San Antonio sidekick, Allen.

As Larry and I returned to our room, I felt for the first time that I might actually be able to survive here.

But to survive, I decided, the time had come to get down to business. I pulled out my chemistry book and tried to make sense of the homework assignment. The text remained senseless. I asked Larry if he understood chemistry, but he just shook his head. I picked up a book on personality traits I'd brought along and started reading the intro a second time. Larry played records until we finally got ready for bed and turned the lights out, exhausted from the ordeal of the day. As I was falling asleep, I heard a chuckle from the other bed, and I had to laugh all over again.

CHAPTER ELEVEN

The next day, Tuesday, played a decisive role in my still tender military life. After the fun we'd had the night before, I remained indecisive about the whole Roxwell experience. While I could learn to march, follow the rules, and even put up with idiots like Gibbons, none of these issues equaled my main concern. These remained obstacles to be overcome but would be achieved in vain if, in the end, I did not pass my classes and graduate. Math and science courses weighed me down like anchors, each class having far too much precision and detail for one with an unscientific mind who preferred the humanities—on the plus side, having Larry as a buddy made much difference. Until now, I'd given the school the benefit of the doubt, realizing my few days there had been too short to reach any realistic conclusions.

Then came Tuesday. By the end of the day, I hated the place and decided I wouldn't stay here the entire year.

My first-morning class, Algebra II, started the day's descent. Math isn't the subject one wants to face right after breakfast. I flunked geometry in tenth grade mostly because the teacher had kept me in a somnambulistic state throughout the semester. As I'd told the Dean, I hadn't had algebra since junior high school and barely remembered how all those letters and numbers played out. To make matters worse, they held the class in a bungalow that had remained unused throughout the summer. When the teacher opened the door for the class to enter, a burst of stale air choked several of us. The powerful odor of god knows what remained after we entered, and though still early in the morning, the accumulated heat from all those summer days had me drenched in sweat in a matter of minutes. The teacher opened every outside window right off the bat, but the air that entered the room felt hot and humid, rendering his action futile. This chubby teacher had a brightly colored, open-throated, short-sleeved shirt on, but we cadets in our khakis and ties began melting from the starting bell. And to make matters worse, I'd worn a t-shirt beneath my khaki shirt to stop the cloth from itching.

Aside from having learned nothing during the hour, I exited the classroom as wet as if I'd spent an hour sitting in a Turkish bath. And that terrible odor that had filled the room kept me company as I departed.

I wondered if I had time to change shirts before going to the next class. I didn't. At least the Geometry class was conducted in a building with a reasonable temperature. Once the class ended, I realized we still had an hour before lunch formation. On a casual stroll back to my room, I noticed cadets running toward the field where we did formation. I raced alongside them with a sudden turn, remembering that this hour wasn't free but devoted to marching. Once we had settled into our formation, we were marched out onto the field one company at a time. Each company occupied a specific marching area, and the field proved large enough to accommodate every company. Our lieutenant, Foghorn, I nicknamed him, spent the hour teaching us basic positions, attention, at ease, and rest. And marching steps. These went left, right, left, one two, one two, cadences; left face, right face, about face. My already-soaked shirt managed to absorb even more sweat. Sweat poured off my reddening face in buckets. "LEFT FACE, HARCH, RIGHT FACE, HARCH, ABOUT FACE, HARCH. Take a break."

A company of drenched cadets collapsed on the ground briefly before starting back at the drill. Right before we marched into the mess hall for lunch, a pimply-faced cadet handed out the mail. A letter from my mother arrived. I folded the envelope into my soaked back pocket as we marched into the mess hall for lunch.

Before afternoon classes began, I had a brief break, using the opportunity to shower, change into dry clothes, and read my mother's letter. The handwritten two pages on her monogrammed stationary, slightly blurred from storage in my damp back pocket, turned out to be full of chatty information. My brother was doing brilliantly (big surprise) in school, meeting interesting people, and dating "nice" girls. She asked me to send my exact mailing address, unsure if this letter would reach me as addressed. After reading all about my dear brother, I almost wished the letter had never arrived. The rest of her jottings updated me on her activities, and the final paragraph said she realized the adjustment would be difficult but hoped I would do my best, that she had faith in me, and knew that as long as I persevered, the year would turn out all right. But then again, Mother had never taken chemistry.

As I put the letter down on the nightstand beside my bed, to my surprise, tears welled up. Her letter emphasized she only wanted the best for me. My uncle had convinced her that this school experience would be the best. As a single woman raising two sons, she had listened to those close to her to get the help she wanted for me. I had been blaming her, but now I realized she had done her best, even if the choice made for her had been a lousy one.

Larry noticed my expression and asked about the contents of the letter. I didn't want to discuss the details. He didn't press me, but from his expression, he knew all was not right.

We hurried off together for afternoon formation and role call. I struggled through my afternoon classes, a repeat of yesterday. By four o'clock, when the torture finally ended, I felt fed up with the entire situation. The schoolwork alone would present a year-long struggle, one that no doubt would flatten me faster than Rocky Marciano's left jab. The icing on the cake, so to speak, came after dinner that evening. I had to go to study hall for a couple of hours while the guys in my dorm section wasted the entire study time engaged in a shaving cream fight; two hours of fighting with my homework exhausted me. Around ten, I headed back to our room, crawled into bed, and closed my eyes. Before I went under, Gibbons popped into the room.

"Hey, Hollywood Cal," he said, sitting down on my bed. "I want you to do something for me."

He had brilliantly deduced that since I had come from Hollywood, and my name was Cal, he should call me "Hollywood Cal." His face lit up like a pinball machine when he'd first put those two words together.

I rolled over to face him. "I'm going to sleep. What do you want?"

"Wal," he twanged in his cracker voice, "I'm in the mood for a burger. I want you to run over to the snack shop before they close and get me a burger and some fries."

"That's what you want. I want to go to sleep." I rolled over, facing the wall.

His voice raised an octave. "Freshy, what you want don't matter. If I want you to get me a burger, then by God, you better go get me a burger. Don't care what grade you are in. You're just another freshy around here."

I rolled over again and shot a look at Larry, hoping he could save me. His expression told me he could say nothing, as this was how things ran here at Roxwell. "Are you sure Frenchy's is still open?" I asked Gibbons.

"Shore 'nough is," he answered, thrusting a dollar bill in my hand. I crawled out of bed, threw on my pants, a shirt, and my shoes, and started out the door.

"Hey, Cal." Larry's voice caught me on the way out. "Since you're going, would you get me one too?"

He reached into his pocket to hand me another dollar. Irritated, I walked slowly across the parade ground to the snack shop, hoping the place would close up before I arrived—no such luck. I sprang for a burger for myself, just in case anyone asked; I could say I'd wanted one, and brought the others back as a favor. But the pissed look on my face would have told anyone the true story. Other freshy cadets stood around waiting at Frenchy's to fill late-night orders. They had arrived before me, and I didn't feel quite so bad waiting in their company.

I gave Gibbons his burger, fries, and change, and he left the room. Larry sat up in bed to eat his, and I crawled back under the covers before eating mine. That became the decisive moment, the moment of truth when I realized that I intended to stick out Roxwell as long as I could, though chances remained slim that I would survive until the end of the school year. I bit into my burger. Then, my usual thought process began. Maybe I hadn't given the school a chance. Maybe classes would ease up. As long as Larry stayed, I would have a friend, even though he'd pissed me off tonight. Why didn't he walk to Frenchy's with me to ease the humiliation I felt? Another bite reminded me that the world contained so much good: good books, music, theater, and good people. That world is the one I sought, not this one oriented to fighting and patriotism. I'd always taken the world I knew for granted, what I had for granted. Now, shut off from my former life, I thought about my future. That brought me back to Hugo, the psychiatrist. If only mother had stayed with him, I wouldn't be in the pickle I found myself in now. Hugo inspired me. He had turned me on to psychology, music, and the theater. He had proved himself a good person. Like Hugo, I wanted to help people get better. A lot of people needed help. Just look at the guys in this school. They could all use a shrink. I decided the more logical path was to pursue psychology because Hugo had explained that in order to become a psychiatrist, you first needed to become a medical doctor. With a final bite of the hamburger and all this future thought spinning in my brain, I slid down under the covers and instantly fell asleep.

Wednesday was uneventful and boring; the minutes dragged by as if the clock had a rusty hour hand. At least the afternoon offered some relief, a study hall class followed by another nightmare, Military Science and Tactics. Thursday afternoon, after another chemistry class followed by boring English, I rushed over to the office of the Dean. I needed to have a change of program, and despite our mutual dislike, he remained the only person who could change my program.

He tapped his fingers together as he sat behind his desk, staring at me. "What seems to be the problem, Cadet Carter?"

I laid the problem out for him. "This is the first week of school, and I'm already falling behind in Algebra and Chemistry. I'm studying them, but I just don't get what they are about. I'm okay with English and geometry, but I don't want to end up failing classes because I don't understand the work. I just don't have a foundation for all this science and math."

Silence followed by more finger tapping. "I thought you Jews were good at these academic subjects," the Dean said.

"Not this Jew," I responded, narrowing my eyes to remind him that he'd just revealed himself as another fucking anti-Semite.

"If I change a math or science class, you will find that will affect the colleges you can apply to," the Dean warned me.

"That's fine with me."

His expression clearly showed that he detested everything about me.

"Well, I can change one class," he said.

"But it's Algebra and Chemistry. I'll flunk them. I know it."

"One class," he repeated.

"Chemistry," I said. "With luck, I'll figure out Algebra."

"What would you like to take as a replacement?"

"Do you have any classes in psychology?"

The Dean's face froze. Nobody had ever asked him a question like that. "You have to wait until college to study psychology. This is a high school."

"Another English class?"

"We have no elective English classes. However, we have a public speaking course, which might be of interest, both educational and somewhat connected to English."

"Okay, that sounds interesting. What time is it at?"

The Dean consulted the schedule on his desk. "The public speaking class meets at 13:30 hours on Wednesdays and Fridays. What time do you have Chemistry?"

"One-thirty, I mean 13:30 hours, but on Tuesday, Thursday and Saturday. Then I have English."

"And what do you have on Wednesday and Friday at 13:30?"

"Study Hall."

The Dean's expression relaxed. "Excellent. We will switch your Study Hall to 13:30 hours on Tuesday, Thursday and Saturday, and then you can go to public speaking in place of Study Hall beginning tomorrow. Since you are here, Carter, there's one more subject I need to discuss with you."

My heart jumped.

"Tomorrow is Friday. You will have to attend your first evening of Synagogue in town. As I told you before, you are the oldest. You will be in charge of the group of Jewish cadets. I have a list for you with the name of each one. They will be instructed to meet you after mess hall, and you will walk into town together. You must take roll and make sure each cadet stays with you from the time you leave until the moment you return. They'll listen to you, as they are between ten and fourteen. Here is a list of their names and dormitory rooms. That is all."

He handed me the sheet of paper. "Yes, Sir," I said, and left without thanking him. I really felt like beating his thin face into a hamburger, but I understood such an action would most likely not help in my life endeavors.

Friday arrived, and all through the morning, I wondered about my new class. Would there finally be a class I actually enjoyed? My previous public speaking was limited to making wisecracks during class, which had often rewarded me with laughs, but extra time after school and occasionally a trip to the vice-principal's office. Now, I might actually learn how to speak in front of a group.

As difficult as the morning classes proved to be, the afternoon classes now looked much better. Public Speaking followed by English, and alternately, Study Hall, and that stupid Military Science, which wasn't that difficult.

Before lunch Friday, I received two letters, one from Hugo, who had stayed in touch with me even after my mother divorced him. I had written to him from Houston telling him about the school. He urged me to make the best of the experience at hand and said that what I might gain at Roxwell could help me in the future if I decided to pursue a career in psychology. I didn't quite get his logic on that point of view, but I sure got the ten-dollar check he'd included for me to spend. Little did I know how useful that check would be down the road.

At five minutes before the 13:30 bell, I entered the public speaking classroom, which turned out to be a reasonably cool room inside a building. The teacher was already seated behind a big wooden desk. A baldish man, his face showed beet red from too much sun, which immediately made me suspect he was not a local. He sported a brightly colored shirt with funny designs of different hues going in a variety of directions. You could call the shirt style "chaotic". He looked like a zombie as he sat in a trance, and I had to wave a hand in front of his face before his faded blue eyes looked up to take notice of my existence. "You're Carter," he stated, and I nodded in agreement. "Take a seat anywhere," he told me, and I took one in the front row to the right of his desk. As the bell rang and cadets wandered in, I noticed that many of the students taking the class were officers. That raised my suspicions that this would prove to be an easy class, which I desperately needed. Cadet officers had a reputation for being extremely lazy. Sure enough, as soon as class began, a few students laid their heads across their desks and went to sleep. Others read or visited. Finally, the teacher, Mr. Fleming, stood up and said loudly, "Shall we begin?"

My eyes went to his potbelly, which became noticeable when he stood up. He waited patiently for about a minute until the hubbub died down. Fleming smiled at the class, showing all his pearly whites, and said loudly and clearly, "Good afternoon, gentlemen."

The class responded like a group of Pavlovian dogs. "Good afternoon, Mr. Fleming."

"Excellent," the teacher beamed. "Clear and concise. However, Mr. Rollins, you can enunciate more clearly if you lift your head off your desk. Rollins, sitting at the desk next to me, had entered the room at the same time as me and headed straight to dreamland. Fleming's comment did not seem to disturb his slumber.

"Well," Fleming noted, "it appears that Mr. Rollins has had a difficult night. Perhaps I should send him to the Dean's office. I'm sure the Dean has a nice couch he can sleep on."

Rollins's head jerked up, and the class broke into loud laughter.

"You will note we have a new class member with us," he informed them. "His name is Calvin Carter. We are happy to have you aboard, Mr. Carter. Aren't we class?"

When the class did not respond, Mr. Fleming repeated the part about being happy to have me aboard to additional silence. He returned to his desk and picked up a book. "We will take up where we left off in our book on Wednesday. As usual, I will read it first. Listen to how each word is enunciated, as you will be asked to read after I finish. Today, your stress should be solely on pronunciation, though Mr. Dale Carnegie has many important points to make. Shall we begin?"

As Fleming began to read, most cadets returned to what they

had previously been doing: sleeping, reading, or whispering to each other. Fleming pretended not to notice.

The way he spoke fascinated me. Each word came out clearly and precisely, emphasising the right syllable and a certain dramatic tone dictated by the content. I had a sense that I could actually learn something from this guy. After he read for half an hour, he asked one of the students to take a turn reading. The cadet, a lieutenant according to his stripes, grimaced as if he'd been shot but put down his newspaper and picked up his copy of the Carnegie book.

"Begin on page 84," Mr. Fleming said, "But alas, if you had been paying attention, you would have known that."

In a thickly accented Southern voice, the student began to read. He mumbled some of the words, and others he read far too quickly. Several of the words he mispronounced or appeared to, as his accent made his pronunciation difficult to understand.

"Do we have any corrections or comments?" Mr. Fleming asked.

Since most students were paying little attention, no one raised his hand. So I raised mine, bringing a look of surprise from the teacher and several of the cadets.

"Well, it looks as if our new student has an idea. What is your analysis of his reading, Mr. Carter?"

I cleared my throat and suddenly felt the sweat beneath my shirt. "I think he read the words too fast like he was hurrying to get the assignment done," I began. At that instant, the reader cut in with the comment, "You're damn right about that," and the class roared with laughter. Fleming waited for them to settle down before he motioned for me to continue talking. "That's all, except some of the pronunciation of words had the emphasis on the wrong syllable."

Fleming's face lit up. Perhaps I was the first person who had ever said anything in that class.

"An excellent analysis, Mr. Carter. Have you taken public speaking previously?"

"No, Sir."

"Then, you have done amazingly well. I believe we will begin the class reading with you next time. But that concludes our lesson for today. Good afternoon."

I started to respond but bit my lip when I realized nobody said a word, merely shuffled out of the room, talking noisily with one another. Alone with Fleming in the room, I approached his desk.

"I don't mean any disrespect," I began. "But that Carnegie book isn't the most fascinating book to read aloud. I wonder if I could bring a book I'd like to read. Maybe if everyone could read from a book he liked, the class might get more involved."

Fleming, who had been busy putting away his books and papers while I spoke, finished his task, then shot me a look as if I'd just arrived at Roxwell on a spaceship from Mars.

"I have taught this class for years," he began, and I could anticipate what he would say next. I had this bad habit of opening my mouth when I should keep my yap shut. "I have always chosen books to read to the class and for the students to read aloud. As you could see today, my choice generates little interest or enthusiasm. You are so right, Mr. Carter. When someone reads a story that interests him, there should be far more enthusiasm to read the work correctly. I am willing to try your little experiment for the rest of the semester. I don't know why I never thought of that myself." He made a cluck-cluck sound, snapped his briefcase shut, and we walked out together. "Where did you say you come from, Carter?"

"Los Angeles."

"Well, you are a welcome addition to my class. Thank you." And with that he walked away, a weary man fighting desperately to save himself from drowning in despair.

A dinner of pork chops dripping with gravy, a kitchen favorite, along with mashed potatoes and canned string beans made for a perfect introduction to the Sabbath for Jewish cadets at Roxwell. At the end of the meal, the Dean stood up to make a few announcements.

"Letters R through T are assigned to study hall tonight. There will be a meeting of the rifle club tonight at seven at the firing range clubhouse. Get a pass from Mr. Stanton. Jewish cadets assemble under the oak in front of the mess hall directly after dinner. Raymond Salisbury, see me after dinner. That's all. Dismissed."

That bastard! He had separately informed the Jewish cadets about meeting me under the tree, but he had to announce our meeting place to the whole school so those good Christian cadets leaving the mess hall could all glance at whoever stood under the tree. And naturally, I had to be the first to arrive, the non-Jew Jew, to stare any of them down as they whispered to each other when they passed by.

"Are you Calvin Carter?"

"Yes, that's me. Who are you?"

A shrimp dressed in khakis, standing as high as my chest, approached the tree. His dark skin and coal-black hair made him look like he came from Mexico.

"Lenny Rosen. You're supposed to be in charge of me tonight," he said, then his voice deepened as he added, "That's fucking stupid. I went to this synagogue all last year. I know how to get there."

"Good," I told him. "Cause I don't, and we're supposed to walk there. And cut the swearing. You can't be more than nine."

He looked me in the eye like he wanted to blacken it. "I'm eleven, and you ain't in the swearing patrol, so cut the crap."

You wouldn't have to be a psychologist to figure out why this kid's parents shipped him off to a military school.

The other three cadets under my control arrived. They looked to be of various sizes, and as a group, they were much quieter than the verbose Lenny. We set off, leaving the school grounds and walking down the residential street in a group leading us toward town. The moment we left the school behind, one kid put on a yarmulke he carried in his pocket, and Lenny pulled a pack of cigarettes from his pocket. He passed them around, and everyone but me lit up.

I almost cracked up. No wonder they all looked so short. Little Lenny puffed away like a veteran, inhaling deeply and even blowing a smoke ring. I told them they looked ridiculous walking down the street blowing smoke, but they ignored me, and Lenny flipped me the bird. Watching them reminded me of the first time I smoked. At about age fifteen, I picked up a butt off the street while walking with a friend, lit up, and inhaled. The smoke made me cough like hell, but at the same time, to my surprise, I produced an erection. Smoking felt so grown up.

After a walk of about twenty minutes with Lenny in the lead, we reached the center of town and soon arrived at the front of the Synagogue. A few people, mostly well-dressed older people, were entering.

I stopped the group out front. A couple of them began to fidget like they didn't know what to expect. I didn't know whether to lecture them about being quiet and respectful or just let the chips fall where they may. "Listen, Lenny, since you've been here before, maybe you can tell the rest of us what to do."

"Aren't you Jewish?" Lenny asked, surprised.

"Yes, but I haven't been inside a synagogue for years." That brought a rumbling from the others. "I ain't never been in one," one said.

"You just listen, that's all," Lenny advised. "The Rabbi talks, the cantor sings, and they serve some refreshments after. Sometimes, you will sing songs. Just do what everyone else does." Lenny straightened his shoulders and marched ahead of the rest of us, reassured that despite his size, he should have been the one in charge.

We sat as a group in a single row about halfway back. The service passed slowly and much the way Lenny described the process, except for the introduction of four or five boys by the Rabbi, for they formed this year's Hebrew study class leading up to bar mitzvahs.

As Lenny had explained, the service concluded with coffee, soft drinks, and cake in the next room. I took some refreshments and sat by myself in a corner of the room. The kid with the yarmulke in our party went up to speak to the Rabbi. The others huddled together except for Lenny, who evidently knew some of the people attending. His confidence increased by the moment.

Glancing around every couple of minutes, I hoped to spot a good-looking girl attending with her parents. None my age could be seen. So I just sat back in my chair, balancing my dessert on my lap, sipping my coffee, and enjoying the momentary feeling of being a normal person. An attractive middle-aged woman in a fashionable gray dress approached me. Her hand, with its manicured nails, reached out to shake mine as I stood to receive her. I had placed my cake and coffee on the floor beside my chair. "Are you the young man from Roxwell?" She asked, though my uniform should have made that obvious to her.

"Yes, Ma'am. There are five of us here from Roxwell."

She smiled a warm smile, which accentuated her high cheekbones. Her husband, a balding man with a slight paunch, joined us, though he stood a few feet behind her. "You appear to be the oldest boy in the group."

"Yes, I'm seventeen. The others are fourteen or younger."

"Seventeen," she repeated.

"Almost eighteen," I continued, straightening my shoulders a bit after tossing out that bald-faced lie. I wouldn't be eighteen for another nine months, but eighteen sounded so much better than seventeen.

"None of the cadets who attended last year were as old as you," she informed me.

"I think there's only one here who attended last year," I told her.

She paused in a way that made me suspect she debated whether to ask a question. I like to try to anticipate people. She glanced back at her husband before she spoke. "Would you like to join us for dinner tomorrow night? We always have a nice dinner when the Sabbath ends."

A real meal sounded tempting. "Gee, that'd be nice, but I have school tomorrow. I don't think they allow us to go out in the evening, but I'm not sure."

"Well, how about Sunday afternoon then? Say, I don't even know your name."

"Cal, Cal Carter. Sunday would be okay, I guess."

"Wonderful Cal. I'd like you to meet my daughter."

There's always a catch to everything in life. I'd learned that, and so her comment came as no surprise.

"Is your daughter with you here?"

"No, she couldn't come tonight. Frankly, I can't get her to come very often. We've been living here a year now, and there are so few Jewish boys living around here."

"What's her name?" I asked.

My question brought a broad smile. "I know your name, but you don't know ours. I'm Sarah Stein, and that's my husband, Fred." Fred gave me an obliging wave. "And our daughter's name is Sandy. She's finishing her last year of high school."

"Me too," I interjected.

"Would three o'clock work for you tomorrow? If you bring your bathing trunks, you could swim since we have a pool. We usually eat around five on Sundays."

"That sounds fine."

Mrs. Stein wrote down the address on a sheet of paper and explained how to get to their house from the Synagogue.

After the Steins left, I stared at the piece of paper in my hand. Her offer, no matter what her daughter looked like, beat hanging around the school or doing nothing on a Sunday afternoon. To visit a private home for a Sunday dinner with a local family would give me a better idea of how people, other than my relatives, lived in Texas. A pool and a home-cooked meal could more than compensate for an overweight, possibly boring, daughter. And who knows? I might luck out and find her halfway decent-looking or someone of interest. Mrs. Stein looked attractive enough, so myriad possibilities existed.

I asked a helper in the Synagogue to call a cab for us. As we stood in front waiting, the kids lit up again. They continued puffing the weed in the back of the cab while I rode in the front. My charges, these midget Jews, proved a hoot, especially Lenny, who talked all the way home in his cocky New York style, telling us about how the best part of the ceremony had been the lemonade and cookies. He'd managed to hoist several cookies, hiding them in his pockets for future use.

The idea of attending class on Saturday made me want to throw up. At home, I might be watching the World Series between the Dodgers and the Yankees or a football game. I wasn't a great baseball fan, but I liked the excitement of a championship series. This match between the Yankees and Dodgers was the first to be televised in color. I had a friend whose parents had a color set. I could have watched the game with him. Instead, here I sat all day in hot, humid, disgusting Texas, listening to dull teachers teach boring subjects. No wonder I wanted to barf.

Once we finished classes and roll call, a couple of free hours remained before dinner. I could have visited the Steins on Saturday night. I didn't know we were free to do so. All I needed was a pass. But after all day in school, in the heat, I felt lousy, irritated, and probably wouldn't have been very good company. I used the time before dinner to walk into town and locate the local bookstore. I polished off almost all of the remaining money Mom had given me. I stocked up on half a dozen books, mostly psychology, and a few novels, including *Catcher in the Rye*, which I had decided to read again, now that the publishers had put out a cheap paperback edition. I would add this new group of reading material to the books I'd sent here in my trunk, mostly books I'd already read once, to get something positive out of this experience, even if that knowledge would be obtained on my own. That night, while Larry went off to a movie, I stretched out on my bed and read. My reading kept being interrupted by my thoughts. I wondered what the following day would be like, if the girl would be nice or obnoxious. Would she look down on me as a cadet? This process of interrupted thought represented typical me, always working myself up ahead of time for an event, even reaching a kind of emotional frenzy. Once, as a kid in San Diego, where we were visiting my aunt and uncle, I remember being so excited about a fishing trip on a boat that I thrashed around in bed the entire night. At thirteen, I'd never been on a boat before, and my uncle had agreed to take me sport fishing. We had to wake up at five in the morning. Not only did I toss and turn, but started to yawn, not from exhaustion but excitement. Finally, at three in the morning, I fell asleep on the living room floor. And we almost missed the boat when my uncle made a wrong turn trying to find the pier.

I'm calmer now, but my mind still gets active, and I think about all the possibilities.

I read straight through curfew until midnight, using a flashlight, before I fell into a deep sleep. As I didn't have to go to church on Sunday morning, I slept in until ten. When I awoke, the others had departed for their weekly visit with Jesus. Quiet made my barracks, or whatever they called this firetrap, actually feel peaceful. At about eleven, the guys started drifting back from church to prepare for role call and lunch.

Larry told me that if I planned to miss a roll call and dinner, I better get a pass, which I did.

I couldn't concentrate after lunch. The time ticked by at a snail's pace. Since the school required uniform dress with a tie whenever a cadet went off campus, I made the best of a bad situation, checking myself in the mirror several times before calling for a cab at twenty minutes to three. With my swimming trunks in hand, I gave the cab driver the address Mrs. Stein had written down, and he drove me there in a few minutes.

The Stein house sat on a lovely street in an upscale section of town where the lawns loomed large, and the yards appeared manicured. The expansive two-story house with a white stucco exterior had painted green shutters framing the front windows. A rose garden ran between the driveway and walkway on one side, while a high hedge separated the impressively deep front yard from the neighbor's house on the opposite side.

I stood at the curb and fiddled until my watch said three, and then started up the walkway that led to the porch and front door. Thoughts raced, along with a little heart flutter, as this unknown girl danced about in my mind. I knocked softly, in a way hoping no one would answer and I could be on my way. No one answered. I rang the bell.

A Negro woman in a maid's outfit opened the door. "You must be that boy from the school," she said.

"Yes, can you tell Mrs. Stein that Cal Carter is here?"

She opened the door for me to enter, and I stood in the

hallway while she went off to announce my arrival. A new thought entered my head. Since so many people had maids, did the maids adopt the same religion as the people they worked for?

Before I could reach a conclusion on that issue, Mrs. Stein entered the hallway with a welcoming smile. "Cal, how nice to see you again. Please come in."

Even in her housedress, Mrs. Stein maintained an elegance that would have made her at home and comfortable anywhere, including Los Angeles. She showed a natural style in her gracious manner, her appearance, and the way she spoke; all her actions echoed her sense of self-worth.

I had removed my cap when I entered the house. "How are you today, Mrs. Stein?" I asked. I wondered if she could pick up on the nervousness in my voice.

"I'm just fine, thank you. Come in. I want you to meet our daughter, Sandy."

As we walked through the living room and dining room toward the backyard, I admired the modern furniture, similar to the furniture in our apartment in Los Angeles. In addition, the artwork displayed on the wall was abstract. I had no idea if these were real paintings or copies, and I dared not ask.

Mrs. Stein pushed open a screen door leading out to a large backyard with a lap-sized rectangular pool directly behind the house. A large hedge surrounded the yard on two sides, and fruit trees grew beyond the grassy area along the back wooden fence. Directly behind the pool area stood a small pool house made of the same stucco material as the larger house.

"Sandy" lay stretched out on a chaise beside the pool, a book covering her face. Her one-piece bathing suit revealed she wasn't overweight, and her slim legs had a rich, tanned sheen that came from a liberal application of suntan oil.

"Sandy, can you come over here and meet Cal?"

I made an effort to keep my mouth clamped shut for fear my jaw would drop open. Sandy put her book down, stood up, and walked toward me. The girl who came to greet me was a knockout, an 11 on a scale of 1 to 10. Her brown eyes sparkled, her face and body tan from head to toe, and her light brownish-blond hair curled down to her shoulders. Even before we greeted each other, I had fallen in love.

Her smile radiated warmth, as her lips parted, exposing straight white teeth. "Hi," she said, briefly taking my hand. Hers felt warm to the touch.

"Hello. Nice to meet you." I felt oafish and inadequate standing there in my stupid uniform. Fortunately, Mrs. Stein broke the awkwardness of the moment.

"I'm glad you brought your suit, Cal," she told me as she motioned to the small changing room past the pool. "You can use that dressing room to change. Dinner won't be ready for an hour or so. Enjoy yourselves. I'll have Essie bring you some drinks." With those words, she returned to the house. Sandy went back to her lounge and stretched out while I headed for the dressing room to change.

The mirror in the dressing room revealed a crew-cut head on a young man with brown hair and eyes, a young man lacking absolutely any hair on his chest. At least my body didn't look flabby in a swimsuit; remnants of the tan I'd cultivated over the summer remained even at the beginning of October. I took a towel from a shelf beside the shower and ventured into the intense heat of the afternoon, settling down on the chaise lounge next to Sandy. She had resumed reading her book while I changed. Once I stretched out, I tried to catch the title of the book she read.

"This is called *The Rise of Silas Lapham*," she told me when she noticed me staring, "A novel I'm reading for a book report," she informed me, assuming my ignorance.

"By Howells," I said with a smile. "I did a report for English about a year ago. What do you think of the story?"

My response seemed to please her, judging from her smile. "I think the story's all right. I don't think that all those people should feel they need money to be happy. And Boston is the worst place for people like them." She paused. "I'm surprised you know this title. I'd never heard of the book before the teacher assigned the book report to us."

I answered with a shrug of my shoulders. "I think the story is pretty well known in literature. When I read the plot, I thought the book resembled an Americanized version of *Pride and Prejudice*."

The surprise showed on her face. "You're right. The characters have a certain type of stuffiness about them that resembles characters in English novels. You sound as if you've read a lot."

I didn't respond right away, in part because my mind sought

a way to shift gears. Fifteen minutes ago, Sandy had been an undefined fantasy. I'd stood on her street, hesitant to even enter the house, and now I found myself seated beside a gorgeous babe wearing a swimsuit, with enough of a mind to carry on a conversation about literature. Dreams do, on occasion, come true. "You're right. I learn a lot from reading, Sandy. I mostly read books to do with psychology, but I like literature a lot. I even do some writing. I'm surprised to find you so interested in books. Most pretty girls I've met don't know one end of a book from the other."

She smiled, revealing a dimple I hadn't noticed before. Her round face appeared strong and confident. "That's probably just a stereotype you have about pretty girls, Cal, but thank you for the compliment," she answered with a blush. "Where are you from? You certainly don't have a Texas accent."

"I'm from Hollywood."

"Oh, really. We went out there during the summer last year. What a nice place. But why are you going to school here? My mother said you go to that military school, Roxwell."

Essie, the maid, interrupted us momentarily as she brought out two glasses of iced tea, the Texas national drink.

"How I ended up at Roxwell is a long story, which I'll tell you later. First, tell me where you come from. You don't sound like a Texan, nor do your parents."

She laughed, or should I say the backyard brightened from her easy laughter. "Goodness, no, we're not from Texas. My father used to be in business in New York City. That's where I grew up. But he had some health issues with his heart, and on the advice of doctors, we moved to the west."

My expression must have shown my confusion. Arizona, New Mexico, California, those places were my idea of the West. Texas, they called the Southwest, and Cullen, nothing more than another small city in Texas.

Sandy picked up on my confusion and explained. "We lived in Houston first because my dad had a cousin living there he'd grown up with. Houston still turned out to be too hectic a pace for him. I don't know why he and mother settled on this place, but we moved here a year ago, right before I began 11th grade. I'll graduate at the end of this year, and I plan to move away, maybe back east, to go to college. I can't wait."

"I know what you mean. I've only been in town a week, and I'm fed up with the whole experience. You're the first ray of sunshine I've encountered."

That brought another blush, which inspired a surge of confidence. She gave me a look of curiosity. "If you feel that way, what made you decide to come to a military school here?"

I relayed the whole sad story, ending with a bit of self-analysis. "I thought the experience might turn out to be an adventure, a radical change from life at home. I haven't really found a direction in my life. I thought this might help. I have learned this much already that I wasn't cut out to live this kind of life. I understand now that I need to focus better and move in my own direction; otherwise, I'll probably end up caving into what other people want for me, as I did this time. If I escape here alive, Sandy, I intend to go to college to study psychology and to work with people."

She nodded as if she understood and then asked, "Do you want to take a dip in the pool before we eat dinner?"

"Sure. But I haven't been in a pool since I left home. I hope I still remember how to swim."

She laughed again. How at ease her laughter made me feel. I walked over to the diving board, and tested the spring by bouncing up and down on the end. I also wanted her to see how I looked on my feet. Then, I took a running start and completed a half-assed dive. The water felt perfect, lukewarm, and refreshing. As I paddled about, Sandy followed me up on the board and executed a perfect jackknife into the water. Wisdom dictated not making another dive. I thought instead to challenge her to a race, until she glided the length of the pool at a pace that would put me to shame. I floated, swam about, delighted in the full impact of being in the water alongside the beautiful companion that shared her pool with me.

After a while, we pulled ourselves out of the pool and laid down again side-by-side on the chaise lounges to let the heat and sun dry our bodies. Eventually, we began to chat, this time about art, a subject I knew little about beyond enjoying Van Gogh and some of the Impressionist painters. Sandy liked modernism, Picasso, and those types. Just as she began to explain her preference for that kind of work, the maid opened the screen door and told us that Sandy's mother wanted us to get dressed and come in for dinner.

Sandy went into her room to change, while I returned to the pool house, took a quick shower, and changed back into the ugly Khaki outfit that had become my destiny. I left my tie off for the time being. I combed at what remained of my hair in the mirror and studied my face. I had been told that my bushy eyebrows and round cheeks created a cheerful look. On a couple of occasions, my mother's friends commented to her about her handsome son. But, seeing my reflection in the mirror gave me pause. This girl came from money. This girl had class. This girl had sophistication. Did I have enough going for me to appeal to her?

Sandy and her parents were already seated when I arrived at the table. Mr. Stein sat at the head, the women on each side, and me, as the guest, at the opposite end. Sandy's father looked more relaxed than he had in the Synagogue reception. He offered a short prayer in Hebrew, and we started with a delicious salad served to each of us by Essie, the Negro maid. There followed a meal to die for. Pot roast with gravy, done to perfection, mashed potatoes, creamed spinach, squash, and hot biscuits. Mr. Stein offered me a glass of dinner wine, but I informed him that I didn't drink. That seemed to score some points, though my response brought a question from Sandy as to why. "I don't know. I don't like the taste of alcohol. I'd rather drink a Dr. Pepper, mentioning a Texas favorite. As if on cue, Essie, the maid, brought in a bottle of Dr. Pepper and a glass filled with ice and sat them down in front of me.

Dessert consisted of apple pie a la mode and coffee. The conversation throughout the meal consisted of the kind of small talk that comes when a stranger disrupts the normal flow of a family. Mr. Stein commented on the Dodgers win that day, but when he heard of my lack of interest in baseball, he changed the subject. They showed curiosity about my background, and I caught the reaction on Mrs. Stein's face when I mentioned that my mother had married five times. Perhaps a product of such instability was not what she had in mind for her precious daughter. Her expression made me wonder if I would ever be invited back.

"Did you enjoy the meal, Cal?" Mrs. Stein asked when I'd consumed the last bite of dessert.

"Enjoy it?" I asked. "That's an understatement. Must be the best food in the state of Texas."

That drew a smile, which bore a strong similarity to her daughter's expression. "Tell me, Cal, how do you like Roxwell?"

I bit my lip, unsure how to respond. Maybe Mr. Stein had been an old military man before he made his fortune. "I don't think I'm the military type," I ventured, opening the door.

Sure enough, Mr. Stein perked up at my comment. As a slow eater, he had only finished half of his slice of pie, but he put his fork down. "What exactly do you define as the military type?" He asked.

I cleared my throat. "Well, Sir, I believe many people are comfortable with the order that a military life provides for them. They want everything in their lives to be laid out in black and white, clear-cut. That's not me. I don't have any problem with others thriving on discipline and order, but that has no appeal for me."

Mr. Stein laughed. "With an answer like that, you should think about a career in the State Department. At your tender age, you are a master of tact and diplomacy."

That brought a laugh all around the table, and mine sounded perhaps the loudest. Somehow, I'd gotten through this without them knowing the real reason for my careful responses.

Mr. Stein continued. "When I entered college, the First World War had begun, and America seriously considered entering the fray. A lot of us in college discussed what we would do if we did join up. So many of my classmates were gung ho to become cannon fodder in that horrible war. I resolved I'd run off to South America before I'd be drafted."

"Did you?" I asked.

He shook his head. "No. When it came down to a decision, I did my turn. Lucky for me, I spent the war in an office in Washington. I had a talent they needed."

"Daddy, would it be all right if I took Cal into my room to show him my record collection?" Sandy asked before her father could elaborate.

He smiled. "Sure, you young people go off and have a good time. We'll talk later, Cal. I like your thinking."

I followed Sandy into her bedroom, wallowing in the approval her father had bestowed on me. As Sandy led me to the shelf of 33 rpm records she had neatly stacked, I marveled at her sense of organization. Every item in the room sat in a specific place. The bed would have passed a military inspection. A bright wallpaper with alternating white and yellow stripes, covered the walls while the open closet door revealed clothes neatly hung, shoes lined up side-by-side on the floor, while knick-knacks covered the top of the dresser, and books sat on a shelf surrounding the records.

A closer look at her records revealed tastes close to my own. The shelf contained a section of classical, popular singers of the day, Frank Sinatra and Sarah Vaughn, jazz greats like Earl Garner, Chet Baker, and Louis Armstrong, and even an album of the hottest addition to the world of music, Bill Haley and the Comets. Seeing these albums reminded me how much I missed my record collection, which I'd left at home in my room. I couldn't wait to hear *Rock Around the Clock* again, and we spent the next hour or so listening to records and talking, just small talk, but to sit on the bed beside her made whatever we discussed feel important and meaningful.

When I glanced at my watch, the hands informed me of the bad news…six-thirty and time to go back. Reluctantly, I told Sandy goodbye, then went into the living room where the Steins were watching a program on their television. The reception on their small set looked grainy.

"Thank you both so much for inviting me," I said. "The dinner was delicious, and I really enjoyed meeting Sandy."

Mrs. Stein stood up. "Do you have your swimsuit?"

"Thanks for reminding me," I responded, going out in the back pool room to retrieve the still-wet suit. My initial plan had been to forget the suit, which would have given me an excuse to return. But to my great joy, just as the taxi pulled up to the front of the house, Mrs. Stein said, "If you are free next Sunday, we would be pleased to have you join us again."

I didn't need a taxi to return to the school; I could have floated there. The world had tilted over in the right direction, all in a single afternoon.

The smile on my face must have given away my state of mind when I returned to the room. Larry was stretched out across the bed. I knew the smell that permeated the room at once. We had lots of weed in LA. "Great day, huh?" He asked, sporting a slightly goofy smile on his face. He offered me the joint, which I turned down.

"Aren't you afraid of getting caught?" I asked.

"Nah. It's Sunday night. Nobody ever comes around. So you had a good time?"

I took off my tie, which I'd put back on in the cab. "Larry, they are the nicest people I've ever met. And their daughter is a doll. We have so much in common. They even invited me back for next Sunday."

He nodded his head, before he asked, "Do you have everything ready for inspection?"

"What?"

"I thought you knew. Tomorrow morning, before drill, the platoon leader makes a room inspection of every cadet. Every item in the drawers has a certain order. You stand at attention next to your bed while they inspect the room. Every item issued needs to be in the right place, or they will give you demerits."

I must have looked lost. I didn't have a clue about what went where. "Will you show me?"

"Let me finish my joint," he said. When he did, he stood up, and we spent the next hour or so putting each piece of clothing in the proper order. That night, I fell asleep with a grin as wide as the Grand Canyon.

CHAPTER TWELVE

Reality intervened soon after the Monday morning bugle sounded the wake-up call. After roll call and breakfast, we returned to our room for inspection. Our dress, bed, clothes, and each and every issued item we had been given caught the sharp eye of the platoon leader, who, by coincidence, was in my speech class. He pretended not to recognize me as he poked through my drawers, looking very self-important. I couldn't help but notice that after my thorough inspection, he gave Larry just a quick cursory look as if he'd been given orders to go easy on him, though Larry had everything in order as well. With Larry's help, thankfully, I avoided any demerits.

Next came the morning drill. Three hours on an increasingly hot drill field proved to be exhausting. We marched up and down with our rifles on our shoulders. We practiced left face, right face, about face, column left, column right, at ease, and attention.

Two guys in our company collapsed from the heat. They were laid out under the only tree at the edge of the drill field while the marching continued. Around and around in circles, we went, rifles on our shoulders. About an hour or so into the drills, I received special attention. I managed to remain constantly out of step, not on purpose, but because my head and feet possessed divergent ideas. Even worse, on the about-face, I kept kicking myself in the ankle, making about-face one painful drill. My incompetence was spotted, and one of our squad leaders took me aside. We spent the rest of the drill period practicing the art of the about-face. Life became a carousel as I spun around and around and around. Though my ankle felt sore by the end of this special attention, I eventually mastered the art of the about-face.

Lunch proved a welcome respite from this morning's torture, for the meal signified the beginning of an afternoon devoted to total freedom for the non-demerit person. Larry invited me to go for a spin in the Ferrari, which he had moved to a garage in town, as he thought the car needed some exercise. I begged off. Sandy had loaned me a book she said I should definitely read, her well-thumbed copy, titled *The Fountainhead.* Eager to dive into the story, I looked forward to an afternoon of peace and quiet prior to the six o'clock roll call.

The paperback appeared to be thick and wordy, but once I dove into the story, I didn't want to put the book down. When Larry returned after a couple of hours, he found me so engrossed in the plot that I didn't realize he'd entered the room. What hooked me was the actions of the main character. How I longed to be like him, this Howard Roark, a pillar of strength, without fear, a man who could take on all the social norms and defeat them.

When roll call arrived, Larry had to practically drag me from the room. I wanted to go back to read after roll call, but Larry insisted I have dinner with him. After dinner, I made a beeline for my room, hopped on my bed, and didn't put the book down until I'd read every word, the last part completed by flashlight, after I'd undressed for bed, under the covers, sometime after midnight.

Larry had drifted off to sleep earlier. After I put the book down, I undressed, climbed under the covers, and, lying on my back, began a night daydream. My thoughts flowed free; free association we call this process in the world of psychology. They went along this line: "I'm only seventeen, pretty young. Lots of kids in certain parts of the country marry at seventeen; at least, I think they do. Sandy Carter. Sounds odd, not very odd, though. Her parents are sure nice. I wonder what my mother would say if I came home with a wife. She wouldn't mind-oh, yes, she would, but not if she met Sandy. Well, we wouldn't need to marry right off. I mean, we need to get to know each other better, don't we? The whole idea is silly but fun to think about. I better go to sleep."

I switched off my night-light and fell asleep at once. That night, a weird dream woke me up, and I remember every bit of the action. In the cockpit of a small plane, I was in the process of landing when several jets sped above my head pursuing a single jet. As I landed, I almost hit a rocket on the runway about two feet long. As I jumped down, the door of the rocket opened and a small bug appeared. I reached down and snatched up the bug, holding the little guy firmly but gently between my forefinger and thumb. I hitched a ride with a friend to a science laboratory. When we arrived at the lab, I showed the little bug to a woman scientist. Together, we watched as the bug changed first into a ladybug, then into a kitten, and finally into a man. The bug attempted to leave in his man disguise while we were distracted, as the woman scientist injected me with a drug to prevent any ill effects from my encounter with the bug. Just then, I woke up in a cold sweat. I sat up in bed for a while trying to figure out what the dream meant. Dreams have psychological implications. Did Sandy fit in there somewhere? She certainly wasn't the scientist taking care of me, because she disliked science as much as I do.

Tuesday proved much more pleasurable than Monday. We only drilled for an hour. Wednesday and Thursday dragged by as all thoughts centered on the upcoming weekend. Minutes passed at the speed of hours. Nights tended to move faster than days. An evening in study hall allowed me to catch up on my homework. During the imposed evening study periods, when we were supposed to be in our rooms studying, almost nobody did. Instead, we played cards, held discussions, or had shaving cream fights.

Thursday night found us all convened in Gibbon's room. We moved from room to room nightly, depending on who wasn't present in the night-enforced visit to study hall, and who wanted to host. This night five of us crowded in: Gibbons, his roommate Allen, Larry, myself and a kid from downstairs named Harold. This kid wasn't supposed to be upstairs, but at Roxwell Academy, cadets tended to do with they wanted and only hoped they didn't get caught. Roland and his roommate Charlie were missing; the kid actually studied every night, and no one had bothered him since he'd stood up to Gibbons the week before.

The conversation started when Gibbons complained about the heat. "Sure 'nuff is hot as hell these days. Damn weather better get cool soon. I spend too much time changing shirts, and getting Allen here to take them down to the laundry."

Harold from downstairs piped in. "I hate it. I get to sweatin' so bad when we drill, I begin to smell like a nigger workin' on the docks." Harold came from New Orleans where they had docks.

Every time I heard that word, "Nigger," I wanted to throw up…right on the chest of the person using that pejorative. To my surprise, that kind of talk didn't surface too often, perhaps because those around us knew Larry and I had strong feelings. Harold from downstairs obviously didn't have a clue.

Gibbons, seeing some support, sympathized. "Better not get too tan, Harold boy. Someone's liable to mistake you for a nigger around here and try to integrate ya'all somewhere. Those big shots in Washington are on the lookout for little niggers to integrate the schools with."

"Yeah," Allen agreed. Then again, he always agreed with Gibbons.

Harold piped in his agreement. "I don't know why those Northern Commies are pushing the niggers off on us. I bet they don't integrate them up North. You know, Chicago, New York, they have lots of race riots."

"Yeah," said Gibbons.

"Yeah," agreed Allen.

Encouraged, Harold continued. "I don't know why they are always pickin' on the South. They had nigger slaves in the North too. At least we stuck to our principles. We didn't think much of niggers a hundred years back and we still don't. Those two-faced Northern bastards think they can have slaves one minute and fight against slavery the next."

"I thought the Civil War had ended," I piped in.

"I figured you were for that integration, Hollywood boy," Gibbons began, waving his arms as he spoke. "Maybe you don't care about niggers out there in Holllllywoood."

I tried to bite my lip, but no luck. "No, it's different in California. We respect every person based on his ability, not on his skin color. People are people no matter if they are black, white or purple. You Southern guys are still looking backwards. The Constitution says every person has the right to make the most out of his life. Your backward thinking just stops progress."

Gibbons face began to redden. Then he put his finger to his lips, as the sound of footsteps told us someone was ascending the creaking stairs.

In a flash, Gibbons had given each of us a book, and we sat engrossed in our studies by the time the platoon leader entered the room. We all stood at attention.

"What are you'all doing in here?" He demanded.

Gibbons showed an amazing cool. "Why Harold, Larry and me is studying for a test together, and Allan and Hollywood here they's going over their military science material." If the platoon leader had looked closely, he would have seen that Gibbons had tossed me a book on botany.

"Well, it's almost curfew, so Harold, you better get your ass downstairs, and you others get back in your room before lights out."

With that, he stalked off, as everyone breathed a sign of

relief.

Gibbons, for once, looked proud. "Guess I saved us all a demerit," he announced, and we had to agree.

Before we broke up, Allen put his two cents worth in on the discussion. "Ya know what I think?" Allen added, as if anyone might care. "I think we ought to let all them niggers marry white girls. Then in a while all them babies would be white and we wouldn't have niggers anymore."

I could only shake my head, while Larry broke out in a loud laugh.

Harold from downstairs looked shocked, unfamiliar with examples of Allen's thinking processes. Even Gibbons couldn't believe what he'd heard. "You are one dumb bastard, Allen. That ain't no answer. There ain't a nigger from Texas to Africa that's good enough to kiss a white girl's feet. "

"Damn right," Harold added.

To my surprise, Larry finally spoke. "What you guys don't seem to get is that there are as many whites who are just as bad or lazy as niggers. My Daddy runs an oil company in Venezuela, and he's got all kinds of workers there. Some work well, some are lazy, some like to cause trouble. Doesn't much matter what color they are, or religion, or anything else. You just sound retarded when you say any race is bad because you don't like their skin color."

Larry had a way of cutting off the opposition.

"You guys would be amazed how different people can work

together," I added. "I got invited to join this group sponsored by the Los Angeles Examiner, one of our morning papers there. All you had to do to join was be interested in covering high school sports, which I did for my school paper. Every Friday night, each high school has someone who calls in to report on the football games after they are over. Other high school students come down to the paper to write up the results of the games that are called in. The stories appear in the paper on Saturday morning. These sports writing kids come from all over the city, kids of all races and religions and they get along great because they all have a common interest, following and reporting sports. I know some of them and they are great guys. If we had more programs like that, there'd be less trouble in the country."

While Larry had shut Gibbons up, I didn't seem to be able to do so. "I think if we had more lynching's there'd be less trouble," Gibbons said.

"How about we start with you?" Larry said, moving toward where Gibbon sat on the bed.

He jumped up so fast he fell flat on his ass, and everyone howled.

Gibbons turned red, picked himself up and left his own room.

"Well, that sounds pretty good," Harold said. He'd obviously never thought about another approach to race relations. "Only I can't see sitting in a room working next to a nigger."

"What have they done to you?" I wanted to know.

Harold paused as Gibbons re-entered the room and went to

his record player to play

an album of country music songs.

"Nothin', really. I don't know any of them. I'm sure they'd do somethin' though if they had the chance. You know they hate us."

"Do you blame them? Listen to how you talk about them."

"Well, when I was growin' up, my pappy warned me about them. 'Boy,' he told me, 'you watch out for niggers and Jews. Niggers'll beat you, and Jews'll cheat you."

The others looked at Harold in surprise. He obviously had no clue about my supposed religion. "Well, Harold," I told him. "Your Pappy was a smart man. See, he knew how smart Jews are and how dumb you are, so he warned you to be careful."

While the group was trying to absorb this unexpected comment, Larry broke into a loud laugh. "Hey, cracker, your leg must be getting longer because Cal here is pulling on it."

Harold looked lost. The conversation had moved past him, and he suspected Larry's comment might have been an insult. Then he smiled, as he looked at me to share a sudden realization. "Just as I thought. You're prejudiced against them Jews just like me."

That brought the house down. Gibbons, in the know for once, took Harold by the arm and led him into the hallway to share the news. He returned white-faced with Gibbons behind him, sporting a big smile.

"Jeez, I didn't mean to insult you all. I didn't know you were

Jewish. Really. I'm sure they're all not so bad. I knew one once in my school. He was an okay guy." He shook his head in the affirmative. "Yeah, an okay guy."

"I know a lot of bad Jews," I told him.

His eyes narrowed.

"Yeah, and a lot of rotten Christians, racist Christians just like you."

Harold had had enough. Before I could add another word, Harold shouted, "curfew" and suddenly bolted for the door. Next, we heard the sound of his feet clattering down the shaky stairs toward his room on the lower floor. Or maybe when he hit the ground he headed straight to Frenchy's to drown his sorrows in a Dr. Pepper.

Walking to my room with Larry, I felt great, as if I had become a little David, tackling and vanquishing my foe, Southern stupidity. As we readied ourselves for bed, I found myself drawn closer to Larry. Not in a sexual way of course, but I felt a respect for him, though I usually have disdain for the super rich. In addition, my mind harbors stereotypes about wealthy South Americans. Yes, I confess that I have my own set of prejudices. Larry defied most of my stereotypes. While he didn't show flashes of genius, he stood on the right side of most issues, big, confident and unafraid. And similar to drinking from a well filled with magic water, I could draw strength from him. I admired him, and secretly wished that I could be more like him. Larry saw life clearly, and at the same time knew how to place his needs above those of anyone else. In some ways, he resembled Howard Roark in that book I'd just read.

Friday night, on the way to synagogue, an unexpected event shook the group as we walked into town. We had assembled underneath the tree after dinner. As we left the grounds to walk to Synagogue, the boys all lit up. As mentioned, they were all shrimps, led by the all too cocky Lenny, who pranced his way along the sidewalk, a few paces ahead, as if he was the farmer leading a group of cows back to the barn.

As we approached the town, two local boys came walking along the sidewalk in our direction. They looked to be about fifteen or so, and they dressed the way these locals dress: sloppy plaid shirts, cowboy boots, and greasy hair. The two of them covered the sidewalk and were intent on making us move aside so they could pass. While we complied, one of them noticed the yarmulke one of the boys, Jacob, had put on once we left the school. Since this kid never spoke, we didn't know he was religious until he had pulled from his pocket his own yarmulke on that first Friday night. His yarmulke must have been a family heirloom because he had his name sewn inside. Though he put the yarmulke on the moment we left the school, this didn't prevent him from lighting up a cigarette along with the others. Evidently, his God had no objection to peewee smokers.

"Hey, look at this," one town boy said to his friend, as they passed close enough to Jacob to grab the yarmulke off his head. "One of those Roxwell boys wears a beanie."

"Give it back," Jacob said. His face paled from the confrontation.

Instead, the boy, laughing, put the yarmulke on his own head. The other one stopped and turned back toward us.

"You must be Jew boys going to church, huh?"

Lenny turned bright red; even in the fading light, his cheeks glowed. "You assholes give that back or I'll beat the shit out of both of you," he informed them with an intensity to his words that floored me. For a minute, the boys hesitated, and then broke into laughter. "Cool it, punk," one of them answered in his Texas twang, "or we'll pick ya all up and toss you like a football."

That response brought a sudden whirr of motion, kind of like the way a propeller winds up faster and faster before the plane takes off. Before anyone could react, Lenny rushed one of the boys and, with a flying leap, planted both feet solidly between the mocking boy's legs, causing a loud squeal of pain as he dropped to the sidewalk. Before the other kid could react, Lenny had turned towards him and, with his knees planted on the sidewalk, grabbed both the kid's ankles and upended him. The kid dropped to the sidewalk faster than a cut tree falls in a forest. An instant later, Lenny jumped on top of him, pounding both fists into his face. I had to pull Lenny off before he killed the guy. The yarmulke had fallen off during the melee, and the first kid had already taken off down the sidewalk, limping and holding his groin with both hands. Using every ounce of strength, I could muster to hold Lenny back, I gave the other kid enough time to pick himself up and, with blood running from his nose, make his way down the street to catch up with his friend.

Once this little tiger calmed down, I let go of him. He brushed himself off, picked up the yarmulke to return to Jacob, and then calmly lit a cigarette. The group walked on as if nothing had happened, but I made a mental note about which kid I wanted to watch my back in the future.

Before we reached the synagogue, my curiosity got the best of me. "Tell me, Lenny, who taught you to fight like that?"

Without looking around, he said, "my aunt."

Now, I had to know the story.

"We lived in an Italian neighborhood in Brooklyn," he explained. "I used to get picked on. One day in second grade, I came home bloody, and my dad started to teach me how to fight. My aunt lived with us. She didn't say nothing, but later, she called me aside. She said I was too little to fight fair. I had to make things happen fast if I wanted to win. She showed me some tricks."

"But how did she know these tricks?"

We were walking a little ahead of the others. Lenny paused and looked up at me. "She told me she used to fight those fucking Nazis. She was in, I don't know what they called them, but she said they lived in the woods. They learned all the tricks. They killed Nazis. I wish I could find a few fucking Nazis. I'd kill them, too."

I took him at his word.

At the Friday night services, Sandy remained a no-show. I began to wonder if she shared my anti-religion ideas. Mr. and Mrs. Stein visited with me during the refreshments. Since our talk, Mr. Stein acted much more outgoing and friendly, asking about my week, and what I'd done at Roxwell, not that I had much to tell him. I did tell him about the incident with Lenny, which brought up a comment about how Jews had to stand up for each other.

Marching and classes occupied a boring Saturday, which led us into Sunday. While the others attended Church, I took the opportunity to once more sleep in until 10:00. Soon after, the returning cadets woke me, making loud noises.

After I washed up, I climbed back into bed and began speculating on the afternoon ahead, the only time of the week that made life worth living. I looked at the clock on the desk.

Three hours and fifteen minutes before I could ring that doorbell. I so wanted to wear one of Larry's imported suits, though I knew none of them would fit, while requirements stated I wear my miserable khakis. I began to speculate on what Sandy would be wearing, then somehow started to think about what she wouldn't be wearing, that is, how she looked with her beautiful tan body in a bathing suit. That reminded me to bring my swimsuit. The clock reminded me I still had three hours and twelve minutes left.

I needed a faster way to pass the time. I took up *The Fountainhead* again and began to read excerpts, pages where I'd inserted torn pieces of notebook paper to reference passages when I discussed the book with Sandy. I planned to return the copy she'd lent me during my visit.

Thoughts kept interfering with my reading. Finally, irritated, I put the book aside, stood up, and went into the bathroom down the hall to shower. Then I dressed in a fresh shirt and khakis, put on a tie, and went to the mess hall to have lunch. At one o'clock, free for the afternoon, I walked into town to buy a box of candy at the drugstore to bring Mrs. Stein. She deserved a reward for producing a daughter like that. I had time for a coke at the counter before a quarter to three arrived, and I walked the short distance to where the Stein family lived. I went up the walkway and, with no hesitation, loudly knocked on the front door.

The afternoon began much like the previous Sunday. Essie opened the door, showed me in, and the Steins greeted me. I gave Mrs. Stein the box of candy, and after she thanked me for "a thoughtful gesture," she told me that Sandy was once more lying out by the pool. In an attempt to be cool, I thanked her and headed towards the back porch. I spotted Sandy stretched out on the same lounge chair she had occupied the previous week. The book in her hands differed from the Howells book she'd been reading the previous week. I couldn't catch the title, but I said a quick hello before going into the changing room. I put on my swimsuit and took a towel to dry myself off after the swim.

"I've returned *The Fountainhead,*" I told her once I joined her at the poolside. "Thanks for loaning me the book. I thought Rand's book was a great read." Her expression indicated she hadn't expected me to finish so quickly.

I wanted to start a dialogue about the details, but before I could decide which aspect of the book to discuss, she asked, "How about a swim? I'm dying from the heat."

When she swam, the water around her barely moved, whereas my swimming resembled a thrashing shark in the middle of a kill. Finally, I just retreated to the side as she did laps back and forth with the ease of a pro or at least someone on her high school swim team.

"How did you learn to swim so well?" I asked when she finally slowed down and pulled up below the diving board, the edges of which she gripped with both hands.

"I had a swim coach in Houston," she said. "He helped me compete when I was in school there. I learned a lot from him."

"You are really good. Did you compete statewide?"

She laughed before she splashed a handful of water at me. "No way. I'm not that good."

I splashed her back, and a moment later, we were engaged in a full-blown water fight, the waves lapping against the sides of the pool. I moved closer to her, sending a constant spray of water in her direction.

Suddenly, she dived down, emerging behind me and splashing me as I turned around to defend myself from the attack. By the time we exited the pool, we were both out of breath and laughing aloud.

I stretched out, lying on the lounge chair next to hers. "That was the most fun I've had since I arrived in Texas," I told her.

She smiled, revealing those teeth as bright and straight as the ones shown in the Ipana ads. I felt the strongest urge to reach over and kiss those lips. I wanted to take her in my arms and hold her body next to mine. I kept those urges inside my brain.

I know that understanding the opposite sex is essential, but

I'm a flop. More than once, I've taken friendly horseplay for being more than that. Girls have always told me they liked me "as a friend." The girls in my high school could confide in me about their relationships. So, I have always had a hard time reading signs. Sandy indicated she liked being with me, and we seemed compatible, but if she sent out any message beyond that, my receptors didn't pick the message up. And my fear of rejection (I'd read a lot about that subject in my psychology books,) as always, hung around my neck like a garland of needles.

After she flashed that smile, she leaned back and closed her eyes, allowing the sun to dry off her golden skin and light brown hair.

I thought back on all the ideas I wanted to share with her about the book she'd given me, ideas that would reveal what an original thinker I'd become, even before reading the book, how I lived in a world of ideas, of the mind, of areas that made life worth living. Instead of talking, I followed her lead and closed my eyes as well, and what seemed like a moment later, the maid stood at the back door to tell both of us to get ready for dinner. In the changing room, I noticed a light redness on my chest and legs and a bit of sunburn.

At the table, Essie, the maid, brought in a big roast beef while Mr. Stein sharpened up his carving knife to serve me, the honored guest, a large slice. A bowl filled with crispy brown potatoes was passed around, as were the string beans.

"How was your week, Cal?" Mrs. Stein asked, just as I'd stupidly taken a too large piece of meat into my mouth. I chewed as fast as possible. "We didn't have much of a chance to talk at Synagogue the other night," she added before I could answer.

Still chewing, I shook my head in agreement. Then, I relayed the story of Lenny, the Jewish dynamo. That brought a good laugh from the table, including Sandy.

"And what about the school?" Mr. Stein asked. "Are you feeling more comfortable there as you've gotten to know the routines?"

Again, I produced a negative shake of the head just as I swallowed. "No. If anything, it's worse. I mean, the classes are okay, though they're hard for me because I'm not great at science or math. It's the cadets themselves, the kids. They call themselves Christians, but they sound like a bunch of racists spouting off about Negroes all the time. They think they're so much better."

"I hated that attitude when we first moved to Houston," Sandy piped in. "But in Houston, there were at least a few liberal people who didn't feel that way. Here, in Cullen, I have learned the best response is just to keep my mouth shut."

"You young people have every right to be upset," Mr. Stein said just before consuming a very rare bite of roast beef.

"I don't understand their reasoning," I confessed. "They talk about lynchings and how all Negroes are shifty and lazy. The stereotyping is disgusting."

"Please take some more potatoes," Mrs. Stein urged, passing me the bowl. With no desire to disappoint her, I used the spoon to scoop up a second helping.

"This is so different from New York," Sandy said. "I think Southerners are some of the most backward people I've ever met, though a few I've come to know are wonderful."

"That's ironic," I said with a smile. "You've been here a year or so, and I've been here a couple of weeks, and we are already prejudiced ourselves."

Sandy looked surprised by my response, while Mr. Stein smiled. "I don't understand what you mean, Cal."

Essie came around with the iced tea and filled half-empty glasses. She stopped to stare at me for a moment before returning to the kitchen.

"I simply mean that we're here in one small place in one Southern state. I'm certain there are people every bit as concerned with racism as we are, people who have lived here all their lives and are working to try to make life better for everyone. Maybe there are places in the South where black people and white people are working together at great risk to make improvements. I just don't know, only that I've made this snap judgment based on a very small survey of the population."

"Bravo," Mr. Stein said. "I like the way this boy thinks."

I turned my attention to him. "Sandy told me you came out West for your health. I wonder why you chose to settle here in Cullen, of all places. If you don't mind me saying so, and please take what I say as a compliment because I just wonder, well, you all seem so out of place here."

Mrs. Stein's sudden expression, which just as quickly passed, made me realize I'd hit a raw nerve that indicated she hadn't landed here by choice.

Mr. Stein didn't answer right away. He'd just about polished off his slice of roast beef, and he took another bite or two while he thought out his response.

"I'm sure Sandy filled you in on why we settled in Houston. I had a cousin I had grown up with who was very successful in business there. He wanted me to help him expand, and I wanted to get away from the rat race in New York. At the time, the slower pace appealed to me. Now, living here, I must confess I long for a little more action."

"What kind of work did you do there?" I inquired. Though my questions were innocent, they seemed to evoke a mystifying response.

"Oh, just the usual business," Mr. Stein said.

I nodded and let the subject go. I concluded this man had moved here for a reason, and if my relationship with Sandy developed, I would eventually learn that reason sometime in the future.

Essie brought in the dessert once she'd cleared the table. We had an all-American dessert: Ice cream with a homemade cherry pie.

I could barely stand after we finished the meal. I asked Sandy if she'd like to take a walk, joking about how I needed to walk off some of this dinner. My heart pounded when she smiled and said she'd enjoy walking and that they had a nice wooded area about a mile from the house we could walk to.

Sandy had changed into a flowered dress that seemed to

mirror the fall colors that started to show themselves on the trees around town. Brilliant reds, yellows, and browns reminded me that we weren't in Los Angeles, where all the seasons seemed to offer nothing more than mild variants on an endless summer. Not that I minded. I liked sunshine, and if the temperature wanted to hit 80 in January, who was I to complain?

We walked side by side along the street. With her hand by her side and only a few inches from mine, I longed to take hold of hers. Doubt shadowed me like a hunter following prey. What if she pulled her hand away? Or worse, slapped mine for trying to take hers? What if she turned to me and said, "you're a nice boy, Cal, but I don't like you like that." What if? What if?

We walked into the park, which had benches and shade trees surrounding a small pond. We sat side by side on a bench facing the pond. Finally, I had a chance to bring up the *Fountainhead* and that crazy Howard Roark, who would not compromise no matter the consequences.

"He seemed too much like an anarchist," Sandy explained. "The way he torched those houses for poor people just because his partner in them had made some changes. His thinking proved to be too rigid for me."

I couldn't disagree. Roark had raped Dominique, and though he made beautiful buildings, he wouldn't give an inch in his convictions. "I always feel like the expectations of society are like a weight on me, pulling me down like an anvil," I told her. "This school is like that. The training is all about serving God and country. There's no room for individual thinking or ideas."

Sandy turned her head toward me and flashed her smile. "That's one goal we share in common. We both want this year to end so we can escape Cullen, perhaps for different reasons, but we are both eager to move on."

"I'm ready to move on," I agreed. "I'd be ready to move on today if I didn't know you and my friend, Larry, at school."

She opened her mouth as if she wanted to respond, but no words emerged. At that moment, I reached over to where she had placed her hands together in her lap and took one of them gently. Just as gently, she pulled the hand away as if the action had never occurred.

When we reached her house, Sandy said she needed to study, and with a little peck on the cheek, she took her leave. I was left in the living room with her parents. Before I could leave, they set me down and had Essie make us all a glass of iced tea.

The Steins sat side by side on the couch while I'd been given the flowered easy chair with the soft cushion. I stared at a painting above the couch. The image looked familiar as if I'd seen a reproduction somewhere in a book, but I had no idea if this was the original or merely a copy sold at Woolworth's or somewhere else.

"Tell me, Cal," Mrs. Stein asked, "What do you think about the Rabbi?"

I immediately suspected a trap. "He's okay," I said. "He's a little long-winded, but I guess they all are. They have a captive audience."

Mr. Stein laughed at this until a quick look from his wife silenced him.

"I noticed when we sing or recite prayers, you don't follow along."

"No, Ma'am. At Roxwell, we are required to attend either a church or a synagogue whether we have any interest in doing so or not. I'm not much for religion."

"Hear, hear," added Mr. Stein.

The dynamics in this family were becoming clearer fast. I wondered where Sandy stood on the subject, though I suspected her absence on Friday nights made her position clear.

"I feel we all need to respect God," Mrs. Stein said. "If we didn't have guidance from our traditions and teachings, we would be as lost as those wanderers in the wilderness."

I sipped my iced tea. "I should be heading back. They have a roll call before dinner, and if I miss that, they will give me demerits." I stood up.

"Please visit us again next Sunday," Mrs. Stein said. "I know Sandy really enjoys your company. She told me you were so different from the boys she's met here."

After thanking them for the afternoon, I left the house with mixed messages. I had given myself enough time to walk back to the school as I wanted to attempt to sort out how Sandy really felt about me. On the one hand, she appeared warm, friendly, receptive, open, and seemed to enjoy my company. On the other hand, she had withdrawn her hand the moment I took hold. What did that mean? Did she see me as many other girls in the past, just a friend, but not one she could feel romantic towards? Howard Roark never had that problem. To confuse the situation further, she discussed me with her mother in a positive way.

CHAPTER THIRTEEN

After an afternoon visiting paradise, I returned to another week of military school hell. I returned, though, with more energy than I had felt in a long while. Love must do that, release those endorphins or whatever they are called. Brimming with energy, I decided to spend the whole week trying hard to catch up on my classwork and work to receive decent grades. I didn't plan to repeat my senior year again, and certainly not here. I knew the time would pass faster if I concentrated on my work and spent less time thinking about Sandy. Besides, a plan had begun to formulate in my mind.

Every night that week, I went to the assigned study hall, which any cadet could do on a voluntary basis. I took advantage of a tutoring program they offered, where advanced students in a field made themselves available to help the slower ones. The courses like Algebra II and Geometry that had so mystified me at the beginning had become more clear. I can't say I enjoyed them. Military Science was mostly memorizing information. English and Speech were no problem. Not that my grades moved toward brilliance. But I pulled myself up to a C in my worst courses, and I had an A from the admiring teacher in public speaking. He had adapted a plan of having the student who read that day in class bring his own book for the event, and the interest in the class developed exponentially. Our current assignment consisted of preparing a talk to give to the class, and I had chosen a theme that I suspected would be both provocative and challenging, titled *The Role the Military Plays as a Deterrent to Peace.* I thought a discussion on that subject might shake things up a bit.

Because of my new energy and approach, this week differed from the previous ones. No time spent hanging out listening to the sounds of racist chatter, and no bullshit sessions. Instead, I took a nose to the grindstone approach, leading to a feeling of achievement and, ironically, my first demerit. On Thursday, while studying for a Friday test in my room, I missed the pre-dinner roll call. One demerit meant an hour of marching on Monday afternoon with the demerit squad.

Friday night, after dinner, I led my contingent to the Synagogue. The Steins told me how much they looked forward to my visit on Sunday. I reached my room around nine, and Larry looked as if he'd been waiting for my return. We'd barely spoken during the week, as I'd spent all those evenings in study hall. His first action coincided with my entrance. He tossed his car keys in the air and caught them, which drew my attention.

"Hey, Roomie, you've been hitting the books too damn hard. Time to have some fun."

I looked up, smiling. I assumed that meant another shaving cream fight.

"Listen, you remember that little chaquita, Jill. I met when we went to the soda fountain a couple of weeks ago." I nodded. "Well, I talked to her a couple of days ago, and I'm on my way over there now to see her."

"But, we have school tomorrow. You're not supposed to go out."

"Fuck that," he said, surprising me with his inflection. "I've had enough of the stupid rules in this place. I'm going. And she has a friend over who wants to meet you."

Larry turned to our shared mirror to comb his hair while I contemplated an answer. "You know, there's this girl I like," I said, hesitant.

"So there's a lot of girls I like," he said. "We'll have some fun. Come on. You're not married yet."

I laughed. "How can we go over there without getting caught?"

"Just wait." He went into his closet and pulled out a device I'd never seen before.

"This here is called a timer. I'll set the clock for ten-thirty. The light in our room will stay on until then, and then, at curfew, the timer will turn the light off. They never check a room unless they spot a light that is still on after lights out. We'll be fine."

Thirty minutes later, we were cruising down the street in Larry's Ferrari. He'd called a cab to meet us in front of the school and take us to the garage in town, where he'd housed the Ferrari once classes started. This adventure thrilled me. I felt like we were two guys giving the school and all their stupid rules the middle finger. And, I'd forgotten what a strange feeling of power I felt riding in a car so expensive. Somehow, sitting in the front seat made me feel as if the car belonged to me as well. Larry drove slowly and carefully, not wanting to attract police attention in his fancy car. He seemed to know the way to the girl's house, and we arrived on her block soon after nine-thirty.

Jill lived in what looked like a small, square wood frame house, at least from what I could make out in the dim street light, in a neighborhood where the houses generally looked far shabbier than the block Sandy lived on. The street had an eerie quality, almost pitch dark, with a few dimmed streetlamps the only source of light.

"Her parents are off somewhere," Larry announced as he parked in front of the house.

All the way over, I had been weighing my conscience, concerned I'd done the right thing considering my feelings for Sandy. Yet, she had offered no clear reciprocal signs. Perhaps she wasn't the least bit interested in having a relationship with me, whereas, for my part, I was prepared to go steady, get engaged, or even marry her. As the song goes, you need two to tango, but at the moment, ever hopeful, I was dancing alone. Not very realistic perhaps, but one has to follow his heart.

Later that night, I drove the car back to the school. Larry had me park the Ferrari on a side street, saying he'd return the car to the garage the next evening when we could go out. We were safely in our room by midnight. I laid down on my bed in my clothes, still in shock from the events that occurred at Jill's house. How can I describe what unfolded before my eyes except to say the evening exploded with unexpected surprises?

First, when we parked in front of the house, Larry opened the trunk to pull out a bottle of vodka. He carefully carried the unopened bottle to the front door. Jill answered, wearing a pair of shorts and a halter, an odd outfit for so late in the evening. On the couch, in semi-darkness, sat her friend, Ruby. When we entered, Ruby stood up. Upright, she towered about half a head taller than me. She had the slim build of a basketball player with dyed blond hair curled in the fashion of the day. After introductions, Jill pulled a bottle of orange juice from the fridge for those who wanted screwdrivers. She filled a juice glass half full of straight vodka for Larry and poured another for herself. They clinked glasses, downed the vodka, and disappeared into the bedroom, shutting the door behind them.

Ruby and I stared at each other across the breakfast room table where the bottle of orange juice, the vodka bottle, and our two empty glasses sat.

"Should I mix you a screwdriver?" She asked.

"Okay."

We stared some more. I couldn't tell much from looking at her, her age, for example, if she was still in school, actually I couldn't read anything at all. She wore a flannel nightgown with little bunnies all across the front and back, a one-piece that ended just above her knees. Possibly, she and Jill had planned a sleepover, and she had borrowed Jill's nightgown, as Jill was quite a bit shorter. Ruby poured a glass half full of orange juice, leaving plenty of room at the top for the vodka. "How much?" she asked.

"Just a pinch," I said.

"Okay." She poured in a shot, took the fourth glass in her hand, and poured in the vodka almost all the way to the top. "Bottoms up," she said, clinking her glass against mine and drinking down the contents in a few hasty gulps as if she'd swallowed a glass of water. What followed next froze me.

She carefully set the empty glass back down on the table and stared intensely at me. She reached down with both hands to the hem of the nightgown and then used a single motion to lift the fabric over her head and toss the nightgown on the floor. She continued standing in the same position with the same intense stare, stark naked.

"What's your name again?" She asked.

"Cal," the word stumbled out of my mouth.

"Drink up, Cal. Let's go sit on the couch."

I took a sip. She came around the table to take the glass out of my hand. After carefully placing the glass on the table, she gripped my hand to lead me over to the couch. She sat down, reached up, and pulled me down beside her. "You're cute," she informed me, and I could taste the residue of vodka as her lips folded themselves over mine and her tongue explored the fillings in my teeth.

My heart pounded while total internal confusion reigned. Obviously, I could move in any direction with this girl, but I didn't know how I wanted to move. I felt like an object she wanted to use for her pleasure and discard, like an old shoe or a torn piece of clothing. At the same time, I'd never had an opportunity like this before, and this girl who pressed her lanky naked body against mine was far from unattractive.

Sex, for sex's sake, came to mind. Did I want that? Did I have a choice? And this scene, so unexpected, was taking place two nights before I'd see my beloved Sandy. Lust came to mind. Her intense, passionate kisses left me temporarily mindless. She forced my hand onto her breast (or did she?) and then moved my fingers down between her legs, moaning and groaning as she guided my hand back and forth, thrusting the fingers inside her as if she had found a wind-up doll to perform the necessary duties to satisfy her.

With a relaxed, experienced hand, she unbuttoned my military pants and pulled them and my underwear down around my ankles. She stretched out across the couch, put her head into my crotch, and performed a most unmilitary action, except, of course, for the aggression involved. With my pants now gathered around my ankles, my shirt unbuttoned, and my underwear somewhere, I experienced for the first time a sensation performed by a tongue and mouth that far surpassed those past attempts at self-gratification in the shower at home. At the same time, I despised myself for betraying Sandy. But, was I really, if this was only some kind of an experiment? Or what if Sandy didn't really care about me? Why was I going on about this amidst so much pleasure? This girl delivered sex plain and simple.

Beyond my growing enthusiasm, initially, nothing physical seemed to grow larger. With the movements of a skilled surgeon, Ruby brought me to arousal with a few deft movements of her hand. This girl had been around a few blocks. With tongue and hand, she performed an act that would have impressed any magician who pulls rabbits out of hats for a living. At the moment of climax, where the explosion from inside wiped away all thoughts and analyses, I moaned so loud I heard a laugh come through the door of the bedroom.

Panting, flayed across the couch like a martyr in a religious painting, I reveled in this new and exciting experience. For a moment, I lay there, relishing the power of the moment. When I had sufficiently recovered (though I had difficulty looking at Ruby out of embarrassment), she said with a pointed forefinger, "the bathroom's there."

Using the bunny hop to move forward, as my pants still clung to my ankles, I made my way across the living room to the bathroom in the hall and shut the door. I took a washcloth off the rack and, with cold water, cleaned all the goo that clung to my stomach and any other area as a result of this encounter. I washed myself carefully, dried off, and finally reconstructed my underwear, pants, and shirt, which now showed patches of sweat. I rinsed my mouth with a mouthwash I located in the cabinet, then opened the door to return to the living room and whatever adventure Ruby might have in store for me next. Only, much to my surprise, no Ruby remained. The nightgown had vanished, and the girl who had so brazenly flung the item off her body had vanished as well.

I searched the kitchen, each of the other rooms except for the one Jill and Larry occupied, calling her name softly, but not a trace of Ruby. I thought maybe she'd gone into the backyard to cool her passion in the night air, but in the small backyard with dying grass, not a sign of her. I had to wonder, had all this been a dream? Had I only imagined this in the form of a wet dream? I might have opted for that theory, but for the feeling of total satisfaction that remained so vivid beneath my underwear, a feeling different from any I'd experienced before.

There had been a Ruby. Her glass and mine remained where she had placed each one on the kitchen table before we'd moved to the couch. So thinking she still might return from some unknown hiding place, I turned up the light, took a book from one of several leaning against one another on a small bookshelf, and read. I read about fly-fishing for well over an hour until Larry emerged from the bedroom looking happily stupefied. He tossed me the car keys.

Yes, as I said before, I drove the Ferrari back to the school following Larry's directions. The sensation of being behind the wheel, feeling that raw power at my beck and call still played second fiddle to the other feeling that lingered in that strangest of encounters.

CHAPTER FOURTEEN

Saturday passed faster than expected. After all, during my boring classes, I returned to the previous night or anticipated the following day. Every time I thought back on the previous evening, I could not quite believe what transpired at Jill's house. In my classes, I felt different somehow, though I couldn't exactly nail down the origin of that feeling.

Saturday night, Larry vanished, but I went into town with several of the cadets to see a lousy movie at the Cullen Theater. The movie helped pass the time and brought me an evening closer to Sunday dinner with the Steins.

The following morning, church morning, in the quiet of our house, I woke up early and spent time reading and trying to decide if I should bring Sandy a gift, a token of my affection, so to speak. All morning, I gravitated back and forth about how to approach such a delicate subject as my feelings for her. I would have planned a full-out advance if she had offered me any serious encouragement. On the other hand, I didn't detect any sense of rejection. The fact that she removed my hand from hers the previous week when we sat together on the park bench could have had a simple explanation; she wasn't yet ready to advance the relationship. Sandy certainly didn't indicate any displeasure with me, even after she removed my hand. She appeared to enjoy my company as much as I enjoyed hers.

By lunchtime, I had decided to pop a question. At the appropriate moment, I would ask her to go steady. Once we'd settled that, the rest would fall into place. She might say she didn't feel ready to commit. Fine, I could wait until she felt more comfortable. At least, this would allow me to get a sense of how mutual and deep our affections were for each other.

On the way into town, I remembered a tattered cookbook that my mother owned with a saying on the cover: "The way to a man's heart is through his stomach." I decided that perhaps the way to Sandy's heart went through her parents. They both seemed to like me. Instead of bringing Sandy a gift, which I finally decided might be too premature, I used a few extra dollars I'd received from my mom at a florist shop in town to buy a dozen red roses for Mrs. Stein. She'd gone out of her way to be nice, and though I probably didn't come across as the ideal match for their precious Sandy, they still accepted me and treated me with great kindness.

Essie answered the door. When she saw me holding the roses, her lips parted into a wide smile. "Mrs. Stein loves roses," she whispered in an almost conspiratorial manner before leading me into the living room.

Mrs. Stein stood up to greet me when I entered the living room. I gave her the roses, which elicited the kind of response Essie had led me to expect. I told her she had been such a wonderful hostess; bringing flowers was the least I could do.

I could smell dinner cooking in the kitchen. To my surprise, Mrs. Stein invited me to sit down. I took a seat on the patterned couch across from her.

"Sandy isn't back home yet," she explained. "On Friday, after school, she went to Houston to spend the weekend with a girl friend from her old high school. She had promised to be back by noon today, but she called. There had been some delay, and she had to take a later bus. She should be back within the hour. Would you like to have a swim while you wait?"

"Yes, Ma'am," I said. "Is Mr. Stein out too?"

"No, he's off in the den watching some game. I don't know what kind. Would you like a glass of iced tea? I could have Essie make you one."

I thanked her, went out in the back, and changed into my trunks. I stretched out on the chaise lounge. A few minutes later, Essie brought a tall glass of iced tea, which I placed on the small table beside me.

I stared at the pool. Sandy had gone to Houston. I'd almost forgotten she'd lived there for a year or so. She probably loved to visit friends there, but I felt sure her mother had insisted she return in time to be here for me. And she hadn't complied. What, if anything, did that imply?

The humidity soon forced me into the pool. Swimming first, then stretched out in the shallow end up to my neck in water, I mentally went through a variety of conversations that would either lead to my goal to make Sandy my steady or perhaps inform me that I had been wasting my time, or possibly learn she needed more time to commit, though a future possibility existed. To bring this subject up, I needed to find an appropriate opening, perhaps a conversation that would set the stage properly and put us both in a good mood, but then, well, I couldn't see clearly past that point.

Half an hour later, after finding no opening gambit and finding myself once more stretched out on the chaise lounge, the screen door to the backyard opened, and Sandy appeared. She looked gorgeous. Her hair curled around her neck, held in place by a head scarf; her short-sleeved blouse set off her tan arms; her black skirt, with a pink poodle prancing on one side, was cut just below the knee, and she wore small heels. She flashed a big smile.

"Cal, please excuse me, but I missed the bus this morning and had to wait a couple of hours for the next one. I had intended to be here when you arrived."

I melted. She sounded so sincere and gracious.

"Should I change into my suit? And we can have a swim. I think dinner is going to be an hour or more from now."

I nodded, and she disappeared inside the house, returning a few minutes later wearing a two-piece suit new to me, all white in contrast to her deeply tanned body. She gave me her hand in a warm greeting as she stretched out on the chaise beside mine.

"I see you've already had a swim. I'm so hot. I'm going to jump in and cool off."

With that, she mounted the diving board and, with one high jump off the end of the board, executed a beautiful jackknife into the water.

She moved across the length of the pool like a mermaid, eating laps as she moved from one end to the other. After about a five-minute swim, she waded out of the shallow end to flop back down in the chaise she'd first occupied.

"That felt so good," she said. "How was your week?"

"Fast," I said. "I spent most evenings in study hall trying to catch up with my class work. I may hate the place, but I'm determined to graduate. Can I ask you a question?"

"Shoot."

Essie came out with a glass of iced tea for Sandy, and I waited until she returned to the house to pose my question.

"Every week when I go to Synagogue, your parents are there, but you aren't. I know you were in Houston this weekend, but I wondered why you didn't attend."

She sipped at her iced tea before answering. "I just don't have any interest in attending. Fortunately, my parents let me make up my own mind about that."

I nodded, and remembered I'd told her family about our crazy eleven-year-old cadet, Lenny, but not about his background and how he learned to fight. That might be just the opening I needed. His saga might be the perfect story to get her laughing and a way to lead into a more serious discussion. So I told her more about Lenny, the Brooklyn boy who grew up in an Italian neighborhood, and whose aunt had taught him how to fight dirty.

Sandy giggled and laughed constantly through the story. When she laughed, her white teeth flashed and she showed her dimple. I felt the greatest urge to kiss her.

"That's a great story," she said when I finished. "I can just picture him with that cigarette dangling out of his mouth. He must be an amazing kid."

I smiled. "When I came to Roxwell, I told the Dean I was an atheist and didn't want to go to church or synagogue. He explained the school requires you to attend some place of worship. He didn't look too favorably on my views in general. I could have gone to a church or synagogue, it really didn't matter to me, but now I know I chose the right one because if I hadn't gone to Friday night services, I'd never have met your wonderful parents, and of course, I'd never have met you."

Her smile masked an expression of curiosity as to where this conversation was headed.

I continued, perhaps rushing the words a bit too much. "Since the first day we met, you've made my attending Roxwell a bearable experience because in my free time, I can think about you and look forward to the following Sunday when I'll see you again. You must know I have strong feelings for you, Sandy."

As the words jumped out, my heart jumped with them. Sandy's face reddened, and not from a sudden burst of sunshine.

"I'm not very good at pretending," I continued, eager to get all the words out before she responded. "The truth is that I dream of us going together. I'm not sure how you feel about me or if you think I'm moving too quickly, but I need to know if you would consider going steady with me, if not now, at some point. You'd make me the happiest guy in all of Cullen."

A nervous laugh before asking, "Not in the state of Texas?"

"In all of Texas and Oklahoma, too," I smiled, encouraged by her response. Then her eyes narrowed to reflect the sudden serious expression that crossed her face.

"Cal, I think you are a really sweet person and a good friend. You are the only real friend I have here. I also suspect that you are someone who can keep a secret."

My smile had vanished. I could keep a secret, but did I really want to hear the secret she wanted me to keep?

Desperate, I nodded yes.

"Swear?" Sandy asked.

My heart thumped. I almost wanted to cover my ears, though curiosity got the best of me. "I swear."

"I just spent the most wonderful weekend in Houston."

A flood of relief replaced my anxious moment. "I know. Your mom told me you went to visit your girlfriend. Did the two of you do something you shouldn't have?

Sandy shook her head. "It's not that."

My heart tangled with my windpipe.

"My parents think I went to stay with my girlfriend, but she's my cover. I went to visit my boyfriend. He's a year ahead of me, so he graduated from my former high school last year just as I moved here. He goes to Rice University now. My parents know him, but they don't know we are still involved. In my one year of high school in Houston, he became my boyfriend, but my parents thought I'd broken off with him when we moved here. He isn't Jewish, so they, and particularly my mother, weren't thrilled by the relationship, though they both acted very accepting as long as we were together. But I could tell they felt a sense of relief when we moved here.

"Dale and I are in love. When I graduate in June, we will announce our engagement. I know my parents seem liberal to you, but they would be very unhappy if they knew we had stayed together. I'm sorry to upset you with this. You are a terrific person. I tried really hard not to lead you on."

For a moment, I remained silent. I felt like a boxer who just received a pop on the chin, and I stood teetering on the brink, ready to hit the deck at any moment. I reflected on our previous meetings, how Sandy had always been friendly but, at the same time, how she remained distant, at least on an emotional level. Her whole balancing act suddenly made sense.

The fantasy had been mine. For a moment, I imagined what my brother or Larry might have done if they had been sitting here listening to this. Masters of smooth talk, knowing just what to say, in the end, either of them might have convinced Sandy to break off with Dale to take up with either of them. They had this knack for getting girls to desire them with barely the flick of a wrist.

"I wish you all the best," I mumbled. "Dale is a lucky guy."

An embarrassing silence followed. I wanted to change into my clothes, tell her parents goodbye, and walk out the front door. I wanted to run away and hide. I wanted to break out in tears. I wanted to bang my head against the nearest wall. I wanted to jump in the pool and not come up for air. Inside,

I felt as if my brain had been injected with Novocain.

Sandy sat up, pivoted her body around, and reached over to take my hand in both of hers. "Cal, I'm so sorry. We get along so well. I really love being with you. If the situation had been different, I'd have been more than happy to be your steady."

The words came with such sincerity, and her hands felt so warm, clasping mine that I melted once more. As much as I wanted to strike out, to hurt her, to walk in and tell her parents, "Sorry, I can't stay for dinner. Sandy just spent the weekend with her boyfriend in Houston, and she doesn't have any time for me. Have a good life." As much as I wanted to do any of that, all I could do was manage a faint smile and say, "I hope he is good enough for you. You deserve only the best."

She pulled her hands away, stood up, and gave me a quick kiss on the cheek before she walked to the screen door to enter the house.

Dinner proved a challenge to get through, but we both pulled off our roles, acting as normal as possible in an incredibly awkward situation. Fortunately, Sandy's father spent most of the meal discussing politics, which allowed both of us to listen.

When Mrs. Stein invited me back for the following week, I said my uncle was coming to take me out to a football game for the weekend, but I would be in touch. I said I'd see them on Friday at synagogue, though that thought sent a chill through me.

When I said my goodbyes, perhaps seeing Sandy for the last time, I stood out on the street in front of the house for a moment. I had arrived at Sandy's house in love and excited, and now, a few short hours later, I had departed to a different future than the one I dreamed about and so longed for.

CHAPTER FIFTEEN

One of the first books Hugo had suggested I read after he learned of my interest in psychology was *Man's Search for Meaning* by Viktor Frankl, a psychologist who found himself trying to survive in a few of Hitler's death camps. Hugo explained that Frankl's real-life experience caused him to split with Freud about his primary purpose in life. Freud believed life was a search for pleasure, while Frankl felt that the primary object of life was for each person to seek and find meaning. If no God existed, then each person had the responsibility to find a meaningful existence for himself.

I had been searching for such a purpose. I hadn't yet discovered that purpose for my life when my uncle convinced my mother that the way for me to find a focus was to spend a year in a Texas military school. That didn't exactly jive with my thinking, but to my surprise, after arriving here and meeting Sandy, I have gained the first insight into meaning. If we could have become a couple, she would have provided me the motivation to conquer the world. She had every quality I didn't know I wanted in a woman. Even her compassionate rejection of me fit the bill.

Now left with a feeling of rejection and emptiness in the pit of my stomach, I came to the realization that finding love, in and of itself, cannot be the primary purpose of any person's life. Love offers a richness to the moments you share with the one you love, but I have learned now that love alone can't give your life meaning because you remain dependent on the love of that other person to achieve meaning.

When I returned to my room shortly before roll call and dinner Sunday night, Larry picked up on my mood in an instant. I spilled out the story, trying to hold back tears. He reminded me of the events of Friday night and how unpredictable life can be. He told me I'd certainly find someone else to love, that one day in the future, my life would be fine, and I'd look back on this and laugh at my reaction. After dinner, he went off to play poker in another room.

Sunday night, after Larry left our room, I stretched out on the bed to spend time absorbing my loss and thumbing through a few of the books I had on psychology. My greatest weakness has remained a lack of confidence, which in turn previously led to a lack of motivation. The short time Sandy became my dream girl, I'd felt more of an incentive to accomplish something significant, to encourage her to be more appreciative and supportive. If there was a lesson for me here, I had to find a way to unlock that same energy I felt for Sandy but for myself.

The next day, I spent one free hour of my precious Monday afternoon marching off my demerit in the hot afternoon sun. While the rest of the school went into town, napped, or played cards, I joined the group of demerit losers. Fortunately, I had only an hour of the grueling march around the parade grounds while others marched through the entire afternoon. I don't know how they survived, as my uniform had soaked through by the time the sergeant in charge dismissed me.

Back in my room, I peeled off the wet clothes, took a shower, and relaxed with my books for a quiet afternoon. I had a lot of stuff to figure out. The most important had to do with what exactly made a person successful. What model did I need to follow? On the other hand, no one came to mind, certainly not my friend Ray, who floated through life much the same way I did.

Larry appeared to be the primary subject for my study. He displayed so many qualities I admired, which in a way I found odd, considering in many respects he resembled my brother, whom I detested. But they both put themselves first, seized each moment, knew what they wanted in life, and both appeared to know how to get whatever they wanted. The problem with the selfishness of that model, which reminded me somewhat of the character of Roark in *The Fountainhead,* is that selfishness offered little appeal to me.

The answer arrived in an unexpected way later in the week.

Monday night, after dinner, I went to study hall and continued to use a tutor to help deal with my math issues, the two of us huddling quietly in the back of the room. Since most people didn't use their forced study hall to study, our low voices hardly mattered.

After study hall, I returned to an empty room. At first, I assumed Larry had gone to Frenchy's for a burger, but as the 10:30 curfew arrived, no Larry. I prepared for bed, turned off the lights so the room would not attract attention, and read by flashlight under the covers for half an hour. At eleven, exhausted, I fell asleep. At one in the morning, I heard an angry voice and a banging around. I turned on the light.

Larry looked a little drunk. He was thrashing about the room, undressing in the dark, but with my bed lamp on, he sat down on his bed to take off his shoes.

"What happened?"

"Fuck," was the only word that sprang from his lips.

When nothing more came out, I asked again.

"Oh, I met this girl this afternoon when I was in town. We set up a date to meet tonight. On the way back to school, one of the staff showed up at the same time and nailed me. He took my name and told me that he had a duty to report me to the Dean. Being caught off grounds without a pass is four hours of marching in the fucking afternoon sun."

"That's rotten luck," I said. "You know, I had to march an hour today, and even marching that extra hour exhausted me."

To make matters worse for Larry, who had been directed to report to the Dean the next morning, he'd been dressed in civilian clothes rather than his uniform. "I don't know how many hours they'll tack on for being out of uniform. I guess I'll find out tomorrow."

On Tuesday, Larry learned he had received 8 hours of demerits, all of which went against our platoon. If I'd received those demerits, the platoon probably would have murdered me, but I wasn't' as sure how they'd deal with Larry. The school required him to march two Mondays in a row, four hours each Monday afternoon after lunch, on top of participating in regular Monday morning drills.

The penalty impacted him. The fun-loving, outgoing, Larry

dove into a shell. He went to classes, but in the evenings, he refused to get involved in the nonsense that went on daily. He didn't play cards, didn't visit other rooms, and just kept to himself.

Though still feeling pain from my loss, I tried to bring my roommate out. A couple of times, I suggested Frenchy's, but he showed no interest. One time, Gibbons came around trying to entice him into a card game, and he almost physically tossed him out of the room. Most of the time, he just laid down on his bed listening to jazz records on his phonograph.

I decided to leave him alone until he felt better, suspecting all that marching might keep him irritable for a while. So the week passed with me keeping to myself, going to classes, studying hard, and trying not to dwell on what had happened at Sandy's house the past Sunday. I thought about Jill's weird friend a bit, and though Ruby had overwhelmed me with her aggressiveness and disappearing act, she hardly struck me as someone I would want to get to know better.

Then came Friday, the day I would have to face Sandy's parents in Synagogue and pretend that all was cool. While in class, I thought of maybe telling the Dean I felt flush or some such thing so I could be excused from attending Friday night services. The Steins might pursue my visiting the week after next, and that would require another lie. The more I thought about what to do, the more Sandy came to mind, and the more she came to mind as another boat I'd missed in life, the more upset I felt.

Classes ended at four Friday, and I headed back to my room,

preoccupied with making a decision about the evening. The moment I entered, the shift of appearance in the room drew my attention. Somehow, the room seemed off, as if someone had removed certain items. The record player and records remained. But other items that belonged to Larry had vanished. My first thought was we had been robbed. I immediately suspected Gibbons. That thought quickly vanished. He wouldn't dare. I opened the closet that Larry and I shared. My miserable collection of civilian clothes still hung there, but Larry's expensive suits, ties, and shoes were no longer present.

Then I spotted an envelope on the dresser with my name printed across the center. By now, I recognized Larry's writing. Just as on Sunday, my body reacted in fear and rejection. Larry had abandoned me. I knew he'd taken off.

Dear Cal:

I'm having a hard time writing this. You have been a good friend, and I feel lousy that we haven't really talked all week. But this school and its fuking (sic) rules have just got to me again. When I left before the end of last year, I had no plans of returning. Then, my father and I talked, and I agreed to try the place again. But getting busted and thinking about a year of this crap just doesn't suit me. And other than you, I find the place boring. I've left you my record player and records.

This morning, I had Mr. Roxwell call my Dad, and he agreed to let me come home. There is a decent high school for foreigners in Venezuela that I can finish up at. I know I should have spoken to you about this after lunch, but I had to pack and get out of here, and I expect to be halfway to

Galveston (where they'll ship my car back home) by the time you get this. Cal, you've been a pal, the only thing that has made this place livable. I hope we'll stay in touch. I'll write you once I return home to send you my address and see how you are doing.

Your Pal,

Larry Thompson

I took the letter to my bed, stretched out, and read the words again. I tried to make them sink inside my skull, but they refused, bouncing right off my forehead. How could Larry have done this to me? And how could he leave without saying a word? What kind of friend did that? I didn't care about his damn record player and records. I wanted him.

A week ago, Roxwell felt bearable. I thought I had a girl and a friend. I'd accepted the challenge of passing my classes. I had an incentive to make my way through. Then, with no more than a snap of the fingers of fate, I had no girl, no friend, just me. My hatred for this place welled up suddenly, more than ever. I hated Cullen. I hated struggling with my schoolwork. And most of all, I hated my responses. Whenever anything goes wrong, all I do at first is read, as if the answer to every problem can be found inside a book. After that, I analyze. What good does any self-examination do me? I feel like a freak, set apart from the rest of the world. And I understand that feeling is my own damn fault. I always assume too much, as I did, about Sandy and Larry. I build ideas up about situations, and then those situations blow up in my face. When I return home, I'm determined to be different. And I'm determined to find my way home. The feeling overwhelmed me. I want to go home NOW.

I felt my body begin to shake. Nobody wanted me. Nobody in LA cared that I had left. My family thought me worthless and wanted to ship me off to this place. Nobody here cared whether I lived or died. Tears began welling in my eyes. A week ago, I'd felt on top of the world. How could my life shift so suddenly and dramatically?

My brain didn't want to function, and before I realized it, Grooper's roommate, Charlie Harris, knocked to ask if I was coming to roll call and dinner. He waited for me, and we walked out together. Though I'd never talked much with him, he seemed like a good guy. All the way over, he kept glancing at me with a sympathetic expression, like a doctor checking my pulse. Finally, as we reached roll call, he said, "Sorry to hear about Larry leaving."

I just had time to nod my head. Then, we needed to line up with our platoons.

After dinner, I gathered the squirts for Synagogue. During the service, staring at Sandyt's parents two rows in front of me, my thoughts returned to last Sunday. While listening to the rabbi with one ear, I tried to figure out what to say to the Steins at the reception afterwards. To my surprise, when the service ended, they passed by without a glance at where I sat with the kids. Looking straight ahead, they marched out the front door as if I no longer existed. That really raised my curiosity. Had Sandy revealed the truth about her boyfriend? Or had Sandy asked them not to invite me back again, making them embarrassed to acknowledge me?

With the squirts safely back at school, I returned to my

empty room. My impulse was to pack my bag and get the hell out of town. With nothing left here, what could possibly be worth staying for? All I needed to have was a plan.

Despite my upset, I realized leaving with a suitcase in the middle of the night carrying a total of around $20, most of it in checks, might not be the smartest decision. I decided to sleep on the situation and see how I felt about leaving the following morning. Saturday meant another day of school, and if I planned to leave, keeping up with my schoolwork wouldn't matter. I could use the day in class to work out my plan of escape.

By the end of dinner, Saturday night, I had decided to leave. When I returned to my room, I took the small bag I'd brought with me and packed my suit, pants, shirts, and a couple of pairs of underwear and socks. In my state, I forgot to shut the door to my room. In the midst of the packing, a voice interrupted my thoughts.

"Going somewhere?" The voice belonged to Charlie Harris, the cadet who lived with Grooper across the hall from me.

"Maybe," I said without looking around.

"Where would you go to with a suitcase on a Saturday night?"

I glanced at him, then sat down on my bed. "I don't know. I just need to leave."

Charlie entered the room and sat down across from me on Larry's bed. "Listen, you don't want to take off now. You've heard what happens to cadets who get caught going AWOL. The demerits aren't the worst part. It's what the company does to you. I have a better idea. Why don't we go into town tonight? We can have a little fun, and get away from here for the evening."

I hesitated. The truth hit me hard. I had no plan. I had no place to run to. And this guy, whom I barely knew, had reached out to me.

Charlie's intense brown eyes belied a soft-looking, almost baby, face. Like Larry, nobody tangled with him. A rumor had circulated last year after he first arrived; you didn't want to mess with Charlie because, at sixteen, he'd earned a karate brown belt, whatever that meant.

He continued speaking in his soft Texas accent while I stood up and fiddled with closing the suitcase, which I returned to the closet. "I hated the place when I came here last year. I'm from Houston, so the school's right around the corner from me, so to speak. After about a month, I decided to leave. There is a process for doing that, like your friend Larry did. You go into the Dean and tell him you want to leave. You have to be determined, or he'll try to talk you out of going. If you are determined, he sends you in to see Mr. Roxwell. He's the one who will call your parents. When I got my dad on the phone, he was a retired army officer; he asked me to stick the year out. He knew I'd been dying to go to Europe during the summer, and he promised to take me on a trip to anywhere in Europe I wanted to go, provided I stuck the year out and got passing grades. Eventually, I got used to the place…everyone does after a while. This year has been much easier, and we had a great time traveling in Europe."

Europe remained a far away dream. Nobody would trade me

a trip to Europe for staying in school. I had no hope of getting there in the future.

"Okay, I'll go into town with you. What do you want to do?"

We called a taxi to take us into town. We didn't do much. After checking out the double feature, we went for cokes at the drugstore. We talked some more. Charlie liked sports a lot. He followed the Houston Buffs, a Texas league team. He liked Rice in football. But he didn't sound like a jock. He talked and acted far from that kind of person, which made me wonder if he'd come up with the karate story just to be left alone.

The next morning, Sunday, I still had my small bag packed and ready. While the others were out visiting Jesus, I spent the morning weighing what to do. If I followed the procedure for a normal withdrawal, as Larry had, I weighed what I would say to my mother over the phone to convince her that I'd learned my lesson, that this place could no longer serve a useful purpose for me, that I now understood what I wanted to do with my life, and would be willing to do whatever work that required. Maybe, if I said the right words, she would agree to let me return home.

The truth is that the prospect of being able to return home legally and by airplane appealed to me far more than the uncertainty of taking off randomly, unsure of where to go. By the afternoon on Sunday, after a great Sunday dinner, I had developed a plan of action for the following morning.

CHAPTER SIXTEEN

Crommy, that is Dean Cromwell, let his left hand tap a rhythmic tattoo on the desk in front of him. His face remained frozen in a stern expression as he listened to my explanation on why the school had failed me, and how I wanted him to call home to get permission for me to return.

I had come to his office after the room inspection and just as the Monday morning marching began.

"I only have one question," he told me, his voice colder than any day I'd experienced in Texas once I had finished my comments. "Does your leaving have anything to do with Larry Thompson going home on Friday?"

"We were friends," I answered, not surrendering any information.

The Dean tapped a solo on the desk with four fingers, as his mind worked. He pulled out my file and thumbed through the pages.

"You aren't doing badly in school. You are passing all your courses, and you have an A in public speaking. I don't understand your motivation. I must warn you leaving like this is a grave mistake. To graduate from Roxwell is to open many doors. You appear to need the kind of direction this school can provide."

"Excuse me, Sir," I responded, "But I have found my direction, and that direction isn't here."

"Carter, the success of this school is built around tradition, principles, and honor. When a cadet wishes to withdraw, the problem lies with the cadet, not the institution."

"Perhaps." I felt sweat mounting under my arms. I just wanted to finish the damn thing. "But military life isn't what I was cut out for. I know a lot of people respond to the order and regiment, but not me. The sooner I get out of here the better."

He glared, his face tightening into what might be termed a Jew-hating expression, one I'd experienced before in Junior High School. He probably couldn't admit he'd be really happy to rid the place of another Jew, but as a good soldier, he had to do his duty and pretend I would be better off staying put.

"Are you insistent on leaving?"

"I am."

He hesitated, before forming his next line of attack. "You know, we have a draft in this country. You will be obliged to serve. Many Roxwell graduates become officers. They command men. They are men. When the army calls you, you must obey. You can't tell them you don't like the place and want to go home. What will you do when you're drafted?"

"I don't know what I'll do. That's a black cloud hanging over my head. I'll deal with that problem when the time comes."

Getting nowhere, he cleared his throat. "There is a procedure. Anyone leaving prematurely must first see Mr. Roxwell. He's a busy man. So if you are not serious, please don't waste his time."

"I think you understand I'm serious. Please arrange for me to see Mr. Roxwell."

Without another word he stood up, assuming a kind of straight military stance, and walked stiffly across the room to open the door to an adjoining room. He shut the door behind him. A few minutes later, he returned.

"Mr. Roxwell will see you now." As he seated himself back at his desk, Crommy pointed to the door he'd just re-entered the room from.

Without a word, I stood up and walked through the doorway. On the other side, I found a small room with a young woman in a bright colored dress sitting behind a typewriter at her desk. A couch and coffee table with a neatly stacked pile of magazines faced the desk. A coat rack with hangers occupied another corner. The girl behind the desk looked up as I entered and flashed a smile. She said, "You can go right in. Mr. Roxwell is expecting you."

The secretary's desk sat beside the door that led into Roxwell's office. I had only seen him one time, during orientation, when he gave his welcoming speech to the cadets on that first day. I entered a large rectangular office with high ceilings painted a light brown. The room held quality brown leather furnishings, one painting of the West, which hung directly behind the couch, and another larger painting depicting cowboys and Indians hanging on the wall directly behind Mr. Roxwell's impressively expansive desk. Papers in neat stacks filled the in and out baskets on one corner of the desk, alongside a table lamp, a pen set, and a telephone which had Mr. Roxwell's attention, as I entered.

Against the wall to the left of the desk stood several large four drawer wooden files.

With a wave of his hand Mr. Rockwell motioned for me to sit on the couch while he continued his conversation. As I sat, I noticed a corner cabinet that contained several trophies.

When Roxwell finished his call, he hung up the phone and turned his attention to a file that Crommy had probably left for him to go through. After he perused the contents, he closed the cover, and stared silently at me for a moment while I squirmed, a bit nervous about this encounter.

Up close like this, I picked up the same softness in his expression that I spotted that first day Roxwell spoke, just some sense of another person existing beneath the exterior he maintained in a school that bore the family name, for the school had been around for 50 or more years, and I assume had been started either by his father or grandfather. Perhaps, beneath that stern exterior, was someone exactly like me, a person who didn't want to be here either, but had fallen into the position and tradition he upheld, and didn't know what else to do. He regarded me in a very different way than Dean Crommy, and there almost appeared to be a twinkle in his bright blue eyes.

"The Dean reports that you are unhappy here and wish to return home." His baritone voice filled the room.

"That's correct, Sir."

"I have briefly examined your file. You seem to be passing your classes. You have had only one demerit. You've only been here a brief period of time. Can you perhaps explain the source of your unhappiness?"

I wanted to answer that I'd fallen in love with a girl who was in love with someone else, and the only person I cared about at the school had suddenly left. Instead, I responded. "I just don't feel as if I fit here, Sir. I grew up very differently. When I left home, I told my mother I was willing to try, but there is a very different culture in Texas than in California."

This brought a smile to his face. "When I was in college," he told me, "I spent a summer working in California. Believe it or not, I didn't attend a military college. I am an administrator, not a military man, though I did serve my country in the war. California is like a flame that draws moths from everywhere. If I had not made family obligations to return here and assume my responsibilities, I would have happily lived in a place like California with your beautiful weather, amazing mountains, and a coastline that stretches on forever."

That speech amazed me. My mouth probably dropped open, for I could see my response had made him laugh. "Yes, we can surprise others sometimes. I assure you that if you ultimately change your mind and decide to stick Roxwell out for the remainder of your year here, you will find yourself becoming a different person, even if you never pursue the military again. A man grows in mind and body through confronting and overcoming adversity."

I wondered if his adversity had been to surrender any opportunity for a normal life in order to run this place.

"Your point is well taken, Sir. The problem is I don't fit in. I feel awkward with the marching drills and military aspects, and I have had a difficult time making friends." I paused, then because he revealed some expression of sympathy in his face, continued. "To put this in psychological terms, I can't seem to adapt myself to the mentality of the people here, and an environment so different from my own world. The racial issue is extreme here, and my views are so completely at odds with the other cadets that I feel a separation, as though a chasm exists between me and my classmates."

I had guessed correctly, reinforced by the sympathetic nod of his head. "You've made a very articulate and interesting observation, Mr. Carter. You may find this difficult to believe, but I have tried on more than one occasion to introduce members of the Negro race to the program here. Not all Southerners fit a racial stereotype. In 1948, President Truman issued Executive Order 9981 integrating the United States Army. But that is the army, and this is Texas. I have discussed the issue with faculty, students, and my board. To my great disappointment, Roxwell Academy is not yet ready to launch such a transition. I do appreciate both your honesty, and your sensitivity to this issue. Tell me what you'd like me to do."

"I would like you to arrange for me to return home."

"I will do that. It is often the out-of-state students who have the most difficult time adjusting, especially students who have been raised in a more tolerant environment. I am glad you chose to leave honorably rather than just running away. That approach has never been a favorable one, and there are severe repercussions for those who fail. I'm sure you've heard about that."

I nodded to signify I knew the drill.

"If you do decide to stay, you will always be welcome in this office. You seem like an intelligent and insightful young person and I would be more than happy to visit with you whenever you need a friendly ear."

This conversation had turned a 180 degrees away from what I'd anticipated coming into the room. Thrown off, I didn't answer right away, for having someone like Mr. Roxwell for support could make all the difference.

"You don't object to my leaving?" I asked.

Roxwell stood up, took a cigarette from a package in his pocket, and lit one, as he walked over to the couch where I sat. He seated himself in a plush leather chair directly across from me.

"No, the issue is not about objecting, Mr. Carter. You and I both understand that any early departure reflects badly on a school, especially when the school is unable to fulfill the needs of a student. On the other hand, I understand there can be compelling reasons for wanting to depart. If that is your ultimate wish, I will stand by your decision."

"Thank you, Sir."

He puffed on the cigarette, and for a minute I sensed something else, something uncomfortable, in the way he smiled and stared at me. "There is a procedure, as I'm sure the Dean informed you. I have to first call your guardian in order to get permission to release you from the school. Since the balance of the prepaid tuition is not returnable with a voluntary withdrawal, once we have approval, we will purchase for you an airplane ticket home, and provide someone to transport you to the airport in Houston in order for you to catch your plane."

He intended to call my guardian. The thought made me shudder. I doubted if my uncle would let me go home; not the way he had talked during my visit. "Sir, if you would, can you call my mother? She is my permanent guardian, and I'm sure if I explain what's going on to her, she would be sympathetic."

"I wish I could do that for you, Mr. Carter. But your file states that you have an uncle here in Houston who is your temporary guardian. This is a protocol I am forced to follow. Despite the fact the school bears my family name, and I am the ultimate decision maker, I am bound to follow the same rules as everyone else. If I began to break them, what right would I have to ask others to follow them? I hope you see my point. Do you want, perhaps, to sleep on the issue until tomorrow? I will give you a pass so you will not be penalized for missing Monday morning drill. You can have a nice afternoon to relax, and perhaps we could speak again in the morning."

The room seemed hot, even though a ceiling fan did its circular thing and sent cool air throughout the room. "I'm sorry, Sir. I may as well find out now. I'm not optimistic my uncle will approve my leaving whether he receives a call today or tomorrow. I'd just as soon find out where I stand so I can move ahead."

"You're a very level-headed young man," Mr. Roxwell said, flashing another of those smiles that made me feel uncomfortable. I tried to put my finger on what bothered me, but my mind kept flipping back to how trapped I felt. I knew when asked, my uncle would never allow me to return home.

Mr. Roxwell lifted the phone off his desk and trailing a long extension cord, placed it down on the coffee table between us. Holding a sheet of paper with a number in one hand, he manned the phone, while I crossed my fingers behind my back trying to give myself a bit of luck. Roxwell dialed my uncle's home number, and they spoke. After a brief explanation of why he called, Roxwell told me my uncle wished to speak to me.

"Cal, what is this crap?" My uncle Sid's voice sounded irritated. "You want to leave school now? You just got there."

"I know," I responded. "The place just isn't working out, Uncle. I've been trying really hard. My grades are okay. I just feel so out of place here. I can't seem to make friends. I want to go home. I need your permission."

"YOU DON'T HAVE IT." His voice almost blew out my eardrum. "Now cut this crap out. You will stay there until the end of the year and you'll do well. Do you hear me loud and clear?"

"Yes, Sir."

"Now, let me talk to Mr. Roxwell. And remember I'm picking you up next Saturday afternoon to go to the Texas A and M game. Okay?"

"Yes, Sir."

I handed the receiver back to Mr. Roxwell. I felt like slamming Uncle Sid's voice straight against the floor. I hated listening to the message that receiver had brought. I sat in silence with my arms crossed, as Mr. Roxwell finished the conversation with Uncle Sid.

"Well, Mr. Carter," he said, in a soft voice, once he'd placed the receiver back in its cradle.

"I see a decision has been made for you to stay on. I hope you will make the best of the opportunity you have here. And remember, my door is always open to you."

He returned to his desk and wrote out a note. "Give this to your commanding officer when you line up for lunch. That way you won't be penalized for missing morning drill."

I stood, took the note, and thanked him. Maybe I should have saluted, but I was too pissed to think about that. I held the note in my hand, went out through the secretary's office, only to realize another door in her room led directly to the hallway. I didn't have to see the Dean's face again. Lucky me.

On the way back to my room, I weighed my options. I could stick the year out and make my family happy, and make myself miserable. Or I could take off, and try to hitch back home because I didn't have enough cash to take a bus or plane.

I hated my uncle. The bastard. He thought everyone should be like him. Why in the hell would I want to be like that? He may as well have come out of a cookie cutter. His whole life was just one lousy cliché. At least my family in California was interesting. We weren't like the Texas crowd.

Back in my room, I tried to clear my head. If I wanted to leave, there would be no time like the present. We had a roll call before lunch, but not another one until six, just before dinner. That gave me at least four hours after lunch to get the hell out of Dodge.

Though he came across as a bit strange, Mr. Roxwell's offer of support made me hesitate. What he said about adversity making the man repeated an idea I'd read about more than once in a psychology book. If the truth be told, I knew I could survive the year and graduate. With the help of a tutor and diligent studying, I had turned my classes around. Charlie, Grooper's roommate, seemed like the kind of guy who would make a good friend. My family would be proud of my ability to stick the school out, and no doubt, by the end, I would be a different more mature person, one who had confronted adversity and won out.

Putting off any final decision, I took the note Roxwell had written out excusing me, and went off to roll call and lunch. I lined up, glancing at the other cadets, the student leaders, and a military order that existed all around me. Would these guys walk into the valley of the shadow of death without a thought? Did they really feel ready to die for some stupid war, like the recent Korean war, that some stupid politician laid on them? Did the idea of going to war and killing people excite them?

With Larry gone, I sat alone at lunch, though the table was filled with chattering cadets, excited to have their afternoon free. I had no mail to read, no one to speak to, but I had a hell of an appetite, and went back for seconds, loading up on fried chicken as if I would never have another meal.

In my head, I counted up the money I'd have to cover the trip home, a ten-dollar check, a five-dollar check, and five dollars in cash. If I took that money and left, I'd have to find a way to cash the checks. California seemed on the far side of the moon from here, especially when one had to travel by thumb. Where else could I go? If I survived the trip home, I knew my mother wouldn't force me to return. But a larger question loomed, if to go, then how to go? A Southern route meant hitching south and west to El Paso, while the northern route went up to Amarillo and to Highway 66. If I went at all, and as I downed an apple cobbler for desert, the final decision still remained iffy, I decided to aim for Amarillo, as highway 66 went straight through to Los Angeles.

As I left the mess hall, the answer came to me, but not in the way I intended.

"Hey, Freshy," came the call in my direction. Gibbons, and a group of about ten cadets, stood outside the mess hall. They had half a dozen other cadets lined up. "Get over here, Carter," Gibbons directed. With Larry gone he'd become assertive, acting like a new man.

I walked over to the group. "In line, Freshy," one of the others said. I joined the lineup, standing around while they recruited one or two more freshys. Most of these kids were younger than me, as the school started in the Sixth grade. I towered over most of them.

We stood like a bunch of dummies in the afternoon Texas sun.

"All right, you freshys," one of the group yelled, walking over to take command while the others in the group, Gibbons included, started to laugh. "Now I saw some of you good old boys piggin' out on that chicken there at lunch," the guy began. He had sergeant stripes like Gibbons. "So my boys and me thought you should work some of that lunch off. Now, drop down on the ground in a push up position. I'm gonna count to ten, and each time I count you do a push up. One," and the line, now side by side along the ground, went up and down. "Two." He continued on like that, but he skipped nine and went right to ten. One of the others in his laughing group called out. "Hey, Caleb, they all missed number nine." Caleb barked out to the group. "Did you freshys hear that? Guess you better do it all again."

Groans came from the group, but nobody dared challenge this insanity. I longed to get up and walk away, but during each passing moment I stayed, a decision was being forced on me. The sweat began to accumulate along my back, under my arms, and on my face and neck. "One," Caleb counted, and we all went up and came down again. Some of the kids were struggling, and I could feel the pain in my arms. "Two." When he called five, one friend called out, "hey, time to hit town." Caleb turned and walked off with his group leaving us all hugging the ground, unsure when we should rise. Finally, when I noticed they were out of sight, I leaped to my feet and the others followed and scattered.

Those good old boys had helped make my decision. I would go home. I would go back to my room, pick up my packed suitcase, take a shower, dress as if going into town for the afternoon, and then walk into town. I'd avoid the downtown area, walk to the edge of town, stick out my thumb and hope to get a ride before the cops picked me up, or someone from the school spotted me standing out on the highway. The decision made me light-headed. I had to try to get home. I had to return to a world that, though far from perfect, represented sanity, my world. I would come back the changed person my mother hoped for.

In my room, I took my wet clothes off, jumped into the shower, and dressed in fresh khaki pants and shirt. I knotted the tie, took my cap and checked my appearance in the mirror. I removed the small suitcase from the closet. I decided to leave Larry's record player and records for whoever wanted them. All I wanted was to never see this place again.

I waited a few minutes, as cadets departed for various locations. As soon as the place quieted down, I made my way down the creaky stairs one final time and crossed the field behind our house, valise in hand. I heard voices calling me through the dorm windows. "Carter, hey where you all goin'? Come back, Carter boy? Bye, Carter. Hey, Carter."

As I reached the sidewalk in front of the school, and my feet hit solid cement, the voices faded like the ghosts of past times.

CHAPTER SEVENTEEN

My stomach churned the fried chicken lunch, and my heart beat so hard, I could almost hear the sound audibly. I knew how risky this escape could be, especially with the town full of Roxwell students on a Monday afternoon. Not half a block from Roxwell's front gate, I caught my first break. I had kept glancing back sure someone was following me, when a passing car halted and the driver offered me a lift into town. A middle-aged man with bushy eyebrows, he expressed curiosity about the small valise I held on my lap.

"My mother's sick," I lied. "I'm on my way to see her."

That seemed enough to satisfy him. He dropped me off at the bus station, in the mistaken assumption I'd be taking a bus home. If only…

Once he drove off, I stayed away from the main street, and headed towards the town limits intent on hitching towards Amarillo and Route 66. As a matter of caution, I walked north along the block parallel to Main Street, the street where the cadets usually gathered. I didn't know exactly how to reach Amarillo, but I planned to buy a map to figure out a route. Meanwhile, all my energy was spent looking out for other cadets. A short walk led me to a block of ramshackle hovels on the northern end of town, the area that housed the Negro residents. I hadn't seen any homes like this since arriving in Cullen. Once in the Negro area, I felt comfortable enough to move a block over to the main street, which soon turned into a highway at the end of town. As I passed these miserable dwellings, a burst of anger overtook me. I said, not too loud, and to no one in particular. "I hate you Roxwell and Cullen, Texas. I hate you all." I shook my head. "No, not hate. I pity you and your backward ways. I don't understand why you have such crazy ways. All I want to do is get away."

That felt good. I wanted to scream for joy, but I still felt leery of being captured before I escaped. Fifteen minutes of solid walking in my squeaky military issue shoes brought me to the edge of town and an expanse of countryside. The two-lane highway began with a sign that increased the speed limit. On each side of the road, a gulley about six feet deep paralleled the road, and on each side, past the gulley, a fence separated the highway from an expanse of farmland with a scattering of houses visible in the far distance.

As Cullen had been built along the main route from Houston to Dallas, a fair amount of traffic moved in both directions, including an occasional large truck. I crossed the highway to the side of the road headed north. As I was about to stick out my thumb, I realized that I still wore my Roxwell uniform. That shirt, with the Roxwell patch sewn into the sleeve, tie and cap made me a sitting duck, almost as if the word RUNAWAY had been branded across my forehead. Besides which, I hated this goddam uniform. I made my way to the bottom of the gulley on the side of the road. Undoing my tie, and tossing the cap, I began unbuttoning my shirt including both sleeves, yanked at the now open shirt pulling the shoulder section down until the shirt dropped to the ground. I scooped a sleeve up, then tried to rip the cloth. That took a lot of effort, as shirts aren't the easiest thing to rip apart unless they are old and falling apart already. But I felt determined to destroy this military symbol. I would leave a statement in this ditch for whomever found this Roxwell cadet's remains. They would know all they'd ever want to know about my feelings from seeing a Roxwell shirt ripped into shreds.

With the khaki shirt now lying in tatters on the ground, I opened the suitcase and removed one of my short-sleeve shirts inside. As I buttoned the blue striped shirt, my body transformed. I had joined the human race again, and now, once more, became part of the multitudes. I wanted to change out of my khaki pants as well, but decided to wait until later, as they weren't as much of a giveaway as the shirt had been, especially with the Roxwell patch on the arm.

I made my way back up the gulley to the side of the road, and stuck out my thumb to the passing traffic. How critical this first ride would be. My escape would be complete if I could just get away from the town. Then, in the distance, I spotted a patrol car coming in the opposite direction. I flung myself back into the gulley, lying flat against the side until the police passed. After a couple of minutes, I ventured back up.

Just as I stuck out my thumb, a broken-down old pick up passed. The driver pulled over to the side, and I ran up. To my surprise, the driver was a Negro with a face full of white whiskers and snow-white hair. He wore a pair of faded overalls and a plaid shirt. Without asking where he was headed, I threw my suitcase in the bed of his truck and hopped into the cab beside him.

He shifted gears to start driving, and we chugged along at a snail's pace. Cars lined up behind us, and passed us at the first opportunity.

"Where are you headed?" I asked, talking loudly over the engine noise.

"Goin' to Dallas," he informed me in a gravelly voice, putting all the emphasis on the first syllable.

"Do you live there?"

"Yes, Sir, Boss. Me an' my wife got us a little shack there. Us both pretty old now, and we ain't strong like we was, but we're happy there. I'se just on my way back home from Houston. Gone to visit my kinfolk there."

"Well, I'll be happy to ride as far as Dallas with you," I said, "If that's okay with you."

"Sure 'nuf," he said.

We rode in silence for a few minutes, while I admired the irony of the fates that had directed a black man to stop in order to rescue me from the military school and everything I hated. In all the time I'd been in Texas, I'd never had a chance to speak with a black person about his feelings. A million questions flooded my head all at once.

"Tell me, if you don't mind, how you feel living here in Texas. I'm from California, you see, and this whole way of life is strange to me."

The man glanced over for an instant. His brown eyes regarded me curiously. The loud roar of the engine made talking difficult. "Don't exactly gather what you wants to know, Boss," he finally said.

I raised my voice. "I'm trying to find out how you feel about living here in Texas, how you are treated by white people. And my name is Cal, not Boss."

That drew a chuckle. "Okay, Cal. I sees what you is gettin' at. Us black folks stay out of the white folks way. Do that and they don't bother us none. We's good church goin' God fearin' people and we don't have no call to get in no white folks way. I've lived for a long while now, and I ain't never had no trouble. But, you see, sometimes a Nigger gets uppity, like this friend of my daddy, George Lincoln. When I was still a young 'un, my daddy told me about old George Lincoln and what happened to him when he got uppity. You see, he was workin' the land as a sharecropper for Massa Jim Wilson. Well…"

"What's a sharecropper?" I interrupted.

"I think dat's what you call a farmer who grows crops on land that don't belong to him, and gives part of his crops for usin' the land to the one that owns it like Massa Jim Wilson owned the land George Lincoln tilled."

"I think I get it."

"So, George Lincoln wants a bigger share of his crops. He was one brave nigger man. He goes to Jim Wilson and tells him that he ain't gettin' enough for all the work he's doin' on his crops. He says he's got a wife and four kids to feed and clothe. Jim Wilson looks him back and says, "'George, what you gonna do if I don't give you no more share?'" George, he full of 'mancipation and he say, "'I'se gonna leave your place, that's what I'm gonna do. I got the same rights as you. We is equal. So I'se just gonna go find a boss man who gonna be fair with me.'"

"Jim Wilson, he don't say nothin', but he boiling mad. That night he brings two or three of his neighbors and they visit George in his cabin and they beat old George black and blue with a strap. Lordy, how they beat that man. Well after that George don't say no more about leavin' or bein' equal. He just do his work quiet like. My daddy told me that story long time ago, and he know George cause they was slaves together before 'mancipation."

I had listened in silence. I felt like the past has seized me by the throat, like all the pieces of the puzzle fit into place. The expression on the old man's face was like someone reaching back into his memory bank to pull out a tale from a different world. And yet the hatred for Negroes that I saw everywhere in Texas made me think his world hadn't changed much.

"Say, I don't know your name," I told him.

"Andy, Yes sir, Andy Brown's what they call me."

"Well, Andy Brown, I'm really happy to meet you. Tell me though, why you stopped to pick up a white boy."

He stroked his chin, as if seeking the answer. Finally, he said. "You looked like you really needed a ride."

We both laughed at that one. He was right on the mark.

"When you told me that story, Andy, you used the word nigger. Doesn't the word bother you when you hear a white person use it?"

This time he scratched the back of his head before he answered. "You sure askin' a lot, Cal. Let me say, when I was a young sprout, the word bothered me some. Nowadays, that word don't bother me none at all. I guess I just got used to hearin' it and there ain't a thing I can do to change how white folks talk. I'm seventy-two years old and I worked hard all my life. I ain't got no fight left in me."

"But someone has to fight," I blurted out. "This is all wrong here. Black people are as good as white people, and they are supposed to be equal under the law. Where I come from, everyone's treated the same." When I said that, I realized that I didn't have a clue as to how Negroes were treated in Los Angeles. We barely had any at our school and my few friends were white like me.

Andy chuckled with a kind of warm affection my enthusiasm inspired in him. "You'se right, son. I knows I'se as good as any white folks, but they don't know that. And iffen they don't know, my tellin' them ain't gonna make a difference. There's a lot of young-uns fightin' for equality, but so far not much has changed."

I thought of the man who had stood up for the black woman in the ice cream line. He ended up with a beating and being arrested. He'd received Southern justice. Andy made sense. Rome wasn't built in a day, and it's only been ninety years since slaves were emancipated. One day, the situation will have to change. America was supposed to be the land where "all men are created equal." So far, that is just a fantasy.

If a sheriff came along right at this moment and dragged me back to Roxwell, and my platoon beat the crap out of me, the pain would have been worth enduring, just for the time I'd spent with Andy.

He stopped at a ramshackle excuse for a gas station in the country, surrounded by trees, and with only one working pump. The attendant, fat, Ku Klux Klan sheet white, and fifty, stared at us, the odd couple, the whole time. I bought a Dr. Pepper from the cooler and a Texas map to figure out which roads I should take to get to Amarillo. I also gave Andy a buck from my cash to help towards his $3.00 fill up.

We started off again. The old pick up truck kept a steady forty as he operated the floor shift and chugged along the road, but that wasn't enough for the most impatient drivers who passed us as soon as they could. I studied the map, and when I saw the city of Dallas, a thought struck me. Now, months later, as I sit at my typewriter writing about my experiences, I know that my thought process at that moment was totally dumb, but my state of mind then was different. I had an old aunt and uncle who lived in Dallas. My Aunt was my grandmother's sister. Somehow, the thought entered my mind that if I went to Dallas, I would run across them. They'd call my uncle, he'd call the police, and I'd end up being sent back to Roxwell. I couldn't take that chance.

According to the map, an alternate plan was to leave Andy near a town called Ennis where a road that led directly to Fort Worth crossed the highway we were driving on. I could hitch on that road directly into Forth Worth, reaching the city, with luck, before dark.

When we saw a road ahead with a sign for Fort Worth, I told Andy I'd decided to go directly to Fort Worth and I'd be getting off here to hitch a ride in that direction. We shook hands, and I stood by the side of the road watching the rickety old pickup that had rescued me from possible capture rattle off into the late afternoon. I crossed the road easily due to an absence of traffic on 34, the road that led into the main highway to Fort Worth. Ennis was only about 60 miles from Fort Worth, and I intended to spend the night there.

But to arrive there before dark required cars. I stood on the northwest corner of the intersection waiting for a traffic flow that didn't flow. Ten minutes passed. A car passed without stopping. After another fifteen minutes, another car passed. I began thinking about finding a cheap place in Ennis to stay for the night when an old pickup rambled by and pulled to a stop. For an instant, I thought Andy had returned, but no, this was a frazzled-looking white man in jeans and a faded shirt along with work boots. He had an unlit cigar stub hanging on his lips and his large nose looked bright red, perhaps from too frequent nips on the bottle he kept reaching for in his pocket to take hits all the way to Forth Worth.

He called himself John, and he made a living going from junkyard to junkyard buying up old batteries, melting them down, and selling off the lead content. He let me off in the outskirts of Fort Worth at a bus stop, and told me the bus would take me into the center of town.

A short wait, and I boarded the bus. As I sat looking through the window, the truth hit me. For the first time in my life, I encountered the world on my own with no family person to turn to for help, no structure to retreat to, no rules except the rules I made for myself. Simultaneously, I experienced exhilaration and fear, if a feeling can cover two emotions at once. The bus arrived among the shabby buildings that formed downtown Fort Worth, just as the last vestige of the sun began to sink in the west producing an orange sky over the city.

With my small suitcase in hand, I wandered up and down the main street looking for a place to stay. A couple of blocks from the bus stop, on a corner, I found myself in front of a fancy looking old hotel made of thick stone and several floors high, the Worth Hotel, situated beside a movie theater. A doorman in a red coat stood in front of the entrance with seemingly nothing to do. He glanced at my small suitcase.

As I peered through the revolving door, curious about the interior, the doorman spoke to me. "Why don't you go in and have a look around?"

I shook my head. "I could never afford a place this fancy."

He smiled. "You might be surprised. You can go inside and ask at the desk. The room might not be as expensive as you think."

He moved the revolving door and I found myself in a large plush interior with a high ceiling, a heavy rug on the floor and couches and easy chairs for the patrons. The front desk lined up with the revolving door, placed toward the back of the lobby.. I inquired about a room for the night. The middle-aged clerk behind the desk gave me the once over. He had on a white shirt, tie, and glasses. "Would that be a single, Sir?"

For the second time in a day, I'd been called Sir. I'd entered a new world.

"Yes, just for tonight."

"I could let you have a single with a private bath for $4.00."

"I only have a check," I told him.

"That would be no problem, Sir. Many people pay by check."

A few minutes later, I found myself inside a plush room on the fourth floor with an attached bathroom. This room had fancy wallpaper, a full double bed, nightlights on each side of the bed for reading, and a view of Fort Worth from the window. The large bathroom contained a full-length mirror, glass fixtures on the sink, and a shower in addition to a bathtub.

I spent a long time in that shower, washing my hair and feeling the flow of hot water across my body. I realized I had forgotten to bring along my shaving kit, toothbrush, and toothpaste. No problem. Everything was right there in a drawer next to the sink.

After shaving and brushing my teeth, I unpacked my suitcase, took out the slightly wrinkled charcoal suit I'd brought from home. I intended to wear the suit along with the sport shirt I'd worn since I left the school. I only had the school issued shoes, but looking in the full-length mirror, I ignored my feet, concentrating on the profile of me dressed to look human once again.

With a growing appetite, I took the elevator down to the main floor and entered the coffee shop. A few people were scattered around the room eating dinner at wooden tables with white tablecloths, and I sat down at a table as a waitress brought me water and a menu.

The prices on the menu shocked me. Every dish was priced much higher than what an ordinary restaurant would charge, and I pictured my meager amount of cash disappearing much sooner than intended. I could have kicked myself for not going down the block to some dump that fit my budget. I wanted to walk out, but the waitress had already given me water, a basket of rolls and a menu. I felt awkward walking out. So I ordered the cheapest thing on the menu, a chef's salad, which was good but not too filling. Fortunately, they kept replacing the two rolls each time I ate them, and six rolls plus the salad left me full.

After dinner, noting the evening was still early, I thought about what to do next. I remembered seeing a movie theater next door, and decided to see what they were playing. Fortunately, they featured two western films, my favorite kind of double bill. Even though I enjoy psychology, reading and learning, I love a good western. A western movie with its heroes and bad guys is my way of returning to another time period, maybe a fictional one, but a time when issues were more clearly defined than in my own day to day life.

I paid the admission and went inside. The theater presented a plush interior, like some of the theaters in LA that were built in the Thirties. I wanted a bag of popcorn, but that was a dime I might need later. One of the films had just ended, and I waited in the lobby until people started coming out, and on a Monday night, there weren't many. A newsreel was on the screen when I entered the theater. I stood in the back, trying to adjust to the lack of light.

An usher approached. "Can I show you to a seat?" He asked.

"Sure, thanks."

What a fancy touch, having an usher escort you down the

aisle. His flashlight lit the way down the aisle toward the middle of the cavernous room. For an instant, I paused as he pointed to a seat. My eyes had been on the newsreel, but as I looked over at him I noticed his eyes fixed on me. Then he shined his light directly into my face.

"Cal, Cal Carter? What the hell are you doing here?"

To hear my name called aloud in the middle of nowhere sent a lightning bolt through me. I tried to make out his face in the dark. "Do I know you? Who are you? I can't see."

"Cal Carter, I'll be damned. Come on out in the lobby for a minute."

I followed him back up the aisle, intensely curious. The only thought I had was this might be someone from Roxwell.

In the lobby, I had to blink a couple of times to adjust to the light. Then I saw Howie Brollen, a kid who I knew well. Howie wore an usher's uniform, kind of like the ones they wore in all movie theaters, the fancy ones that resembled Johnny in those Phillip Morris cigarette television ads. Howie's brown-blond hair looked neatly trimmed, his face more strained, but still with the flushed cheeks and bright blue eyes and those protruding ears, I remembered. We were built similarly, not too fat, not too thin, average height. We had belonged to the same club in school in Los Angeles. As a matter of fact, Howie had been one of the guys who had driven to Tijuana with me.

"Howie, my God, what are you doing here? You should be back in school."

"I finished the year in June. Then I got sick of listening to my parents and of Los Angeles, so I left."

Intent on listening, I continued staring, as I couldn't believe my eyes. Howie Brollen, fellow club member, and someone who I'd even gone out on a double date with once…because he had a car. I'd last seen him in school shortly before the semester ended and assumed he would be returning for his last year, the same as me. And here we both were, facing each other in the lobby of a movie theater in Fort Worth, Texas!!!!

"I better get back to work, or I'll get canned," Howie said. "Listen, I'm finished after the second feature. Can you meet me? Where are you staying?"

I pointed in the direction of the hotel. "Right next door. I'm staying at the Hotel Worth. I'll wait for you in the hotel lobby after the show."

With the meeting agreed upon, we went back inside. Howie showed me to a seat, and I sat down. The first western had begun. I tried concentrating, but my mind kept returning to Howie. Though this rarely happens, the idea of encountering someone unexpectedly blows the mind. Most people seem to take a surprise meeting for granted, but I just think of the odds. Here we were, living in the same place on the planet, Los Angeles, in an enormous universe, born around the same time, and then we're both somewhere else at an identical time. What would the odds be of that happening? What are the odds that I would stay in a hotel next to where Howie worked? Or decide to take in a movie in a theater where Howie worked? Or that Howie would be at work this evening? Or that he would even be living in Fort Worth? Or that I would be staying here? And how about the odds he would have taken a job in this very theater? My mind kept spinning. I had planned to continue on to Dallas, where Andy was headed. I could have been sitting on the highway and spent the night in Ennis rather than Fort Worth.

My mind continued to whirl throughout the first film. Howie, who grew up in LA, never struck me as the type who would live anywhere but there. Though always a nice guy, he could be rough and tough. I saw him knock out a kid in a fight after school. I'd met his family. He told me he didn't get along with his dad, but we all have these little problems. I thought about his parents and wondered if they knew where he lived now. I imagined myself knocking at their door, telling them I'd just run into their son in Fort Worth.

I totally missed the plot in the first film, but I'd settled down enough by the second to actually follow the story, not that following the plot is a big deal in a western.

When the lights came on, I walked out to the lobby, and the ten or so people left the theater when the film ended. The clock behind the refreshment counter showed 11:15. Howie was nowhere in sight. I walked back to the hotel and sat down on one of those plush leather chairs in the lobby to wait for him.

A few minutes later, Howie appeared. In street clothes, he looked shabby, almost like a transient with a pair of Levis, a western shirt, and worn shoes.

In our club, he had always been the most meticulous dresser.

"We can go up to my room and talk," I suggested. I didn't

want to spend any more money in the bar if they even would have allowed us to sit there. He didn't object but followed me to the elevator, drawing a look from the night clerk as we passed the front desk.

"Excuse me, can I help you with something?" The clerk asked.

I waved my key in front of his nose, and he shut up. We went up to the fourth floor, and I opened the door to my room.

Inside, I flopped down on my bed while Howie sat down in a chair across from me.

"Who first?" He asked.

"You go ahead," I insisted.

"You didn't spend much time at the club last year, did you Cal?"

"No. I had other stuff on my mind."

"I didn't think so. I didn't see much of you. Otherwise, you'd have known that things came to a head with my parents. School bored the hell out of me, and I wanted to quit at the end of the school year and take a job. Like Albright did. Remember?"

I nodded yes. Albright was one of our club members who had quit school to go to work with his father. He would visit on occasion, showing off his new car and flashing lots of cash. Albright irritated the hell out of me.

"We had a showdown about my wanting to quit once school let out for the year," Howie explained. Then he paused.

"Hey, do you have room service? Can we order a drink?"

I didn't know, but Howie spotted a menu next to the bed, and he thumbed through the pages. "Sure, we can call down for something until midnight. You want something?"

"Everything's expensive here," I warned him.

"My treat," he said. He picked up the phone and asked for room service. A minute later, he ordered himself a gin and tonic and a hamburger. I told him to order me a coke.

Howie settled back into his chair to continue his story. He pulled out a cigarette and lit up prior to speaking. "At the beginning of the summer, I had it out with my parents. I wanted to find a full-time job and start making money, not just take a summer job. They were dead set against my quitting. My old man said I was going back to school and finishing up high school, and that was that. I told him where to go. He didn't like that, and he slugged me. After that night, I didn't talk much with either parent. A couple of weeks later, my parents went off with some friends for a three-day weekend. They wouldn't take me, even though they were staying at a beach resort, because I hadn't found a job yet. Once they left, I packed up my clothes and stuff, emptied my savings, and even swiped twenty bucks they'd left me to pay the milkman. I was damned angry. I didn't even leave a note. I drove through Arizona and New Mexico. I thought about heading for New York. Remember my car?"

"Sure," I said, sitting up on the bed. "We drove in it once. A gray '49 Ford, right?"

"That's the one. The car broke down near Albuquerque, and

I had to have it towed in.

The rings were shot. The car needed four new tires. Overall, the engine was in pretty bad shape. I ended up junking the thing for twenty-five bucks. That left me with about a hundred-fifty and no car. I still had all my junk with me, but no way to carry so much around. So I took a room by the week, right there in Albuquerque. I tried to find a job but couldn't find one. I stayed there through most of the summer; it was hot as hell. I kept peddling my stuff to stay there, even my twenty-two. Finally, I just took off and started to hitch across the country. I figured if I could reach New York, I could nail a job with no problem. I spent two weeks in Texas picking cotton. That almost killed me. Man, you don't know what a backbreaker bending over all day is. Then, I remembered a kid in Fort Worth who lived next to me in Chicago during grade school. His family had moved here, while mine moved to LA. So I hitched into Fort Worth to try to find him. I had a hell of a time. That wasn't easy because his family had moved a lot, but at last I located him. Unfortunately, his family wasn't very well off; they'd always been in bad shape, so the best they could do was to let me share a room with him and feed me. I spent a month living off them while looking for work. When I landed this, at a buck an hour, I moved into a room. Been living like that for the past two weeks, but I'm fed up with all this. I want to head back east as soon as I've got the money saved. So that's my story. What about you?"

I shared my tale of woe, and how fate guided me here to see him this evening. He knew about the issues with my brother and had met my mother, so he got my explanation. I elaborated on the horrible conditions in Roxwell but omitted the part about Sandy and Larry. "I never thought I'd miss North Hollywood High, but I do," I concluded.

He shook his head when I finished. "Man, I never would have figured you for a military school. You were always the smartest guy in the club. I never thought you'd end up in khaki marching around with a rifle, at least until they drafted you."

"Believe me, Howie. I didn't figure on that either."

A knock on the door interrupted us. Howie jumped up and opened the door, and after a couple of minutes in the hallway, he entered, bearing a silver tray with his hamburger and drink from the bar. He handed me the coke, then sat down with the tray on his lap to eat and drink.

In between bites of the hamburger, he asked, "What will you do now?"

A shrug of the shoulders was my response. "Go home, I guess."

"If you do that, you'll probably be sent back to that damn school."

"I don't think so; I mean, I just won't go. I'll tell my mother the next time I run away, I'll head in the opposite direction. Besides, they would have to carry me back bodily."

"Hey, listen, man, why wait to go the other way? Why don't you come to New York with me? We could bum across the country together. Hey, we're free, white, and a few years from being 21. What the hell? We could have a ball, take jobs here and there to get some scratch and see what this country we live in looks like. Then, in New York, we could get an apartment together."

Wow. The thought behind his words overpowered me. Talk about living in absolute freedom; that's the open road. Talk about the very opposite of what I had experienced in the past month. Howie stared at me, his blue eyes looking for a hopeful sign. He must have felt a bit alone, off by himself in a world like this, living out an adventure with no one to share his ups and downs. In an instant, I imagined us hitting the road together, meeting beautiful girls, and having adventures such as the ones I'd had today, which reminded me I was living an adventure right now while poor Howie was stuck here using his flashlight to seat patrons inside a movie theater.

"Hmm, Howie, Jeez, I don't know. This is the first time I've ever thought of taking off like I have. I planned to go back to our old school and graduate in June."

"Hey, you can go to night school in New York. It'd be so cool to hang out in the Village. They have great jazz and lots of chicks there. Just think, having nobody telling you what to do or where to go or what to wear. I'll tell you, Cal, sometimes living this way is a little tough, but I love the freedom. Just to be out on your own. There's nothing better."

He had moved to the edge of his chair, and his hands cut through the air to animate his passion.

"You make the idea sound tempting," I said. "But I have to think about what that would mean for me. I'm trying not to just react but to weigh decisions carefully, to really decide what's best for me. Even leaving the military school, I tried to exit the right way. That just didn't work out."

"Hey, what if I go downstairs and have another smoke, and you can kick the idea around?"

"Sure."

He put the tray on the desk in the room. He'd polished off the drink and hamburger in record time. "I'll be back in a half," he said, shutting the door behind him.

I could have just said no, but the idea did appeal to me. I loved the idea of travel and adventure. That had been my Achilles heel that led me to the military school. In a way, I had taken the same challenge as Howie, leaving everything I knew behind to see how I measured up in the world. And I didn't measure up well, at least not yet; I knew that much. But with travel in my blood, the idea of seeing the country, stopping here and there for a while, and being my own decision-maker, that idea offered an attraction. Today, I had intended to go home. If I left with Howie, I'd be running away from home or maybe running away from myself. After all, I had left with a plan in mind: finish school, go to college, and gain a profession.

That future also had a strong appeal. I'd finally learned how to study and how to focus on my class work. I could go home, ignore my brother, concentrate on my schoolwork, and make something of myself. I had an ambition now. If I left with Howie, I'd be running from all that future just when I'd made up my mind to pursue my goals. I'd be running away from myself.

I hadn't needed but a few minutes to think the issue through. I sat up, patiently waiting for Howie to return. Finally, a knock on the door announced his arrival.

"What's the scoop?" he asked as he entered.

"No dice. I love the idea, Howie, but I just can't do something that crazy right now. I made up my mind when I took off from Roxwell that I'd go home, get my act together, and move forward. I want to finish school this year and apply to college. If I went with you, that could be the end of my family support. So I better head home."

He took one final shot. "Hey, I've got a little money saved. It would carry us for a while."

I shook my head in response. "But, listen, why don't you hitch back home with me? I'm sure you could make up with your folks. They'd probably be happy to have you home if you agreed to finish school. Then, once you were out of high school, they'd probably be more supportive of you doing what you want."

Now, he was the one to shake his head. "I tried. But we just don't get along. I'll be fine."

I extended my hand. "Good luck then. Hey, I'll write down my address and when you get to New York, you can write me and let me know how you're doing." We shook hands, and then I went to the desk and wrote out the information on a sheet of hotel paper. I handed the address to him.

He folded the paper and slipped it into his wallet. He opened the door to the room.

"Well, good luck, Cal, hitching home. Maybe our paths will cross again one day."

"Right, Howie, really great seeing you. Best of luck."

The door shut softly behind him, and I sat down on the bed, conflicting emotions taking hold of me. I wanted to run after him. But then, I thought about Larry, how he suddenly took off. How did I know I could trust him?

I undressed and slipped under the crisp sheets of the double bed. The clock showed the time as a few minutes after one in the morning. I fell asleep at once.

A knock on the door from the maid woke me at ten. I took a long, hot shower, wondering what the day would bring. Here, I sat in luxury, and tonight, I might be sleeping beside the road. I dressed, packed up my stuff, and said goodbye to the room.

The man behind the desk printed out an itemized bill. I stared at the figures and charges on the bill: room, $4.00; a chef's salad, $1.25. A coke, a gin and tonic. And a hamburger, $3.00, plus a quarter tip. $8.50 of the $10.00 check had been used. "Are you sure this room service order wasn't paid for?" I asked. The clerk checked through some papers.

"No, if it's paid at the room, they don't send the bill over to the front desk. This was charged to the room. I'm sorry."

 Anger built inside me as I took my $1.50 change and walked out of the hotel. Maybe I don't know much, but I know one thing, I'd made the right decision about not going away with Howie.

CHAPTER EIGHTEEN

The doorman at the hotel took pity on me when I asked him for directions to the edge of town and the road that led to Amarillo. He seemed to know everything, instructed me on what bus to catch, and where to catch it, and said that if I took the bus to the end of the Diamond Hill line, I'd be right where I wanted to be.

I had decided to wear my suit and a clean sports shirt, thinking a well-dressed look might help secure rides.

On the bus to the edge of town, I tried to decide what had led Howie to charge the drinks and hamburger to me rather than paying for them himself, as he said he would. I concluded that if I'd agreed to go with him, he would have stopped on his way out and paid for them, but since I hadn't agreed to join him, he decided to save the money. Why not? Chances were good he'd never see me again. He'd probably tossed my address into the nearest trashcan.

"Last stop," the driver called out as we came upon a two-lane highway. As the only remaining passenger, I took my bag, thanked him, and headed across the road. The traffic proved to be active, though most of the traffic headed in the direction of Fort Worth rather than away from the city. Still, within half an hour, an old Ford pulled over. The Ford was one of those old '47s with the curved roof that I'd always liked. The driver wore a suit and tie, and the car smelled a bit like toothpaste or tooth powder.

"Take you as far as Wichita Falls," the portly driver said. His face had a red glow, like the lights on a Christmas tree, and he could have steered the car with his stomach, which extended all the way to the steering wheel. "Gotta make some calls there," he went on. "By the way, who is your favorite ball team?" He asked the question in a strange, aggressive way, almost as if he intended to drop me off if he received the wrong answer.

"I live in LA. We don't have any major league teams. I follow the LA Angels in the Pacific Coast League."

"You gotta like a big league team," he told me.

"Well, their parent team is Cleveland. I follow them a bit."

"Oh yeah," the man said, pulling out a cigarette from a pack in his shirt pocket and placing it between his lips. "They're the ones with that Jew third baseman."

I didn't answer. I wanted to say, "Stop the car and let me off, you anti-Semite asshole," but on the other hand, I wanted to get home, and after surveying the wasteland that loomed all around us, I decided to keep my yap shut. "Rosen's great," I responded.

"Hell of a hitter," the man agreed. He pulled a lighter from his pocket to light the cigarette dangling from his lips. "I like the Yankees," he informed me. "Never seen a team so good year after year."

The couple of hours the car took to reach Wichita Falls produced random periods of baseball chit-chat punctuated by periods of dead silence. Just as we parked the car in Wichita Falls downtown area, the salesman announced he would be going on toward Amarillo after he made his calls.

"Be back here at three, and you can ride along," he announced.

We'd parked across from a Woolworth's variety store. I went inside and sat down at the long lunch counter, knowing how cheap the five-and-ten-cent store meals were. I ordered a chicken salad sandwich and a coke. When I finished, I wandered down the street looking at shops. Wichita Falls, full of old buildings, some in decay, looked just like most other towns, like Cullen, for example, as if someone had purposely made them all look the same. I found a magazine and newspaper store and read through some magazines until three o'clock. I returned to the car and waited until I saw a fat man waddling down the street carrying a heavy black satchel, like one of those cases doctors carry on home calls, only larger.

After we'd started on our way, I asked him what he sold.

"Special dental supplies for dentists," he said. And that's all he said. He seemed about as deep as an empty pie tin.

We reached the small town of Childress just as darkness began to set in. The fat man rolled through the town slowly, staying under the posted speed limit, "speed trap," he muttered. At the far edge of town, he pulled off into a motel, parking the car across from the registration area.

"Gonna stop here for the night," he announced. "Leave at eight tomorrow if you want to stick around."

That was that. Off he went to register. I walked out to the street, and as we were still on Highway 287, I crossed to the north side and stuck out my thumb. A beat-up old Dodge pulled over. As I approached, the driver reached over and rolled down his window. "Where you headed?" He asked.

I surveyed this guy. He looked about thirty, skinny, wore an old boy flannel shirt, and had a big scar running the length of his right cheek. His hair went in all directions.

"Amarillo," I said. I almost said Fort Worth so he could tell me I was standing on the wrong side of the road, but I didn't want to spend another night in a town if I could avoid doing so.

"Ain't goin' that far," he drawled. "Take you to Ashtola, though, about halfway."

When I opened the door and sat down in the front seat, my suitcase on the floor tucked under my legs, I noticed he kept an open bottle of beer between his legs. He took off like a shot, squealing his tires against the pavement. He turned up the radio volume to listen to the Okie music he'd turned down when he stopped. He drove fast but not crazy. Every couple of minutes, he took a sip from the beer and soon tossed the empty bottle out through his window. When we passed the next town, he stopped in front of a store.

"Don't you all be touchin' that," he said, pointing to a holstered gun I hadn't noticed but which literally sat in front of the space where my feet rested. "You want a beer?"

"No thanks," I said. I wondered if I should disappear while he was inside, but since he hadn't used the gun on me yet, I had good reason to suspect he might not plan on doing me in. He actually didn't come across as very threatening.

When he returned to the car, he pulled open the glove

compartment, extracted a beer opener, and opened the bottle, which he then placed between his legs just before he took off, squealing down the street doing fishtails. This brought a roar of laughter, after which he turned up the volume on another Okie song and, to my surprise, plunged right into singing at the top of his lungs.

All around us, as we drove, the Texas night crawled in, Texas dark, broken only on occasion by lights from far-off homes. After a while, to my surprise, in the middle of all that darkness, he pulled off to the side of the road. "I turn off on this here next road, so you can git out here," he informed me.

The here he pointed at looked more like nowhere. "I thought you were going to Ashtola."

"I am tomorrow," he said. "It's about ten miles up the road there."

He pointed straight into the darkness that permeated the road ahead. Warily, I opened the door, lifted out my suitcase, and stepped out. I saw his headlights guide the car onto a road about a hundred feet ahead, then vanish into the darkness.

My heart began pounding. I hadn't even thought this possible, to be trapped here in the middle of nowhere Texas, surrounded by rattlesnakes and tarantulas. No town lights showed ahead, and the last town we'd passed was at least ten miles behind. I stood close to the road, not too close, but closer to the road than to the ominous pitch-dark fields behind me. I stuck out my thumb every time a car passed, but the darkness of the night seemed to have killed off the traffic. A car passed about once every fifteen minutes, and each one flew past at full speed. Not one of them slowed down, though a couple of wise guys honked as they sped by, and I jumped about a foot in the air.

I stopped hitching. Any car that would stop in the middle of nowhere could be the kind of car I didn't want to ride with. I tried to think. But my imagination kept returning to rattlesnakes and tarantulas. When I drove in the car with the salesman, I spotted one of those big spiders trying to cross the road. The salesman aimed his wheels, squashed the poor thing flat as a pancake, and had a good chuckle over his conquest. Meanwhile, even sitting inside the car, I jumped when I spotted the critter. Now, I might have one keeping me company at any minute.

I paced back and forth, wishing for a flashlight. I could kick myself for not bringing the one I'd used for reading in my room. I contemplated walking towards Ashtola, but with no lights in sight, I was walking ten miles in the dark alongside a road that didn't sit right with me. Lying down near the road, or worse, lying down far away from the road, had no appeal. Finally, I sat down on top of my suitcase, which put me a bit off the ground, and used every opportunity that the lights of a passing car provided to survey my immediate area for critters. Fortunately, no snakes or tarantulas appeared. I wanted to close my eyes, but every time I managed to close them, I snapped awake as if some creepy-crawly had suddenly appeared on my left foot.

A light, cold wind began to blow across the flat land, and my thin suit coat did little to protect me from the developing chill in the cold night air. As I sat on my little suitcase, I thought about my warm room back at the military school, my warm bedroom at home, and the wonderful warm room at the Worth Hotel where I had spent the previous night.

An hour passed, then two. Darkness remained as the moon appeared to be obscured by some cloud layer. I was shivering now, holding my arms tightly across my chest, and seriously questioning if I would survive this horrible Texas night. In my head, I began to write my own obituary. "Cal Carter, 17, a Los Angeles native, died of exposure alongside a highway in Texas, escaping from a military school he could not endure. Accomplishments little, but great potential." Change that last line. "Showed great promise in helping others achieve their life potential." Much better.

I stood up, stamping my feet against the ground, doing a kind of Indian war dance, my arms still wrapped around my buttoned coat, trying to give myself as much warmth as possible. My hands felt frozen. If only I'd brought a sweater, but who brings a sweater when they move to Texas?

A car approached, a bit slower than most, an old wreck of a car that pulled over to the side of the road just past me. A robbery was the first thing that came to mind. In the extreme darkness, a figure emerged. The figure advanced towards me.

A female voice broke the chill in the air. "Jesus told me you needed help, young man," the voice said.

"I'm freezing," I said.

"Please, come in the car. I'll take you home and warm you by a fire."

The red taillights shined in the darkness, leading us to the ramshackle vehicle, a pre-WWII relic. I climbed into the passenger's side. As the driver entered and seated herself, what I could now make out with partial light was a heavyset Negro lady. She operated the floor shift to move the car back onto the highway, starting us on a journey to God knows where. Not that I cared. My little suitcase and I were willing to go almost anywhere.

I rubbed my hands together to warm them, though the car had a toasty little heater that warmed us both.

"Why did you stop?" I asked when I could finally say a few words.

"You looked like you was freezing, child. And, Hebrews 13, verse 2 commands we help those in need. *Do not neglect to show hospitality to strangers, for by this; some have entertained angels without knowing it.*"

I smiled. "I'm sorry, but I'm not an angel," I informed her.

She let out a hearty laugh. "That's all right, Chile, as long as you ain't the devil, old Hattie don't care a lick."

We turned off somewhere, perhaps at the edge of the town called Ashtola. A sprinkling of lights could be seen in the distance along this pitch-black dirt road, and after a few minutes of driving over ruts and bumps at a snail's pace, the car pulled up in front of a small shack. "You stay here a minute," my hostess said. "I'm gonna get the place all toasty for you."

I sat in the front seat of the old jalopy, thinking about how mysterious the ways of the universe are. I expected I wouldn't survive until morning, and then a lady stopped her car to pick me up because of a bible quote, thinking that she might be rescuing an angel when, in reality, she was the angel who had rescued me out of the darkness. That biblical turnaround brought a smile to my face.

About fifteen minutes passed before Hattie emerged to lead me inside her hovel, one room with a single bed, an old dresser, a two-burner cooking stove, and a big pot-bellied wood-burning heater that occupied the center of the room. Across from the stove stood a heavy armchair with a ragged covering. She plunked me down in the chair. The fire blazed in the big pot-belly stove in front of me, providing both warmth and light to the small room. On the wall over the two-burner stove, she'd pasted a large color picture of Jesus that looked as though she'd clipped the page out of a magazine.

Hattie had something boiling on the stove, and she brought me a bowl of soup that warmed my insides but not as much as Hattie's goodness warmed them. I could see her clearly in the firelight, for the place appeared to have no electricity, and the two-burner looked as if it was connected to a butane tank. Hattie wore a maid's outfit with a little white apron over her ample frame. Her wide cheeks helped to produce a perpetual smile that lit up her face.

"You is one lucky boy," she said. "Every Tuesday, I drives over to Childress to work for a lady. I cleans her house, makes meals for her, and then comes home quite late at night.

The rest of the week, I'se right here so you picked a good night to be stuck where you was."

I smiled at her, sipping the warm soup, content and thankful.

"You saved my life," I told her. "I think you are the angel."

That brought a hearty laugh, a laugh that came from deep in her belly and rolled across the entire interior of the room. "Bless my soul," she said. "Ain't no one called Hattie MacDonald an angel in all these years on earth."

When I'd finished my soup, I asked if there was a bathroom.

Hattie pointed out the front door. "Just go back behind the shack, and you'll see an outhouse. Here, take this stick. If you see a rattler, just give him a poke, and he'll be off. He don't want to hurt you none. And here's a flashlight so you can see."

With my heart banging against my chest cavity, I ventured outside, felt the cold air sting me, swung the flashlight back and forth over the ground in front of me, and moved just far enough away from the shack to relieve myself.

That night, I slept in the big easy chair. The next morning, Hattie insisted on cooking breakfast before I started out on the road. On her little two-burner stove, she produced eggs, ham, and grits that filled my stomach. I wanted to give her some money, but she refused to take anything. After an appreciative goodbye, I took my suitcase and trudged up the dirt road (she wanted to drive me to the main road, but I wouldn't allow her to do so) towards the highway.

The day looked glorious with a blue sky and the sun warming away the chill of the night. I had never felt better. Fate, providence, God, the universe, use whatever term makes you happy, had provided for me, and I'd survived for two nights now with more adventures still ahead.

After about half an hour, a car pulled over, an almost new Plymouth station wagon, the back area filled with women's clothing. This man, slightly balding and maybe forty, looked, dressed, and talked in a normal tone when he asked where I was headed. I told him Los Angeles, and he said he could take me as far as Amarillo. He appeared pleasant and happy to have company during his travels. When we came to a small town, about half an hour past where he picked me up, we stopped for breakfast. The man offered to treat me, and to my surprise, I downed most of an order of pancakes with coffee and juice. During breakfast, we chatted, and I learned he'd moved from Ohio because he'd married a Texan. "They never seem to want to leave Texas," he told me with a smile.

We arrived at Claude, Texas, about 30 miles before Amarillo. A small town with old buildings, Claude, fortunately, had two stoplights. As we drove at the speed limit along the main street, we came to a stop at the first red light. A blue Ford pulled up beside us, driven by a man wearing a sailor suit. When the light turned green, the Ford pulled out ahead of us, and I spotted California plates.

"Maybe he's going to California," I told the driver, pointing to the plates.

The second light, fortunately, also turned red. As we pulled up beside the Ford, my driver honked, and I rolled down the window.

"Are you going back to California?" The salesman called through the open window. The sailor had rolled down his window when he heard my driver honk.

"Yeah, I am," the sailor said.

"Could you take a guy who just got out of the army?" The salesman asked. Since he didn't know my situation, I found his question amusing.

The Navy man looked me over for an instant. "Sure, I'll pull over here," he said. As he pulled over in the next block, the salesman pulled in behind him.

"Good luck, army guy," the salesman said with a wink and a laugh, sticking out his hand to shake mine.

"You brought me some," I said, thanking him as I left the car.

My new chauffeur, Jerry, sported a head full of flaming red hair, cut regulation short, and bright blue eyes that matched his sailor outfit and boyish freckles. I soon found out he had left his pregnant wife off at her parent's house in Alabama and was driving back to Moffitt Field near San Jose, a place I knew well, for I used to drive by the enormous hanger visible from the highway when I was a kid, At that time, after my dad's death, we lived in San Jose close to my grandparents, who had moved out from Texas. Once a week, my grandfather would drive all of us to Oakland to visit my uncle, who was recovering in a military hospital with wounds he'd suffered during the war. On the way back home, driving the Bayshore Highway, we'd listen to a half-hour program called *One Man's Family*, and every week, as I recall, that program played on the radio as we drove past that big hanger at Moffitt Field.

Once we'd finished the formalities and Jerry had learned I

was headed to LA, he clammed up to concentrate on his driving. He didn't say a word about my Army "discharge" or ask me why I was hitching. All he said was I should get off at Barstow, a small town in the desert, not too far from Los Angeles.

A few minutes before noon, he wanted to stop for lunch. He selected a cheap-looking coffee shop in a small town. I ordered a hamburger and a small salad, which was about all I could afford. I decided to live on hamburgers and salads for the balance of my trip. They were favorites, and about the cheapest and most filling dishes I could think of ordering.

We ate together in silence and, once finished, returned to the car parked in front of the coffee shop. When he stopped at another gas station a block up, I wondered if he was going to hit me up to help with the cost of filling the tank, but he said nothing.

In the early afternoon, we hit the border where the sign read, WELCOME TO NEW MEXICO.

Never did I feel more welcome anywhere as I took a final glance back at the state I hoped to never see again. I immediately dropped off to sleep and slept for a couple of hours as we drove along Highway 66 toward Albuquerque. The sailor often fiddled with the radio, trying to bring in stations, but only in the areas close to towns would he have any luck. When we reached Albuquerque after dark, he found several stations to choose from.

We stopped at a place called the University Café for dinner. Jerry told me he'd stopped here with his wife on the drive out from California, and the food was pretty good. I ordered a big chef's salad and, along with the rolls, left the place with a full stomach.

Now, we were on the road toward Gallup. Except for headlights from approaching cars or those from cars in front of us, we were surrounded by almost complete darkness, the only light coming from a pie-slice moon, which made the shapes and sizes of bluffs and hills, such as I could see, appear as menacing.

Around 9 o'clock, I was half-dozing when I heard Jerry.

"Jeez, look at that sonofabitch." He pointed to a Cadillac in the process of passing us up. Jerry was going about sixty, and that Caddy overtook us like we were stopped waiting for a light. As the car pulled in front of us, I saw a young girl, maybe ten or twelve, with blond hair, wave at me from the back window. I waved back, but in a flash, the car disappeared into the darkness of the night. A few minutes later, another car, a big Buick Roadmaster, shot past at a speed that appeared to be faster than the Cadillac. Jerry muttered, "idiot" under his breath.

A few miles up, we found an open gas station. Jerry stopped for a bathroom break. We stretched our legs, bought a couple of cokes, and drank them before we took off again. About half an hour later, we began to slow as a number of flashing red lights warned us of a problem ahead. A few cars were lined up, parked along the side of the road, and others in front of us sat on the highway at a dead stop. Everything remained deathly silent except for the hum of our motor. Ahead, a policeman used his hands to wave cars on our side of the road around the accident, one car at a time. I spotted the

Buick first. The car looked like an accordion, with the front bumper up against the front window and the back end of the car pushed forward toward the rear window. The Buick stood right in the middle of the highway, and the lights from the Highway Patrol cars illuminated the surrounding scene. The Buick's windows had shattered, and much of the glass lay across the ground. I couldn't tell if anyone remained inside; perhaps they'd been thrown out by the accident.

I spotted the Cadillac next, lying sideways in the dirt off the road. The car looked like a junkyard heap with the driver's side caved in and the headlights, in a ghoulish twist, still operating, sending its beams out across the endless stretch of desert. The Caddy made me think of an athlete ready to take off without realizing he had no legs to run with.

Finally, on the far side of the road, a huge truck lay on its side. The cab had shattered glass where the windows were, and the front end looked badly smashed. Then, I spotted a small group of people standing around right past the scene. You could see their breath in the lights, for the night had turned quite cold. That's when I saw the bodies, four of them, laid out on the side of the road, one after the other. They had been covered with any available items, towels, coats, even a blanket. I will never forget, as we passed the scene in slow motion, seeing a pair of black and white saddle shoes with white socks sticking out from beneath the various towels and articles of clothing covering the little girl's body. I felt my stomach wanting to erupt. Several people, probably those first to arrive on the accident scene, stared down at the deceased, seemingly oblivious to the passing cars or the activity around them. They must have all been thinking about how this could have been them, or maybe they wanted to ask, "What's it like? Where are you? You know what it's like now. Tell me."

I fought the nausea. I kept thinking I didn't want to throw up in Jerry's car. As we passed close to the spectators, we heard the wail of an ambulance approaching from the opposite direction. No need to hurry, I wanted to tell him, and Jerry pulled over until the ambulance passed. I rolled down my window and called out to one of the men close to me.

"Do you know how the accident happened?"

The short man wearing a heavy coat turned around. He looked like a local with a stubby beard and cowboy boots. He explained in a straightforward manner that the Buick had tried to pass the Caddy but, for some reason, misjudged the distance of the truck coming the opposite way and ran into him head-on, knocking the Caddy off the road and causing the truck to lose control. The three people in the Caddy were dead, as was the truck driver. They didn't know who was in the Buick, but they couldn't get anyone out at this point. As we edged forward, a state trooper yelled out, "Drive carefully."

I didn't throw up, but continued to feel sick to my stomach. One of those drivers could have been the one to pick me up rather than Jerry, and I could be lying there covered by coats, sweaters, towels, and whatever. Jerry waved at the patrolman, and he drove as carefully as anyone who had a wife back in Alabama about to give birth. We weren't on a suicide mission.

I couldn't stop thinking about what we'd witnessed. That thin line that separated life from death had hit me full force between the eyes. Of all the subjects I dwelled on at various times, mortality had never been one of them. Like most kids my age, I assumed I'd live forever, or at least for a long time. But these guys had been alive within the last hour when they passed us up. A young girl, her whole life ahead of her, had waved at me.

Shortly after midnight, Jerry found a closed gas station, pulled off the road, and took in a few hours of shuteye. He hadn't said a word about the accident or anything else for that matter. As I said, he wasn't the talkative type.

After eating breakfast in Gallup the next morning, Jerry settled down to some steady driving. We stopped a couple of times along the way, but just as the afternoon sun started to set, he dropped me off at the bus station in Barstow. I thanked him profusely, but all I got was a wave of the hand in return. And then his car took off.

Most of the seats in the Greyhound waiting room were packed with travelers. In addition to a ticket office, waiting room, and stalls for the various buses passing through, the place sported a pinball machine center and a poker club. I checked on the next bus to LA, and learned there would be one leaving in an hour that could get me home by ten at night. Only one problem prevented me from buying a ticket. The bus ride cost four dollars. I had a five-dollar check from Hugo, written on a California bank. The Greyhound people took cash only.

I walked outside the bus station and stood there among the town's low life's, trying to decide what to do. I could call my mom collect, and she would probably drive out to get me, but that would be a long trip and a long wait.

I decided to walk down to the main street to see if I could cash the check somewhere. Now, so close, I felt a burning desire to be in the safety of my bed at home tonight. Four days on the road was enough. I spotted a drugstore, went inside, and saw a pharmacist standing behind the counter in the rear of the store where the drugs were located.

"Excuse me, Sir," I said. "I'm trying to get home to Los Angeles. There's a bus that leaves in an hour, but Greyhound only takes cash for the ticket. I wondered if maybe I bought something, you would cash a check from my stepfather for me."

The pharmacist had a friendly face. He wore glasses with thin metal frames. He listened attentively before responding. "Could I see the check, please?"

I had the check folded up in the pocket of my shirt. He unfolded the check and examined the contents carefully. "How much is the ticket?" He asked.

"The bus is four dollars. I've been on the road and only have about fifty cents left, so this is the only way I can get home."

The ring of the cash register became my answer. He reached in with one pale hand and pulled out a handful of dollar bills. He counted out five and handed them to me. "You don't have to buy anything," he said. "Just sign the back of the check for me, then get yourself some dinner before you go home."

I smiled, endorsed the check, thanked him, and left the store, rushing down the street to secure my ticket home. I couldn't believe my good luck.

The bus station cafe looked too depressing to eat in. As soon as I'd secured my ticket, I went down the block to polish off another hamburger, but the place I ate at didn't look all too clean, so I decided to skip the salad.

I returned and waited almost an hour before the bus pulled in late, arriving from somewhere. I joined a line of people waiting to board. By the time I entered, only a single seat remained, and that was next to a lady who appeared wide enough to occupy both seats and, in fact, spilled over into the aisle seat. She wore a hat holding a long feather, a dress that looked like it had weathered the depression badly, and finally, a shopping bag, which she held with great affection, like a baby, in her lap. I sat down, or part of me did, for the rest of my posterior was forced over the side into the aisle. I tried to gently nudge her closer to the window, but there just didn't appear to be any give or anyplace for her body to move.

Once the bus started, the lady in the feathered hat pulled out a small portable radio from her shopping bag and turned the volume far up. I wouldn't have minded a little entertainment, but all this radio picked up was static. Others in front of her turned around to stare but didn't say a word. Finally, I couldn't take the noise anymore.

"Would you mind turning your radio down, please?" I asked as politely as possible.

She cocked an ear in my direction. "Wha, what'd ya say?"

I repeated the question.

She repeated, "Wha, what'd ya say?"

She had me stymied. Before I could think of an alternative approach, she tapped my shoulder, pointed to the radio, and smiled. I shook my head, yes, and she turned the volume way down. "I'm on my way to visit my granddaughter in Los Angeles," she informed me.

I sought a diplomatic way to explain that I had paid for a full seat but was only occupying about half of that seat. I couldn't find one.

"Where have you been?" She asked. She maintained her grip on the radio as if she expected me to grab the little thing directly from her hands.

"Texas," I answered.

"Wha-wha, what'd ya say?" She paused a moment, then spoke again, tilting her body towards me, creating a survival balancing act. "Texas, ya say. I been to Texas, but I didn't go to Mexico 'cause I can't speak no Mexican." With that, she straightened up while I exhaled.

"I can," I told her.

"Can do? What?"

"Speak Spanish."

"Wha-wha, what'd ya say?"

"I said I speak Spanish."

Her eyes narrowed with suspicion. "You're not a wetback, are you?"

I shook my head. "No, Ma'am, I'm Chinese."

"Wha-wha what's that?"

"I'm Chinese, Chinese, like in sneeze."

Her eyes narrowed. "Chinese, you say. You ain't one of them Communists?"

I nodded in the affirmative. Her jaw dropped.

"I'm a God-fearing Communist."

"Are you tuggin' my leg?" She wanted to know. "You Communists don't believe in God. Joe McCarthy said so."

"Some of us do. The ones that are part Indian."

She stared, open-mouthed. I could see her brain at work.

"I knew me an Indian once. He was a Chekee."

"A Chekee?" I asked. "Never heard of that tribe. But if they are American, they

must believe in God."

She put her hand over her heart. She turned away from me and stared through the window at the darkness of a desert night.

About an hour and a half into the trip, the bus pulled into a station to discharge passengers. Two people left, which gave me the opportunity to switch seats before anyone else came aboard. I moved as far back as possible. Once I'd secured my seat, I went inside the station to a bathroom where I could laugh like an idiot, drawing stares from a guy at the urinal. I didn't care. I hadn't had so much fun in months.

From my new perch near the back of the bus, I watched people sitting around the lady trying to get her to turn off the static she seemed to enjoy listening to on her little portable radio.

At last, we reached the city. Driving through the streets of Los Angeles seemed interminable. Finally, we drove through downtown, passing blocks full of alcoholics and homeless people, who seemed to be the principal residents of the center of the city. Downtown Los Angeles has always been known as a disaster area ever since I can remember. Nobody goes there. Despite that, I breathed a sigh of relief when the bus rolled into its designated place to unload its cargo, the passengers.

Though the clock inside the terminal showed close to midnight, I phoned my mother. The relief in her voice overwhelmed me. "My God, Cal. I can't believe you are here. I thought the police were calling with terrible news," she said, sounding as if she was on the verge of tears. "Oh, Cal. I'm so happy to hear you are here and safe. I'll get in the car to pick you up right now."

What a pitiful collection of humanity huddled inside the bus terminal, sitting in the chairs, wandering about. Most of them looked as if they had no place to go.

After a few minutes, I thought I'd find more peace waiting out at the front entrance to the station until my mother appeared. As I waited, I thought back over the entire Texas experience. I felt as if I'd learned everything necessary from the school experience to turn my life around. I'd become a different person from the one who had left home less than two months ago. To hitch home had proved an unexpected eye-opener, and the highlight came when Jesus's best friend rescued me from freezing in the middle of the Texas desert.

"You a marine?"

A seriously scary-looking guy interrupted my thoughts. He had come up behind me, and I had to turn around to see him. I wasn't sure he was talking to me.

"You a marine?" He repeated, looking directly at me this time. As I looked at him, I felt instinctive fear and danger. He seemed young, maybe in his early twenties, but towered over me as he stood above six feet tall, with pockmarks all over his face and a few missing teeth, as if he'd been on the losing end of some fights. His black pants clung to his waist. He wore a white shirt and a bright red cardigan sweater over the shirt. His blondish hair had been combed up towards the top of his head from both sides, then parted down the center, with two spit curls hanging across his forehead, a style I identified with homosexuals. The expression he wore as he repeated his question could be termed malicious, as if he sought any excuse to wail on me. On his right ear, a long red erring dangled down. After a frozen pause, I shook my head to reassure him I was not now and had never been a marine.

"Then what are you doing hanging around out here?" He demanded.

"I'm waiting for my mom to pick me up," I managed to reply. I wanted to run, but my feet had locked themselves onto the sidewalk.

His eyes narrowed, and he studied me before he spoke.

"How old are you anyway?"

I hesitated. "Fifteen," I answered.

That seemed to throw him, for he backed off a step.

"Fifteen," he repeated. "You better get inside. They have a curfew here."

"Yeah?" I could hear the relief in my own voice. "Well, thanks for telling me."

I took off scurrying back inside as if I'd started the hundred-yard dash. The lively movement and noise inside the station made me feel warm and secure. Now, I wanted my mother to show up fast. When, at last, I saw her Cadillac roll to a stop in front of the entrance to the bus station, I made a mad dash for the car. I tossed my suitcase into the back seat and hopped into the passenger seat beside her. "Let's get out of here," were my first words. "The place is full of queers."

Mom stepped on the gas. To my surprise, tears rolled down her cheeks as she drove.

"What is it, Mom?"

She tried to speak but kept staring straight ahead. With her arm, she wiped at her eyes. Then, like a sudden cloudburst, a torrent of words flowed. "Oh, Cal. I thought you might be dead. Four days with not a word. The school called on Monday to say you were missing. I kept hoping you would call. I prayed you were all right, but I was terrified. What if you just vanished, and I never heard from you again? I could never forgive myself for sending you off."

Overcome with all her pent-up terror, she pulled the car over to the side of the road as deep sobs poured out in a way I had never heard before. I reached over and put my arms around her, pulling her close to me. "I should have called, Mom. But all I could think about was coming home," I whispered.

Until that moment, I hadn't clearly understood how much my mother loved me. Warmth covered me like a blanket. I finely had foumd the home I always wanted.